BROKEN
GLASS

Virginia Andrews Books

The Dollanganger Family Series
Flowers in the Attic
Petals on the Wind
If There Be Thorns
Seeds of Yesterday
Garden of Shadows
Christopher's Diary: Secrets
    of Foxworth
Christopher's Diary: Echoes
    of Dollanganger
Secret Brother

The Audrina Series
My Sweet Audrina
Whitefern

The Casteel Family Series
Heaven
Dark Angel
Fallen Hearts
Gates of Paradise
Web of Dreams

The Cutler Family Series
Dawn
Secrets of the Morning
Twilight's Child
Midnight Whispers
Darkest Hour

The Landry Family Series
Ruby
Pearl in the Mist
All That Glitters
Hidden Jewel
Tarnished Gold

The Logan Family Series
Melody
Heart Song
Unfinished Symphony
Music in the Night
Olivia

The Orphans Miniseries
Butterfly
Crystal
Brooke
Raven
Runaways

The Wildflowers Miniseries
Misty
Star
Jade
Cat
Into the Garden

The Hudson Family Series
Rain
Lightning Strikes
Eye of the Storm
The End of the Rainbow

The Shooting Stars Series
Cinnamon
Ice
Rose
Honey
Falling Stars

Virginia ANDREWS

Broken Glass

**SIMON &
SCHUSTER**

London · New York · Sydney · Toronto · New Delhi

A CBS COMPANY

First published in the US by Gallery Books, 2017
A division of Simon & Schuster, Inc.

First published in Great Britain by Simon & Schuster UK Ltd, 2017
A CBS COMPANY

1 3 5 7 9 10 8 6 4 2

Simon & Schuster UK Ltd
1st Floor, 222 Gray's Inn Road
London WC1X 8HB

Simon & Schuster Australia, Sydney
Simon & Schuster India, New Delhi

www.simonandschuster.co.uk
www.simonandschuster.com.au
www.simonandschuster.co.in

A CIP catalogue record for this book is available from the British Library.

Hardback ISBN: 978-1-4711-5867-4
eBook ISBN: 978-1-4711-5869-8

This book is a work of fiction. Names, characters, places and incidents are
either a product of the author's imagination or are used fictitiously. Any
resemblance to actual people living or dead, events or locales is
entirely coincidental.

Printed and bound by CPI Group (UK) Ltd, Croydon, CR0 4YY

BROKEN GLASS

Prologue

Haylee

My mother's dinner date, Simon Adams, stepped out of his car right after Mother started scream - ing at me. She had practically leaped out of the car before he came to a stop when she saw me stand - ing there alone. I had waited as long as I could to walk out, so that I would be one of the last to leave the theater. No matter what my twin sister , Kaylee, thought or what anyone else would think, I couldn't be exactly sure what would happen after she had left to, as she believed, meet my Internet lover and make my excuses. I had a pretty good idea, though. Otherwise, I wouldn't have sent her.

The movie theater we had gone to as part of my plan was one of the few that weren't in a mall these days. Most of the stores on the street in this neighborhood were already closed by the time the movie ended. People scattered quickly to their cars in the nearby parking lot or on the street as if they were worried that it was a dangerous area. Maybe it was. I had no idea what it was like. We had never gone to a movie or shopped here before.

"What are you saying? What are you saying?" Mother shouted after I began to explain Kaylee' s absence. "What do you mean, she's not back? Back from where?"

I started to cry, always a good touch. Mother hated to see either of us cry, always expecting that the other would soon start, too.

"Where is she?" she demanded, stamping her foot.

"I don't know," I said. I kept my head down.

Only hours ago, Mother had seen Kaylee and me go into the movie theater, and now, when they drove up, she saw only me standing there looking around frantically. I was sure that my face was full of enough concern and panic to impress her. I had planned how I should look and sound. When you think ahead to what a scene would be like, it' s like rehearsing for a play. Mother wasn't doing or saying anything I hadn't expected. I could have written her dialogue, too.

I glanced behind me and saw the cashier , a woman probably in her sixties, and an usher who was probably no more than twenty , gaping at us.

We were probably better drama than the movie now playing. Some other people walking in front of and near the theater paused on the sidewalk to look our way.

"How could you not know where your sister is? Maybe she's still in the theater . Is she in the bathroom?"

"She's not in the theater bathroom."

"You checked?"

"I didn't have to, Mother." I took a deep breath. "Kaylee left to meet a man very soon after we got here, but she was supposed to return before the movie ended," I blurted, and continued to cry.

"What? What man?"

"What's going on?" Simon asked, hurrying up to us. He looked at the theater entrance. "Where's the other one?"

The other one? He wasn't sure which twin I was. I nearly stopped crying and started laughing.

Mother looked at him, annoyed, but ignored him. I couldn't blame her. He wasn't exactly what anyone would describe as a strong-looking, take-charge man. He had lost his wife about a year ago in a traffic accident, and either the tragedy had made him meek and helpless or he was always that way . I had called him Mother's charity date, because she had told us she was his first date since his wife's death and that she was going to take extra care with him. I had told Kaylee it seemed more like emotional and psychological therapy than a romantic evening. Mother had gone out with at least half a dozen men since her and our father' s divorce, but none of them was good enough for her to continue dating. I doubted Simon would be.

"What's the matter? What's going on? Where is she?" Simon asked again.

"I'm trying to find out. She says Kaylee left the theater to meet a man," Mother told him.

"A man? Who? What man? Did you know about this?" He grimaced, making it seem like it was her fault.

"Of course not! That's what Haylee was about to explain." She grabbed my shoulders and shook me. "Stop crying and talk," she said.

I took a deep breath, wiped away my tears, and began with "I'm sorry, Mother. I should have told you, but Kaylee would have hated me."

"What are you saying? What should you have told me? Hated you for what?"

"Kaylee was carrying on an Internet relation - ship with some older man. I told her she could get into big trouble, that men like that are dangerous, but she insisted he was all right. According to her , they were talking almost every night for the last month or so on her computer , and she liked him very much."

Mother stared at me in disbelief. She shook her

head as if my words were shower water caught in her ears. Every part of her face seemed to be in motion as she reluctantly digested what I was saying.

"She met someone on the Internet? These things can be bad," Simon said. "So where is she?" he asked me, stepping forward, suddenly more aggressive and manly. "As you can see, your mother and I are very concerned."

He's showing off for Mother, I thought, and smiled to myself. He was still pathetic.

"Talk," Mother ordered. "Quickly."

"She said she and this man finally decided to meet, but she knew you would never approve of it, so she came up with the idea to pretend we were excited about this movie," I said, the words rush - ing out of my mouth like water bursting through a dam.

"Pretend?"

"It was her plan. After you took us here, she left the theater to meet him somewhere. She promised to be back way before the movie ended. Right up to the time she left, I tried to talk her out of it, but she wouldn't listen."

Mother looked up and down the street. "Which way did she go? What else do you know?"

"That's all I know. I went along with it because she said she would hate me forever if I didn't. I couldn't have her hate me. I couldn' t. We're too much a part of each other. I've been so worried." I started to cry again.

"We'd better call the police," Simon said. Mother didn't respond. She stood there almost frozen in place. I was afraid to look at her Sometimes I thought she could read my thoughts. "I'll call the police," he said. He took out his cell phone and stepped back toward the car.

"How could you let her do this? How could you keep it a secret from me? Didn't we talk about how either of you should tell me about the other getting involved with someone dangerous?"

I nodded but kept my head lowered. "She made me promise," I said. "I couldn't betray her."

"Her? What about betraying me?"

I raised my head. "I told her that, Mother , but she said we needed to believe in each other if we were to be forever special sisters. I was afraid of breaking her heart."

"This is so unlike her," Mother mumbled.

I looked up at her quickly "It's unlike me, too."

"Yes," she said, nodding. "Yes."

Simon returned. "They're on their way," he said. "You don't even know which direction she took?"

"She just told me they were meeting at a place he had decided on because it was close enough for her to go to his house and get back before the movie ended," I replied, wiping the tears from my cheeks.

"To his house?" Mother said, the words taking

a strong grip on her worst fears. "She went to his house, to a strange man's house?"

"That was the plan she told me they had made."

"Does he live alone? How old is he? How did she meet him on the Internet?"

"I don't know any of that. She wouldn't tell me that much," I said.

"Men who do this sort of thing know how to find vulnerable young girls," Simon said, nodding like some sort of expert on teenage girls.

I looked at him with an expression that shouted, *Shut up! You're making it all worse.* I guess I was effective. He backed up a step.

"How long has this been going on?" Mother asked.

"Maybe six weeks, maybe seven."

"And you both kept this a secret from me for that long?" she asked, her face now a portrait of disbelief. She looked like a little girl who had just learned that Santa Claus was not real. I had never believed in Santa Claus. Most of life was a fairy tale. Who needed to add a fat man with a beard?

"You were . . ." I looked at Simon. "Busy with your own problems. At least, that was what Kay - lee thought, and I did, too. She convinced me that you'd only start worrying so much about us that you would be unhappy again, and we were both upset at how horribly Daddy had treated you. She said that would all be my fault if I told."

"This is so unlike them," Mother told Simon. "They've never done anything even remotely like this."

"Do you know his name?" Simon asked.

"She told me a name, but I'm not sure it's his real name."

"What does that mean?" Mother demanded.

"He could have made up a name," Simon said, "or your sister could have made one up. Right?" he asked, as if I was now the expert.

"Maybe," I said. I turned back to Mother. "He might be right. I don't know if she wanted to tell me his real name, so she could have made it up just to shut me up because I kept asking her"

"Nevertheless, what name did she tell you?" Simon demanded.

"Bob Brukowski," I said. "It never sounded real to me."

"I can't believe this," Mother said, shaking her head. "This is not happening. It's not happening." She put her hands over her ears as if she could block out reality and return to our perfect world by closing and opening her eyes.

"It's a problem all over the country now ," Simon said. "Young girls being exploited through computers."

She pulled her hands from her ears as if they had been glued to them and made two fists.

"It's not a problem for me! Or it shouldn't be," Mother said. The veins in her neck looked like they might burst. Her eyes were bulging, and her nostrils widened.

He pressed his thin lips together and nodded. A police patrol car pulled up to the curb, and two officers got out quickly. Simon turned and hurried to them, happy, I thought, to get away from Mother. He explained what was happening, and the officers came over to us.

"Mrs. Fitzgerald," the taller one said, "I'm Officer Donald, and this is Officer Monday." He took out a small notepad. "What's your daughter's name and age?"

"Her name is Kaylee Blossom Fitzgerald, and she's sixteen. This is her sister, Haylee. They are identical twins, so you don' t need a photograph to recognize her," Mother said. "Or you can take one of Haylee with your cell phone. There' s not an iota of difference between them, down to how many freckles they each have. They wear their hair the same way, and they are dressed in the same outfit, the same color tonight. They sound the same, too."

Both policemen looked at me, astounded. The shorter one almost smiled at how ridiculous Mother sounded.

"Haylee," Officer Donald said, "why don't you

tell us everything that went on between your sister and this man. Don' t leave out anything because you think it's too small a detail or not important, okay?"

"Okay."

"Why don't you sit in our car?" he said, step - ping to the side so I could do that.

When I started for it, Mother began to follow , but Officer Monday asked her to wait. I knew why. They thought I wouldn't say things in front of my mother. Simon took her hand. When I looked back at them, their roles appeared reversed. She suddenly looked like his charity date. *How ironic*, I thought. *He's the one using psychology on her.* It brought a smile to my face that I wiped away instantly as I got into the patrol car. The two officers got in and turned to me.

"So," Officer Donald began, "tell us how this all started and everything you know about the man. We understand your sister told you his name?"

"She told me a name, but as I told my mother, I don't know if that's his real name. It was Bob Bru- kowski."

"Did he send her a picture of himself over the Internet?" Officer Monday asked.

"I guess he did, but I never saw anything on her computer. I know only what she told me about him. Maybe she thought if she showed me his picture, I'd tell her he was too old for her or something."

"So tonight you just know she was meeting this Bob Brukowski somewhere in this neighborhood, and the man was definitely older, and he was going to take her to his house?"

"Yes. She made a big deal about him being an older man and not a high school student. She was bragging about how much a mature man was attracted to her. I kept warning her, but she wouldn't listen."

"So what happened tonight?" Officer Monday asked. "How was this all set up?"

"She had a plan," I began, and started to de - scribe it. As I spoke, the belief that Kaylee really would never be back grew stronger and stronger . I half wished that I had been there hiding in the shadows and watching, like the director of a movie, when Kaylee had met him.

"Does your sister have a cell phone?" Officer Donald asked.

"Yes, we both do, but we didn't take cell phones tonight." I shrugged. "I guess I should have made sure we did. I was just so nervous about it all that I forgot."

"I've got a teenage sister," Officer Monday said. "Like all her friends, she won't even go to the bathroom without her cell phone."

"We were too involved in my sister's plan. We didn't think," I said more emphatically, and threw in a few well-placed sobs.

I knew now that it was over , that it was hap -
pening. I should have felt more remorse, but a little
voice inside me asked, *If your twin sister is gone, are
you still a twin? Won't people stop mixing you up?
Won't you become your own person finally?*

I had to be careful not to let the policemen see
my smile. They wouldn't understand.

No one who didn't know us and how we were
raised would understand.

1

Haylee

Even with all the warnings and the bad stories out there, whose mother wouldn't have a hard time believing her daughter would do something like this? Everybody thinks they're raising angels. I saw that from the way my friends' parents talked about them. How could their daughter be doing some - thing as terrible as carrying on a romance over the Internet with an older man? And right under their noses? This was all especially true for our mother.

Simon Adams was right. Examples of this were constantly on the news. But our mother was always very confident that we wouldn't do anything that was so forbidden or so stupid. In her eyes, we were such goody-goodies. I hated it when she bragged about us and people looked at us as if we were right out of a fairy tale about two identical princesses, Cinderella clones without so much as a blemish on our behavior or complexions.

When we were little, both of us used to believe that we hadn't been born. We had descended from a cloud of angels and just floated into the delivery room. The stork really did bring us.

Mother had no idea how many things we had done recently that she wouldn't approve of, mainly things I had done and that my dear abused sister would have to go along with or at least keep secret. Kaylee would have been suspected less. After all, no matter what Mother told other people or even what she told us, I knew in my heart that she favored Kaylee, despite her effort not to show any bias.

However, I had no doubt that her favoring Kaylee gave her nightmares. What if I could tell—or anyone else could tell, for that matter—that she really did favor one of us over the other? How horrible for her. All our lives, she had made an effort to treat us equally and to think of us as halves of the same perfect image of a daughter she had created. The smallest thing that could make one of us dif - ferent from the other was vigorously avoided. She was adamant about not loving one of us more than the other.

No one suffered more under this rule than Daddy, who sometimes accidentally and sometimes deliberately tried to treat us as individuals. I pretended to be as upset about that as Mother wanted us to be, but in my secret chest of feelings and thoughts, shut away from Mother's eyes, I was pleased, even when he did something for Kaylee that I might envy . At least, in his thinking, there was a difference, and we weren' t simply duplicates or clones, as some of Mother' s friends occasionally referred to us. It always annoyed me that she didn't mind when people said that. I did. Who wanted to be a clone?

I was tired of hearing how we were monozy - gotic twins developed from a single egg-and-sperm combination that split a few days after conception, that our DNA originated from the same source. I didn't even have my own DNA like most everyone else. I had to share everything with Kayleefrom the moment I was conceived. Mother often told people that we even took up equal space in her womb and that everything that had come from her to nourish us was consumed in "perfectly equal amounts." I never knew how she could know that, but she would say, "How else could they be so identical at birth?"

According to Mother's logic and beliefs, how could I ever even exist without Kaylee? Our hearts beat with the same rhythm. We took the same number of breaths each day . If one of us sneezed, the other soon would, and that was true for every yawn, every ache, and every shiver. We were the mirror sisters; we lived in each other's reflected image.

Well, maybe not now; maybe finally not now. I could walk away, and Kaylee would be stuck in the glass looking out. *Come back, come help me!* she would cry. *Help yourself*, I would say. *I did. That's why you're trapped in the mirror.*

Another patrol car arrived on the scene, and before we went home, we all drove around, Mother in one car and me in the other, searching for any signs of Kaylee. Sometimes the officers would stop to ask a pedestrian if they had seen a girl who looked like me, and I would have to make myself more visible. On one stop, I actually stepped out of the vehicle.

"She's wearing the same clothes," they told potential witnesses. They all shook their heads and apologized for not having seen Kaylee. One elderly man looked as if he might have something to tell them. He was studying me so closely my heart stopped in anticipation, but after another moment, he shook his head and told us his eyesight wasn' t what it used to be.

It seemed like we drove for hours. At one point, we passed the closed-down coffee shop, and I held my breath again. W as Kaylee still there, maybe lying on the side of the road? How would I react to that? It was deserted. There was no one on the sidewalks, no one in the street, and no one sitting in any vehicle. Even the shadows looked lonely.

Simon was left behind to wait at the movie theater in case Kaylee showed up there. When we returned and saw him alone looking confused and helpless, Mother grew more frantic. She wanted more police, more cars, and insisted that they knock on every door within a mile of the theater

"He wanted Kaylee to meet him nearby," she said. "He has to live somewhere in this neighbor - hood."

They tried to reason with her , but she spun around on Officer Donald, the first policeman who had arrived at the theater, and screamed, "Do something! Don't you understand? My daughter's been kidnapped, or she would have been back by now. She's being held somewhere against her will or taken so far away we'll never find her. Every minute that passes is terrible!"

"You've got to stay calm, Mrs. Fitzgerald," he told her, and looked to me to do something to help her, but I just lowered my head and looked as powerless as they felt.

A policewoman arrived, probably called in by one of the other cops to help handle Mother. To be truthful, even I was shocked at how she was behaving. Kaylee and I had seen her upset many times, of course. She used to pound on herself so hard when she screamed that she would have black-and-blue marks, but she was lashing out now and throwing her arms about so wildly that I thought they would fly off her body. She began screaming at me again for keeping Kaylee's secret.

"Don't you understand that you've been kid -
napped, too?" she cried.

Everyone looked at her oddly then. I had to
explain what she meant, how she believed that
nothing ever happened to either of us without it
happening to the other. Of course, it still made no
sense to the police. It was then that I told Officer
Donald about Daddy and how Mother' s insisting
on both of us being treated exactly the same had led
to their divorce.

"It became too much for my father," I said.

They looked sympathetic. They didn' t have to
say it. I could see it in their faces. It would have
been too much for them, too, maybe for anyone.

Officer Monday returned to the patrol car to see
about getting in touch with Daddy.

At one point, Mother broke away and started
running up the street, insisting that the search go on
and that we shouldn't wait for additional assistance.
We were wasting precious time. She had started
toward someone's front door when they rushed
up to her. She was pulling her own hair and had to
be forcibly restrained. The policewoman, Officer
Denker, asked me for the name of our doctor.

"She has to be calmed down. She could hurt
herself," she told me.

I gave her Dr . Bloom's name. Simon Adams
stood off to the side now , looking too stunned to
speak. I laughed to myself, imagining that he was

thinking, *What did I get myself into?* I was sur -
prised when Officer Monday came over to tell me
they had located my father and that he was going to
meet us at our house. I had thought for sure he was
on some business trip miles and miles away.

We hadn't had much contact with Daddy after
the divorce had been finalized. Mother seemed
to keep up with the news about him and his girl -
friend. Apparently, from the last we were told, that
romance had ended, and Daddy was living in an
apartment by himself. We were supposed to go to
dinner with him a week from now . Almost daily,
Mother warned us that he would try to play on our
sympathies.

"Poor him," she said. "He' s alone again. But
he's always been alone. He prefers it, no matter
what he tells you. He's too selfish to be with anyone," she assured us. "Don't waste a tear on him."

Mother had practically passed out by this time,
emotionally exhausted. Officer Denker was with
her in the rear of one of the patrol cars, commiserat
ing. I had heard her tell Mother that she, too, had a
teenage daughter. Mother looked at her and shook
her head. Kaylee wasn't simply a teenage daughter.
Didn't she understand? Kaylee and I were special.

Naturally, all the police activity in front of the
movie theater had drawn a crowd. Anyone who
showed up was questioned, but as I expected and
hoped, no one knew anything. T wo plainclothes

detectives arrived, and I had to tell my story again.
A Lieutenant Cowan asked the questions. He was
older than Detective Simpson, who I didn' t think
was much older than a college student. He was by far
better-looking, with sort of rusty light-brown hair
and greenish-brown eyes. Every time I answered
one of Lieutenant Cowan' s questions, I looked at
Detective Simpson to see his reaction. I even smiled
at him once.

"We'll need your sister's computer," Lieutenant
Cowan said. "Your dad's on his way, and your family doctor is coming to your home for your mother,
so why don't you ride back with us and keep telling
us all you know, all you remember?"

"I'd better ask my mother ," I said, looking at
the patrol car she was in.

"Better to just come along," Lieutenant Cowan
said. "She's calmed a bit. They'll start for your
house."

I shrugged and followed them to their car   .
Before I got in, I looked at Simon Adams. He ap -
peared to be totally lost now and not sure if he
should remain waiting.

"My mother's date doesn't know anything," I
told Detective Simpson. "Maybe you should tell
him to go home. My father's coming," I added, im-
plying that this might be a problem.

He looked at Simon and then at Lieutenant
Cowan, who nodded.

"Get his name, address, and contact numbers," Lieutenant Cowan told him.

I got into the backseat.

The patrol car taking my mother started to leave. When it pulled in front of us, I saw her spin around in the backseat and press her face to the rear window, looking as if she was clawing at it with her hands while she screamed. I looked down quickly, mostly embarrassed by her. *Everyone will see how pathetic she is, but the good news is that most will feel sorry for me,* I thought. *Not only have I probably lost my sister, my other half, but my mother won't be the same.*

They'd be right about that. Mother was going to need me. She'd need me twice as much as she ever had, especially with Daddy not living with us. I'd have to be more like Kaylee sometimes, but that was all right, because I could go right back to being myself. Without Kaylee there, I could do many new things, and everything I wore would seem to be mine alone. There would be no one imitating me, duplicating me.

"Keep thinking about this," Lieutenant Cowan said as we waited for Detective Simpson. "Every little detail that comes to mind will be helpful. Don't think anything is too small to be impor - tant."

"I really don't know all that much," I said. "I didn't want my sister to continue corresponding with him, and she knew it, so she kept most of it from me."

Detective Simpson got in.

"She told you his name, you said," Lieutenant Cowan said as he pulled away from the curb.

"Bob Brukowski. But to be honest, I think she made it up," I said. "She was afraid I might do a search or something and find out that he was a criminal."

"You two are pretty close, though, right?" Detective Simpson asked.

"Two sisters couldn't be any closer unless they were physically attached," I said. "We never kept secrets from each other, but Kaylee was determined to be more of her own person, and I didn't want to stand in her way."

Neither spoke for a while.

"Did she ever print anything out from him to show you, or show you his picture? Maybe you know where that is?"

"No. Everything I knew she told me. I never saw anything. She was possessive about her new relationship. It was the first real thing she had that I didn't."

"You didn't share boyfriends," Lieutenant Cowan said. I was silent. He turned back to glance at me. "Did you?"

"Sorta, sometimes," I said. "W e were very re - spectful of each other's opinions."

The two detectives looked at each other and were silent for a while. Detective Simpson had been checking on the name I had given them.

"There's no one with that name living in the vicinity. The closest one that's come up lives in Cape May, but it looks like he's in his seventies."

"Predators don't seem to be limited by age. Let's see what we can get off her computer," Lieutenant Cowan said.

Yes, let's see, I thought, and smiled to myself.

Daddy and Dr . Bloom were at our house when we arrived. Mother had already been taken in quickly. Dr. Bloom had followed her up to her bedroom.

The moment I entered, Daddy turned to me. "What's going on here, Haylee? Kaylee was involved with an older man on the Internet?" he asked, astounded.

Why would you be surprised? I wanted to ask him. *For years now, you've known less about us than most of our neighbors. You were too busy trying to make a new life for yourself.*

"That's what she told me, Daddy . I told her it was wrong and dangerous. She kept most of it secret," I added. "She made me promise not to say anything. I thought she would grow out of it, realize it was stupid, and that would be that."

"But you worked out a sneaky way for her to meet him tonight?"

"I didn't; she did. I wanted to go along to protect her when she met him, but she thought I was
trying to compete with her for his attention or
something, so I didn't go. I was very worried, but
she promised that if he was strange or anything, she
would come right back to the movie theater."

Daddy looked at the detectives. "What do we
do?" he asked.

"We'll continue a physical search of the vicinity, hoping to find a witness. In the meantime, we'll
need her computer," Lieutenant Cowan told him.

"Sure," Daddy said. "Show them, Haylee."

"How's Mother?" I asked.

"Dr. Bloom's going to give her something to
calm her, and we'll see," he said. "I'll stay here tonight. Don't worry," he added quickly.

"She blames me, but I couldn't stop Kaylee
without her hating me, Daddy. It was hard," I
whined. "You don't know how hard it was for
me to go to sleep every night thinking about the
trouble she might get into. I felt bad about it all the
time, but I couldn't have Kaylee hate me. I couldn't
just tell on her. I couldn't!"

"Don't worry," he said. "I'll stay here until the
situation is resolved."

"I'm so glad, Daddy," I said, and hugged him. I
held on to him tightly.

"You'd better help the policemen," Daddy
whispered.

I let go, sucked back a sob, and led them up to Kaylee's bedroom. They unplugged the computer, and Officer Donald took it.

"We just need the hard drive," Detective Simpson told me. "Do you know how they communicated? Emails, Twitter, Facebook, what?"

I shook my head. "As I said, I never saw any of it. My sister wanted to keep everything secret. It was her thing, not mine. She had to share so much in her life with me, practically everything. I understood why she was upset about it, because it bothered us both. This romance with an older man was her own thing. She told me what she was doing, and I told her how worried I was, but she kept saying she knew what she was doing."

My voice kept cracking when I spoke. I was on the cusp of more tears, but I thought I was doing well, explaining things well.

"I don't understand when you say you two had to share everything," Lieutenant Cowan said. "What exactly does that mean?"

"It's just as I said, everything. We have the same clothes, shoes, games, dolls. Whatever I own she owns, and vice versa, and it has to be exactly the same. We even have identical toothbrushes. That's why we were wearing the same thing tonight," I said. "Mother likes it that way, even at our age now."

The two detectives looked at me with expressions of amazement.

"Why?" Detective Simpson asked.

"We're identical twins, monozygotic twins. We have the same DNA. There are very few like us. Mother brought us up to share. We're two halves of her perfect daughter," I added, and forced a smile as if I thought it was wonderful. Then I changed expression quickly. "That's why she's extra upset. Half of us is missing."

They looked at each other with expressions that said, *We've heard it all now*. I knew they wouldn't blame me in any way after hearing all this. Mother was the kook.

"We'll be back in the morning," Lieutenant Cowan said. "Write down anything that might help us, anything you remember. We can't stress it too much. Details are critical."

"You'll probably find it all on her computer," I said. "That's where she told me it all came about, but I don't know any real details more than I told you," I emphasized.

They left Kaylee's room. I stood there for a moment looking around. *If Mother has her way*, I thought, *she'll turn it into a shrine. Nothing will be touched or changed, but it will be kept as clean as ever. After all, someday Kaylee will return, won't she?*

A new great thought occurred like a surprise bonus. If she did that, I'd be able to make significant changes in my room. She wouldn't want mine to be a shrine. If she tried to duplicate it, I'd stress how important it was to preserve Kaylee' s room exactly as it was, even when I added something to mine or changed something. Finally, I could put up some posters of rock singers and movie stars I liked but Kaylee didn't. There was so much I could do now. New doors were opening every passing mo - ment. I felt like I could breathe better.

Mother was sedated and sleeping. I saw Daddy talking to Dr. Bloom in the hallway . They were practically whispering, and Dr. Bloom kept shaking his head as Daddy spoke. He was probably describ- ing how nutty Mother was, I thought. Dr . Bloom patted Daddy on the shoulder to boost his hopes, and then he left and the house was quiet.

"I'm going to sleep down here," Daddy told me. "Just call me if you need anything."

"Why don't you sleep in Kaylee's room, Daddy?" I suggested. "Sleep in a comfortable bed instead of on a couch."

He considered it.

"I like the idea that you'll be right next door to me, Daddy. I'm not going to have an easy time falling asleep. I'll probably have nightmares. I'm having trouble keeping from thinking about what she could be going through right now, how scared she must be."

"Okay, sweetheart," he said. "I'll do that."

I smiled. He called us sweetheart when he lived

with us, but it was always *sweethearts*, not *sweet-heart*. Tonight it was just me.

And it would be that way in the morning, I was sure.

Everything would be changing now.

I actually felt as if I had just been born, and all that had happened to me before, my whole life until now, was the nightmare I feared.

If I could only wipe my memory clean the way I could delete everything on a computer, life would really be perfect.

I would even be the perfect daughter all by myself.

2

Kaylee

I didn't want to believe him when he told me how isolated we were on his family farm, that I could scream and scream as much as I wanted and no one would or could hear me. But when he left for work in the morning, the only sounds I heard were the creaks in the house above me and the harsh grating noise the chain made when it slid along the uncar - peted areas as I moved through the basement apart - ment. It was attached to my left ankle with a metal bracelet and then to a hook embedded in the wall.

Standing on a chair , I pressed my ear to one of the boarded windows and listened. Not only didn't I hear any people, but I didn't hear any cars or trucks, either. I stood there listening for quite a while, too. If we were close to a road, it was surely a road hardly traveled. A slight breeze played against the side of the building, but the deep silence was not only deafening; it was discouraging, draining out the little hope I harbored. My chest felt like it was filled with butterflies in a panic because they were locked in a jar.

As if his cat that he had named Mr . Moccasin was a double agent, he followed me about and then sat and watched my every move. I wanted to hate him and kick him away, but he looked as lonely as I was and happy to have someone with him. Before he had gone to work, Anthony , my abductor, left me instructions for feeding Mr. Moccasin and told me to be sure he had enough water. Sometimes his words were full of affection, and sometimes they were riddled with threat.

The night before, when Anthony had come to the bed I was forced to sleep in, he had slipped beside me under the comforter and almost imme - diately fallen asleep. He didn't touch me, but I was afraid to move because I might wake him. I didn' t hear him get up. I was so terrified of falling asleep that I didn't close my eyes for hours and hours. I think I passed out rather than fell asleep. It couldn't have been for very long. When I opened my eyes, I saw him at the stove. Just as he had promised, he had risen early and begun to prepare French toast for our breakfast and brew coffee. The aromas quickly filled the basement apartment, which had otherwise smelled rancid and damp despite how clean it was kept.

"Good morning, good morning," he sang, see - ing me awaken. "I hope you slept as well as I did. That's a new mattress. First time anyone's slept on it. How'd you like it?"

He turned back to the stove. As he worked, he babbled on and on about the different dinners he would prepare for us, talking enthusiastically about recipes as if I had come here willingly and was looking forward to spending the rest of my life with him.

"You have no idea how happy I am that you're here. It's so damn sad to have only yourself to cook and bake for," he said. "It's as bad as an artist creating a picture and not having anyone to look at it. Sure, you can be happy about what you've done, but it's pleasing someone else that matters most, don'tcha think? That's what Ma used ta say. Whatcha think? She was right, right? My ma was full of wisdom. Pop used ta say, 'Your mother's so brim full of sagacity that words come pouring out of her ears and eyes.' I had to go look up *sagacity* in the dictionary. I think I told you my father was a big reader, right? He didn't have much more formal education than high school, but he liked to read anything and everything. He'd read the back of a cereal box if there was nothing else around. He wasn't much of a talker, though. I guess he was shy that way, but get him mad, and he'd give you a what-for that could go on for hours, even days."

He paused and smiled. "Look at me going on and on about myself and my parents when you didn't even have a chance to say good morning. Excitement's no excuse for bad manners."

How could he think I was going to say good morning? The moment I awoke, I vowed not to speak to him. Perhaps my silence would convince him that his fantasy romance would not happen, and he would give up and turn me loose. W as that hope a bigger fantasy? W as I deliberately naive because I was afraid of facing the truth that I was trapped and so well hidden that no one might find me? I could be here for years. The night had passed, and no one had come to rescue me. Surely my mother and my twin sister, Haylee, were frantic by now, but I knew the police usually wanted to wait to see if a person had deliberately disappeared, run away. It was typical of teenagers.

And yet Haylee could certainly convince them that this wasn't the situation in my case. By now, as reluctant as she was and as guilty as she would be because it was all her fault, she would have to show them her Internet correspondence and explain how she had sent me on an errand that surely led to my abduction. She'd have to confess that our going to the movie was a ruse, that we—and there was no way I couldn't confess to having gone along with it—were planning for her, not me, to meet her Internet boyfriend.

She'd have to explain that once we were in the theater, she'd suddenly had a terrible stomachache and thrown up in the bathroom, then sent me to tell Anthony she would not be able to meet him as they had planned. She might have a full-blown flu and still be sick to her stomach, but I was con - fident that Mother would force her to explain it all to the police. They would have come quickly to that closed-down coffee shop and maybe located someone who had seen something. If not, by now, Haylee would have surely shown them what she had on her computer.

Mother, I thought—what a panic she must be in by now. There wasn't one day since we were born that Haylee or I was somewhere without the other, even if it meant the other had to sit and wait and be bored. All our dentist and doctor appointments were made back-to-back, alternating between my being first and her being first. For the first time in a long time, I was glad Mother was so intense about us being together. Right now, I'd be the last to complain about her considering us two halves of the same perfect daughter.

"You can get up and go to the bathroom," Anthony said when I didn' t respond. "Don' t forget to wash your hands. If I ever forgot, my mother would seize me on my ear and spin me around to go back and do it. She'd do that in front of my friends. Even when I was eighteen!"

I did have to pee, so I rose slowly and, dragging the chain behind me, went into the bathroom with no door. He could look in and see me, but he was busy preparing our breakfast. I saw that he had put new soap, toothpaste, and a toothbrush still in its packaging in the cabinet above the sink. There were also other typical bathroom items like aspirin, dental floss, Band-Aids of all sizes, itch cream, disinfectant, and other things to treat toothaches. There was a rack beside the sink with clean towels and washcloths. Beside that on the rug-covered floor was a basket for laundry.

What the bathroom did not have was a mirror. Right now, I didn't want to look at myself anyway. I was afraid I might just scream and scream.

After I washed and dried my hands, I came out and gazed around the basement apartment again, an apartment he claimed he had lived in from the age of twelve, something that he said made his friends jealous. He had his own apartment and all that privacy. Perhaps, however, his parents simply wanted him out of their sight. Listening between the lines of things he said, I imagined they hadn' t been pleased with how he was turning out, so they had shoved him downstairs—especially, from the sound of it, his father.

The only two windows down here were boarded

up on the outside. The walls were paneled in light wood. There was an old, heavy-cushioned brown sofa that looked worn like old family furniture, a small dark-wood coffee table all nicked up, and a dark-wood bookcase on the wall behind the sofa. Besides books, there were little figurines and toys on the shelves, model planes and model cars, things you would find in a little boy's room. Next to the shelves were drawings pinned to the walls. They looked like the drawings a child would make of mountains and trees. In many of them there was a cat that resembled Mr. Moccasin. How old could he be? If it was him in the pictures, he would be an old cat, unless those drawings were recent, which would be frightening because they were so childish.

The concrete floor was partially covered with thick, tight area rugs in faded colors. They also looked like hand-me-downs. Directly in front of me was a metal sink, a counter with a linoleum surface, a small two-door refrigerator, and an oven and range with a teapot and a saucepan. There was a cabinet above it, and beside it was a closet without any doors. The shelves were stocked with boxes of cereal and rice, cans of soup, and other things, and on the counter was a bread box. All the pipes and wires were visible, looking like it was all just thrown together.

The bed I had been forced to sleep in was a double with a metal headboard, two large light-blue pillows, and a light-blue comforter that did look brand-new. It had a lilac scent. There were two wooden side tables that looked like a lighter oak wood, and a dark-wood dresser with half a dozen drawers. There was another tight area rug as well, but it was a lot more threadbare than the rest.

He had set the small dark-wood kitchen table. There were only two chairs, one on each end, not matching, both with ribbed backs and seats that had the color washed out of them. He was pouring orange juice.

"I hope you're hungry," he said. "I'm starving." He pulled out what was to be my chair. "Madame," he said.

I stood there staring at him. He really was acting as though I wasn't a prisoner but a guest instead, and that frightened me almost more than anything else.

"Madame," he repeated, raising his voice with more firmness.

His smile was sliding away like a thin sheet of ice. His dull brown eyes looked like they darkened and his sharply cut chin tightened, the tension rip-pling down his neck and emphasizing his Adam's apple. I thought I had better go to the table.

"Comfortable?" he said after I sat.

I stared down at the table and didn't speak. My heart was pounding so hard I thought he might be able to hear it.

"Drink your juice," he ordered, the sharpness in his command revealing his growing annoyance with me. "The French toast is ready."

He stood over me and took a step closer . My throat ached from the crying I had already done. Even though I had finally fallen asleep beside him, I was quite exhausted, my whole body as tight as a fist the whole time and most of the night. It felt like my blood had frozen. With my hand trembling, I reached for the glass of orange juice. He stoodthere waiting for me to drink from it.

"It's freshly squeezed," he said. "I bet your mother didn't give you freshly squeezed every morning."

She did often, but I wouldn't speak. I drank all the juice, and he returned to the stove and brought back a platter of French toast with a small white pitcher shaped like a cow full of maple syrup that you could pour out of the cow's mouth.

"I bought this for my mom when I was ten," he said. "With my own money I earned helping. But my father thought it was too silly to put on our kitchen table, so I brought it down here. You don't think it's too silly, do you?"

I simply stared at it. We actually had one like it in our house.

"Yeah, I knew you'd agree," he said, as if I had replied. "This really smells good, don' t it?" He served a few pieces of French toast to me and then put the maple syrup right in front of me. "Use what you want."

He poured us each a cup of coffee.

"Milk and sugar? I drink it black."

When I didn't respond, he put the milk and the sugar bowl closer to me and then began to pour maple syrup on his own French toast. My stomach was still in knots, but I couldn' t resist the aroma, and although I hated to admit it, it did look good. I poured some maple syrup on mine. He laughed as it came out of the cow's mouth.

"My father thought anything that came out of it was cow puke. He was a hard-ass sometimes, like I told you."

I began to eat, convincing myself that I needed my strength if I was ever going to find a way out of here. But I was also afraid I would heave up anything I swallowed. I knew instinctively that if I did, he would probably become enraged.

"This is great, isn' t it?" He smiled and spread his arms as if he was about to embrace the whole world. "Just look at us, our first breakfast together. Freshly squeezed juice, delicious French toast, or - ganic syrup just as you preferred, and fresh brew . I don't usually eat like this for breakfast, even on weekends, but every morning will be special now. Every day and every night will be, too!

"So here's the plan," he continued, leaning over the table toward me, his voice full of what sounded like a little boy's excitement. His bushy eyebrows lifted as the dark creases ran quickly along his forehead, looking like thin stains of motor oil. "You'll clean up. Normally, I'd help, but I've got to get going. I'm never late for work. Mother taught me that tardiness is a sin. I was never late to school, either, and one year, I didn't miss a day, no sick days. I got a certificate for it. I'll show it to you later, or maybe I'll pin it up on the wall now that there's someone else to look at it."

He sat back, nodding and smiling as if I had not only agreed but agreed excitedly. He leaned forward again, slapping his hands together.

"So. I have three different kinds of cheese in the fridge, turkey slices, mayo, mustard, whatever, and a fresh loaf of honey wheat bread. There are sodas and juices and lots of fresh fruit, too. Make your lunch when you're hungry."

I almost spoke to ask how I would know what time it was. There was no clock in here, and he had taken my watch, but I didn't want to utter a word. *Stick to the plan*, I thought. *Stay mute.* Haylee hated it when I did that to her. I'd make silence work for me. Eventually, it had to work. He'd grow tired of talking, even though right now he ignored my silence, pretending I was speaking.

"I was thinking of eggplant parmesan for dinner with some angel hair pasta. Sound good? Yeah," he said after a sufficient pause. "I thought you said

you liked that. You probably wonder how I became
such a good cook. When you're on your own for so
long, you either become a good cook or you starve.
I never told anyone, but I took some lessons from
a chef I know.

"We'll have a fresh salad, of course. I'll stop at
the supermarket on the way home. Anything spe -
cial you'd like to eat this week? You told me about
pizza, and I promise we'll have pizza at least once a
week. I can pick up some on the way home during
the week, or we can make it a special Saturday night
thing. Any ideas for dessert tonight? You told me
you like anything chocolate."

He paused as though he was listening to me
speak.

"So that's it," he said. "Leave it up to me. Sur -
prises are fun."

I closed my eyes and pushed the plate away   .
Despite my need for energy and strength, I couldn't
eat much after all. When I opened my eyes, he
stared at me, sipping his coffee. Then he continued
to eat.

"You told me this was one of your favorites for
breakfast," he said, his tone of voice strained with
annoyance. "I hope you didn't make up stuff about
food, too, Kaylee."

He was still calling me Kaylee. Why?

A terrible, dark, and very frightening realization
was dawning on me. When Haylee had started her

forbidden Internet romance, maybe she had used my name instead of her own. I first thought that she had mentioned me and he had simply confused our names because they were so similar, but now I was thinking that during their Internet courtship, Haylee had never told him that she was an identical twin. I didn't think she had even mentioned having a sister. Perhaps he wasn't lying about that after all.

When I had gone to meet him on her behalf when she had become sick at the movie theater , he'd accused me of making up a story , playing a joke on him by telling him I wasn' t the one he'd met over the Internet. I told him that my sister was the one with whom he had developed an Internet relationship. Why did he think I would be joking about that, especially then? Why didn't he take me seriously?

All I could think was that she had made up things when she talked with him on the Internet and then admitted she was joking so often that he was used to that. But why had she never revealed that she was an identical twin? Why wouldn' t she have anticipated that he wouldn't believe me when I told him I wasn't her, that I wasn't the one who had started this Internet romance? Why wouldn' t she expect that he would think it was just another one of her jokes, the whole thing, including pretending her sister was sick in a movie theater? Why didn't she warn me that this might happen? Why did she send me to that dark, deserted meeting place with-out telling me he thought *her* name was Kaylee? Was she too ashamed?

All of this had come from her plan to deceive Mother. I knew that I should have risked Haylee hating me months ago and told Mother that she was carrying on this Internet relationship with a man much older than us. Now that I saw him in person, I didn't think Haylee knew how much older he was, because the picture of him she showed me on her computer was obviously a picture from when he was much younger.

When I met him and insisted that I wasn' t the one on the Internet, he simply laughed, and then he grew angry. Of course, there was always the pos - sibility that he did know but didn't want to believe it, or maybe he thought I had told him a story about an identical twin because I had changed my mind about being with him. The reason didn't matter. He wasn't going to change his mind now. As far as he was concerned, he had met the girl he had seen and spoken to for so long on the computer, the girl he had planned to capture and keep.

I had tried to run away and get back to the movie theater, but he'd rendered me unconscious with something electrical and then whisked me off in his van on a street so dark and deserted I had no hope that anyone had witnessed it and gone to the police. I could have gone up in smoke for all it mattered. I awoke in this basement apartment, wearing a nightgown over my naked body and an ankle bracelet with a chain embedded in the wall. There was enough length to permit me to get to every part of the apartment and a little way up the stairway outside the door, but I was like someone's pet kept from wandering off. He was probably afraid that if I could get into the house above, I could use a phone or break out and run for help.

He wiped his lips with his napkin, gulped down the remainder of his coffee, and stood up.

"Got to go," he said. "Believe me, I hate to leave you so soon. We've got so much real acquainting to do, huh? In days we'll know more about each other than we ever could with that computer talk. I betcha in a week it'll be like we knew each other for our entire lives, huh?"

It was then that he told me how to feed and care for Mr. Moccasin. He said he would change his litter box when necessary. He approached me and stood staring down at me. I tried not to look at him, but he stood there so long without speaking that I had to glance up at him. He smiled.

"I think it would be nice if you kissed me good-bye every morning when I leave for work, Kaylee. My mother always kissed my father and wished him a good day . It's important to have someone at home waiting for you, thinking about you, someone you can think about, too, huh? And just

think . . . you'll have something to look forward
to, my arrival. I'll bring you a surprise every day .
I promise. You told me how much you love sur -
prises. So whatcha say? A sweet good-bye to carry
me through the day? And then, when I come home
from work, you can run to the door and greet me
with a kiss, too. It's like putting a frame around a
beautiful picture of us."

He held out his arms. I cringed. He shook his
head.

"You're a lot shier than you made out with all
that flirtatious talk," he said, and leaned down to
kiss my cheek. "Okay. I'm off to see the Wizard."
He laughed and knelt to pet Mr . Moccasin. "You
take care of her while I'm gone, Mr. Moccasin."

He looked around.

"Be sure you do a good cleanup," he said
sharply.

I realized his eyes could click and his whole
demeanor would change from friendly and loving
to harsh and mean instantly. He turned and started
out, pausing at the door to look back at me, smiling.

"I hafta keep telling myself you're really here.
It's a dream come true, a dream I've been having all
these weeks, and a dream I know you've been having, too. Like you said, you'll be free to be yourself
now."

He blew me a kiss and walked out. I heard him
go up the stairs and out an upstairs door

The silence fell like a cold, hard rain. I actually began to shiver and got up to wrap myself in the comforter. As bizarre as it was, everything really was clean and fresh, scented perhaps to make it all seem like it had been in the fresh air and sunshine, or that we were.

During the first hour or so, I simply sat on the bed and waited, praying that Mother and the police would soon come. After that, I got up a few times and went to the window to listen. Once I went out the door, and this time I made sure Mr. Moccasin didn't follow me, because when I had done it the night before, I had left the cat out on the short stair way and Anthony knew I was trying to escape. He wasn't going to sleep beside me the first night, but then, after he had realized what I had done, he had decided to do so.

I went as far up the stairs as I could again and began to yell for help, hoping that maybe a mail - man or some service person would hear me. I yelled until my throat was strained, and then I sat on the steps and cried for a while, before getting up and returning to the basement apartment, which was my prison now. There were books and an old tape recorder with music cassettes, furniture, food, and a clean bathroom, but to me it was the same as a dungeon in some medieval castle. Like a prisoner , I was chained to the wall.

Struggling to come up with a way to escape, I

sat staring at the poster on the wall with the outline of a Valentine's Day heart and the words *Home is where the heart is* inscribed inside it. I had never realized how precious my home was until now . How I longed to be there, safe and happy again. I regretted every moment I had wished I was free of it and away from Mother and Haylee. Every teen-ager has fantasies like that. Now I could tell them not to be so eager to be on their own, to leave the ones who loved them.

So much bothered me about my present situa-tion—the chain, the loss of my clothes, the constant fear that he would come through that door and begin to demand more of me, that maybe tonight he would rape me—but what seemed most annoying now was my ignorance of time, not only what time it was but how much time had passed. I felt like that alone reduced my humanity and made me no better than Mr. Moccasin.

I rose slowly and began to clean up the break-fast dishes and the pans and coffeepot. I was afraid that if he returned and I hadn' t done so, he might get violent. But I also did it just to fill up time and not sit and worry and anticipate my rescue. Mother used to say, "A watched pot never boils." Haylee and I laughed at her sayings and warnings, but how I wished I could hear them now.

I cleaned the kitchen area as well as I would at home, and when I was done, I made the bed. Every once in a while, I would pause and tell myself that this was insane. *You're making it seem like you've given in, agreeing and becoming what he wants you to be.* But what choice did I have? Sitting and crying or screaming wasn't helping me. I did return to the boarded window periodically and listened, hoping for some sound that might indicate some - one close enough to hear a scream, but the silence was like a slap each time. I would come away gasp- ing and starting to sob again and again. Finally, I lay down on the bed, and despite how much I wanted to be ready for any sort of possible rescue, I fell asleep.

I had no idea how long I had slept, but when I awoke, I saw that the little light that seeped through the boards on the window had diminished. It might mean clouds, or it might mean it was al - ready late in the afternoon. Mr Moccasin had come onto the bed and fallen asleep beside me. He lifted his head and looked at me when I sat up.

"Are you the prison guard?" I asked him.

He rose and leaped off the bed to wander over to his food. I watched him for a while and won- dered if a cat felt locked away . Many were never permitted to leave the houses they were in but did sit by the windows and gaze out. W as it curios- ity or longing? I had yet to hear Mr . Moccasin cry at the door. Maybe this was the only life he had ever known. What if it became the only life

I would ever know, no matter how long or short
that might be?

Thinking such maddening thoughts, I stood up
and began to walk in a circle around the basement
apartment like a patient in a mental clinic, mum -
bling to myself, pausing to swallow a sob, and then
walking and walking in a circle again until I had to
go to the bathroom. I felt very dirty , and despite
my reluctance and the way it made me seem obe -
dient, I took a shower. The towels did smell fresh
and clean. After I dried my body, I realized there
was no blow-dryer or hairbrush, but there wasn't a
mirror anyway. I did the best I could to feel human
and reluctantly put on the nightgown again. It was
all I had, and I wasn't going to walk around naked.

I sat on the closed toilet lid and buried my face
in my hands. My chest ached from all the sobbing
I had done. I had been sobbing even while taking a
shower, when my tears mixed with the water that
streamed down my cheeks. My gaze between my
fingers settled on the ankle bracelet. He had thought
of everything, coating the inside of the metal cuff
with a soft material so it wouldn' t chafe my skin
and cause an infection. Nevertheless, the sight of it
seemed to tighten it until it was down to my bones.
It brought a sick, empty feeling to my stomach.
Even if I could break a window or unlock a door, I
couldn't escape. I groaned and then lifted my head
and looked through the bathroom doorway.

He was standing there clutching bags of groceries in his arms, smiling.

"I see you took a shower. That's my girl," he said. "As Ma always said, 'Cleanliness is next to godli - ness.'"

He continued to stand there, smiling madly, waiting for me to say something, urging me to finally talk and accept where I was and what I would be.

I laid my head back against my hunched shoulders and screamed with all the strength I had, "Mother! Help me!"

And then I think I just passed out and dropped like an empty suit to the floor.

3

Haylee

Neither Daddy nor I went to sleep until after two in the morning. After Mother had been settled down, we remained in the living room to wait for any news. Daddy sat in what was always his favorite chair when he lived with us, a soft leather recliner with a footrest and thick arms. Kaylee and I expected that Mother would donate it to the Angel View thrift store, one of her favorite charities, if not simply throw it out, after their divorce. She never sat in it after Daddy left us, and neither Kaylee nor I had the nerve to do so. We both knew that in Mother's eyes, that would make it look like we missed him. Sometimes I teased Kaylee by pretending I would sit in it. Her eyes would nearly explode with fear. I wondered if I would miss teasing her if she never returned.

There was teasing out of love and affection, and there was teasing to drive little needles into some - one you really didn't like. As I lay there on the sofa, I wondered if I had ever done it for the first reason. Surely when we were young and we were forced to spend practically every waking moment, and, actually, every sleeping moment, in each other' s company, we loved each other as much as any two sisters could. I wondered when that had changed. When did I wake up and suddenly wish I had no sister? I never doubted that at one time or another, Kaylee had wished the same thing. She couldn't be that perfectly goody-goody, even though she never showed it as clearly as I did.

If she had only hated me more, I might have hated her less.

I fell asleep. It was getting too hard to keep my eyes open and wait for the phone to ring or a knock on the door. The tension in the air was thick enough to choke someone. I didn' t know if Kaylee would be found running through some strange neighbor- hood after having escaped or maybe found harmed and crying on some street. W e'd get a call from a hospital, perhaps.

Upstairs, Mother was drugged into silence. I was sure she was hoarse from all her shouting. I en visioned her chained inside her own head, scream - ing and pounding on four walls without any exit, at least until she woke. What would the next few days be like, or the next month, maybe the next few years living with her?

"Hey," I heard Daddy say.

I opened my eyes. "Something happen?"

"No, no word yet. We might as well go up to bed, Haylee. We'll both need our strength in the morning."

I sat up slowly . "I'm afraid to go up to sleep knowing that Kaylee is not in her bed, too," I said.

"I promise, if anyone comes to the house or calls, I'll wake you right away . C'mon," Daddy said, reaching for my hand.

He helped me to my feet and put his arm around me as we walked to the stairway. This was already something more between us. Whenever he had put his arm around one of us, especially if Mother was nearby, he had immediately reached for the other. It was impossible to feel special, no matter how Mother emphasized it and bragged about us. I always thought my girlfriends, especially those with no brothers or sisters, were more special, not only to their parents and grandparents but also to everyone else. They didn't have to share love; they owned it all. There was no jealous sister hover - ing over them with eyes of envy whenever they received a compliment or a gift, no mother making sure one didn't get more praise than the other.

We didn't even have our own birthdays. I once proposed, half joking, that we alternate years. One year we'd celebrate mine, and the next year we'd celebrate Kaylee's. I might as well have stabbed Mother in the ribs with a fork.

"And you want your sister to sit there while we sing 'Happy Birthday' to only you?"

"She could sing, too, and the next year I'd sing to her," I said.

I was only ten, but I thought it was a brilliant suggestion. Daddy was smiling, but his eyes were full of *back off quickly* warnings. Kaylee glanced at me and looked down quickly. I thought she was afraid Mother would see how much she wanted that, too.

"Ridiculous and dumb," Mother had said. "I won't hear any such thing uttered in this house. By either of you," she'd added, glaring as hard at Kaylee, who quickly nodded.

How could we be the same kind of person? I thought. My sister had no courage. Maybe now we would discover that she wasn' t real. She was a shadow of me, empty and easily erased with the flick of a light switch.

I put my head against Daddy' s chest as we started up the stairs.

"I feel so sick to my stomach, Daddy" I said. "I should have stopped her from going to meet him. This is all my fault."

"From what you've told us, Haylee, she prob - ably would have found some other way to meet this man. At least you knew this much and were able to help. Otherwise, anything could have been possible, and we'd be wasting so much time and energy trying to figure out what really happened. A teenage girl who runs off on her own could be almost anywhere in the country by now . At least that's been eliminated."

"It doesn't make me feel any better," I said as we reached the hallway.

"Well, you try to get some sleep. I'm going to need you tomorrow and maybe longer to help me with your mother," he said, and kissed my fore - head.

Instinctively, I looked to my right, as if Kaylee was standing there, too, and I was anticipating him kissing her on her forehead. When would I stop doing that? The sooner, the better, I thought. Mostly, I was afraid I would see her even though she wasn't there. We were that imprinted on each other's mind. Who knew? Maybe I really would have to go see a psychiatrist.

Daddy went into Kaylee's room to sleep so he would be close by, and I went into mine. I didn' t even take off my clothes or wash my face or brush my teeth. I fell facedown on the bed and hugged one of my oversized pillows. Contrary to what I had told Daddy, I fell asleep as quickly and as eas - ily as a newborn baby, which was what I thought I was.

Mother's scream woke me in the morning. It was so piercing and sharp that it cut right through my closed door and the bedroom walls. I sat up quickly to listen. Had the police come? Was Kaylee found dead? I heard Daddy speaking softly but couldn't make out any words. Rising slowly, I rubbed my cheeks to wake up my face and opened the door quietly to peer out at them. Mother was standing in the hallway outside Kaylee's room.

Apparently, she had gotten up before either Daddy or me and was shocked to see him sleeping in Kaylee's bed. Maybe she had woken thinking it had all simply been a nightmare.

Her hands were clenched, and her shoulders were hoisted as if she had just had a trickle of ice slide down her spine. Every muscle in her neck and face looked stretched and strained. Daddy was standing in front of her , trying to calm her . She looked like she was staring through him and deaf to anything he said.

"What's happening?" I asked.

Mother turned toward me. "Is your sister in there with you?" she asked.

"No, Mother."

"Let's just try to keep our heads about this," Daddy said, holding his palms up as if he wanted to keep her from charging at him. "We'll go downstairs, have some coffee and something to eat, and I'll call the police to get an update, okay?"

"Where is she?" Mother asked me, ignoring him.

I shook my head and bit down on my lower lip until it hurt and sent pins through my jaw and cheeks, which, as I knew it would, brought tears to my eyes. It was like turning on a faucet. I flicked them away as they started to streak down my face.

"Where is she?" Mother repeated, raising her voice. "Where is your sister? Tell us!" she screamed. Her eyes were wide open, her lips twisted and ug - lier than I'd ever seen them.

I shook my head and looked to Daddy for help. He stepped forward to take Mother's hand, but the moment he touched her, she jerked away.

"This is your fault," she told him.

"My fault? How is it my fault?"

She didn't reply. She backed up a few steps and shook her head so hard and continuously that it looked like she had some sort of palsy.

"Let's just stay as calm as we can," Daddy cajoled. "We won't be any good to Kaylee if we're not."

Mother started to turn away . Her whole body began to tremble as if her bones were rattling. She reached for the wall to steady herself but didn't get her hand against it in time to prevent herself from falling. Daddy leaped forward and managed to grab her at the waist before her body slammed to the floor. Then he lifted her in his arms and carried her back to the master bedroom. Her head was slumped. She had passed out. Or maybe she had died!

"Is she all right?"

"She's all right, but we'd better call Dr Bloom," he told me as he walked by . "I'll get her comfort - ably in bed."

No, I thought. *First, I have to wash my face and brush my hair.* I was not fit to talk to anyone yet, even on the phone. When I left my room, I glanced into the master bedroom before going downstairs. Daddy had put a cold washcloth on Mother's fore- head. She was lying with her eyes closed, and he was standing and looking down at her . He sensed me in the doorway.

"Did you call Dr. Bloom?" he asked.

"Oh, I thought you were going to call. I'll call now," I said. "His cell number is on the kitchen wall next to the phone."

Of course, he knew that, but I felt I should say it so he'd know that not that much had changed in our home since he had left. I nearly bounced down the stairs and, after first preparing the coffeepot, called Dr. Bloom. As soon as he answered, I said, "My mother fainted in the hallway almost as soon as she got up." I didn't even tell him who I was. Of all his patients, who else would be fainting in a hall way this early in the morning?

"Did she get hurt?"

"I think my father grabbed her fast enough, but she's still like unconscious or something."

"I'll stop by on my way to my office," he said. "Was there any news about your sister?"

"Nothing yet, but it's early," I told him. "I'm trying not to think about it. I feel sick, too."

"I'm on my way," he said.

Just as I hung up, Daddy appeared. "She's sleeping again. What did the doctor say?"

"He's on his way. I have coffee going. I don't think I can eat anything, Daddy. All I want to do is cry. There's never been a morning when I didn't see Kaylee as soon as I woke up."

"I know. I'm not hungry, either, but we should eat something. We've got to stay strong," he said.

Stay strong, stay strong. It was becoming a chant. I was sure I would hear it echoing in every room. It was as if he and the whole house knew that there was only bad news coming and we'd better get our bodies ready to receive a very hard blow . He sank into a kitchenette chair as if his body had lost all its bones. He kept his gaze on the floor. I thought he was avoiding looking at me, and I thought I might know why.

When he looked at me, he couldn' t help but see Kaylee, too, or maybe because he didn' t see her, he felt sick to his stomach. Was it like looking at someone who had lost an appendage? Would everyone look at me the same way for at least the first few days or weeks? Maybe everything in the house would feel half used, handicapped. The plates and silverware normally for her would expect to be placed on the table and cry out to me, *What about me?* My one place setting would look awkward, and her empty chair would haunt us all. What a strange feeling to have about your own home and everything in it. It hadn' t felt as bad as this when Daddy had left, maybe because Mother wouldn' t let that feeling in the front door. She even removed his chairs from the dining room and the kitchenette. I avoided walking where they would be, as if there was a gaping hole in the floor.

"We might as well get an update," Daddy said, with a tone of defeat and disaster in his voice. He rose and called the police department, identifying himself and asking for Lieutenant Cowan. He was transferred to the detective' s cell phone. I didn' t think they would be on duty this early, but apparently they were.

Daddy listened for so long that I was sure they had found out something important. "Okay, thanks," he finally said, and hung up.

"What?" I asked.

"Nothing yet. There was one potential witness who said he saw a young girl in front of an out-of-business coffee shop when he drove by. He lives in the neighborhood. From the description he gave, which wasn't much, they think it could have been Kaylee. They are swamping the immediate area in hopes of finding another witness who might have seen more. At least they've centered on an area, if that was her."

"Every time I think about it, about her being with someone like that, I get sick to my stomach," I said. We heard the doorbell.

"That must be Dr. Bloom," Daddy said.

I sat sipping my coffee. When I heard them go up the stairs, I went to the freezer and took out one of the doughnuts Mother had frozen for a future dessert. She hated us eating sweets for breakfast, but she wasn't here to see. I put it in the microwave, and as soon as it was heated, I practically gobbled it down. I was still a little hungry, but I heard them coming back downstairs. They paused to look in on me.

"How is she?" I asked quickly.

"She'll rest. I don' t want you getting yourself sick now," Dr. Bloom told me. "Your dad and mom need you to help. Make sure you eat, hear?"

I nodded. "But I can' t right now, Dr. Bloom. My stomach feels too weak. I'll just throw up what I eat."

"Eat small portions frequently," he said.

"What about Mother? She has to eat some - thing."

"The doctor's giving her smaller dosages of a tranquilizer for now. I'll see if I can get her to eat in a few hours or so," Daddy said.

"Call me if there are any changes," Dr . Bloom said. He nodded at me, and then Daddy followed him to the door, where they spoke some more.

Daddy returned to the kitchen and made some toast for us and poured himself a fresh cup of coffee.

"I guess I'd better call the relatives," he said as he worked.

I doubted any of them would come to help us.

Daddy's parents were living in   a Florida development for retired people and didn'   t travel anymore. Mother's father had died when she was in college, and her mother, our grandmother, Nana Clara Beth, had remarried and lived in Arizona. Her new husband had children of his own, and we sensed early on that Mother resented how our grandmother doted on her new husband's children more than she did on her or on us. Mother was an only child.

Daddy had two brothers. His older brother, Uncle Jack, had gone into the military and was stationed in Germany. He had a wife and two children, a boy, Philip, now eight, and a girl, Arlene, now ten. Daddy's younger brother, Uncle Bret, was a salesman for a drug company. He was married with three children—Tim, Donald, and Jack, who were five, six, and seven. They lived in Hawaii, so we saw little of them.

Daddy served me some toast and put some jam

out. I stared at it. The doughnut was enough, but I couldn't tell him. Actually, I was feeling a little nauseated.

"Try to do what the doc said, Haylee." He took a bite of his toast and jam.

I picked up a piece and nibbled at it. "I could take Mother's car and go looking for her," I said.

"Oh, no. God, no, Haylee. All I need is some - thing to happen to you now."

"At least I would feel like I was doing some - thing."

"There will be plenty for you to do. Y our mother won't be herself for a while."

A while? If Kaylee doesn't return, she'll never be herself, I thought. I was sure he knew that, too, but was just trying to make me feel better. He took a few more bites of his toast, drank his coffee, and rose.

"I'll go up to check on her and make some calls while I'm there," he said.

"Okay," I replied, my voice tiny and thin like a five-year-old's. "I'm going back to my room in a few minutes, too. It feels so strange being down here without Kaylee," I said mournfully. "It's like I feel ... naked."

"Sure. Rest. I'll call you right away if I hear any thing." He left the kitchen.

How should I spend the day? I wondered. Was Kaylee's disappearance news yet? The police had her picture. Would it be on television already? Were newspaper reporters getting ready to interview us? What should I say when my friends found out? They'd be falling all over themselves trying to be the first to speak to me.

I'll pick up the receiver if they call my landline, say hello, and then immediately say I can't talk and hang up. If they call my cell phone, I won't answer and will just let it go to voice mail. They'll be all abuzz about it and might even come over to see me. I won't see them. Not yet, I thought. *I'll have Daddy tell them I can't see anyone.*

Who will they feel sorrier for, me or Kaylee?

Or will Mother be right again and they'll feel sorry for us both equally?

I can't even have my own pity.

Not yet.

But I would. Someday soon, I would.

4

Kaylee

I awoke in his arms as he was carrying me to the bed. He put me down gently. I was still shaking.

"I'm sorry," he said. "I'm sorry I left you alone so long so soon after you arrived. I was dumb to do that and not very considerate. I'm sure it's difficult getting used to a new home, but I don' t take sick days, and I didn't want my boss asking all sorts of questions. People can be so nosy because they're bored sick with their own damn lives. They're al - ways trying to find out what I do, where I go, who the hell I see."

He smiled and nodded again as if I had re - sponded. It was eerie, because when he did that, I almost believed I had. My deliberately forced mute- ness wasn't bothering him.

"Right," he said. "We'll have all night and all day tomorrow and all night tomorrow, too."

I realized I wasn't going to change his mind or frighten him into letting me go by refusing to speak. Besides, I still hoped that I could somehow persuade him to let me go because I was the wrong sister and this wasn't going to work or please him. I wasn't the one who supposedly fell in love with him over the Internet. Just how cozy and lovey-dovey had Haylee been with him? How sick was the whole thing? She was capable of saying some very sexy things.

It was time I confronted him, I thought.

"You didn't leave me alone just after I arrived. I didn't arrive," I said. "You knocked me out and brought me here. You abducted me. You'll go to jail and have to live in a cell that will be nothing com - pared to this, and you won' t have Mr. Moccasin, either, to keep you company. Just let me go home, and nothing more will happen."

He folded his arms across his chest and nodded. "You know what this is?" he said, widening his eyes as if he had just had a brilliant realization. "It's like what performers go through when they first go onstage in front of an audience. I heard about it. It's them butterflies in your stomach sorta thing, right? You're just nervous we won't do well together, but I'm not, and soon you won't be, either. I know this is gonna be just great like we planned. Hey, you came up with a lot of the ideas, Kaylee. Just try to relax, and it'll all work out. I swear," he said.

"Ideas? What ideas? Did I tell you I'd like being chained to a wall? Did I tell you I wanted you to take away all my clothes?"

He held his smile as if he hadn' t heard me. *He hears only what he wants*, I thought. How could I ever get through to someone like that, someone with a built-in filter to keep out anything that opposed what he wanted? I might as well talk to the wall.

"I know all your favorite games, and you're going to teach me some of them modern dance steps, remember?" he asked. "I got the music you told me to get you, and guess what' s in that bag there. That's right, a CD player. Tell you the truth, I never had one. That old tape recorder and those tapes were from when I was a kid and living down here.

"I promise that after a while, when I think you're ready for it, I'll get a television hooked up for you so you can watch them shows you like in the late afternoon, those soap operas. I still don' t get it. Why do they call them soap? Are they clean or something?" He laughed. "Y ou said you were going to find out for me, do some research on your computer, but you musta forgot, huh?"

Teach him how to dance? Choose music for him to buy? Why did Haylee construct so many specific things in this fantasy? How could she not see how sick it was? On the other hand, I knew how she enjoyed playing with boys, teasing them and flirting. She was like Scarlett O'Hara in *Gone with the Wind*, keeping all the men on a hook, promising to dance or eat with each.

"Don't boys look like bees around a flower when they hover near me, Kaylee?" she had asked me more than once.

"They look like idiots," I'd told her.

She didn't like that. As usual, she called me jealous.

"So," Anthony said now, slapping his hands together as if all disagreements were settled amicably. "What say I start on our great dinner? Bet you're hungry. What did you have for lunch?"

"I didn't eat lunch. I didn' t know what time it was. You took my watch, and there' s no clock here."

"You don't need to eat by a clock, Kaylee. You eat when you're hungry. I bet you're twice as hungry as I am because you didn' t eat lunch. I'll get right to it. Glad you took yourself a shower . I'm bringing you some clothes in a while. Y ou should dress for dinner tonight. It's special, being our first dinner. We'll do candlelight. Y ou said you liked that, and I brought the candleholders and candles down. And yeah, we'll play music, and you'll tell me more about yourself. I want to hear why your parents got divorced and how you felt about it. You never said. You just said they got divorced. Conversation. That's what makes a dinner special. So you can imagine what it's been like for me eating dinner alone all these years, huh? Mr . Moccasin doesn' t talk much," he added, and smiled.

He went to the kitchen area, whistling. I lay there thinking, wondering how I could frighten him enough to get him to let me go. Would he ever? Wouldn't he be afraid that I would have the police go after him for what he had done already? Could I ever convince him that he had made a mistake, and if I did, how would he react? Would he be sorry, or would he become the frightened one and maybe do something even more terrible to me?

Think, Kaylee, I told myself. *Think, think, think, and stop feeling sorry for yourself. You'll never get out of here if you don't think.*

When someone is imprisoned like this and has so little choice about everything involving her, she can feel so defeated she simply gives up. I felt like a puppet on a string. The more he pulled and pushed, the less I felt like resisting. What good would it do?

Once, when I was having a discussion with Mr Feldman, my English teacher, about *Huckleberry Finn,* he had made a big thing of Huck' s decision to help the slave Jim even though he believed it meant he would go to hell. That's what he had been taught in the Southern world in which he had grown up.

"What makes him heroic was he was willing. He chose to do it, and making a choice gave him meaning," Mr. Feldman had explained. "It's important to be able to choose. Think of this," he'd contin - ued. "You're caught in a current that is taking you downstream, and you can't fight it. What can you do to keep your identity?"

"What?" I had asked.

"You swim faster than the current. Y ou're the one making that choice. Understand?"

"Yes," I'd said.

Yes, I thought now. *That will be how I deal with this, how I might stop feeling like a puppet.*

I sat up. *Show courage*, I told myself. *Show strength. No more fainting. Swim faster than the current. Embrace his madness, and get him to give up on you.*

"I'd like to see the clothes before dinner," I said in the tone of a demand.

He stopped working and turned to me. "Huh?"

"I want to choose what to wear for dinner. Bring all you have right now. I can't just throw something on. I need time to make it right."

He stared at me a moment.

I held my breath. Would he get violently angry? Would he tell me I couldn' t order him to do any - thing?

He smiled. Then he shrugged and nodded. "Yeah, you're right. Of course. Girls like that. I shoulda known. Sorry. I'll get right on it."

"And shoes," I said. "I don't like walking on my bare feet. Your mother's shoes might not fit me, so bring slippers, too, and some stockings or socks."

He nodded again and started for the door.

"Wait. I need a hairbrush. You didn't put a hair-brush in here."

"Hairbrush? Right. Sorry," he said. "Oh, I don't have any lipstick or nail polish, any stuff like that. It all went bad or got hard or something."

"So you'll buy some. I'll give you a list. My nail polish is worn away, and I don't want my lips to get too dry. Get me a pencil and a pad to write on."

"Buy some? Yeah, right. I'll do that, but not tonight," he said.

"And bringing me a hairbrush won' t help if I have no mirror. There's no mirror in the bathroom. I need a mirror."

He stood there thinking. "I broke the mirror in there years ago and never replaced it. W orried about bad luck, or maybe I didn't like the face look-ing back at me, huh?" He laughed. "It' s a happier face now, so I'll like it. Yeah, I got a mirror I can put up. Sorry I didn't think of it. It's been a long time since I thought about what a woman needs."

Excited, he hurried out, and I stood. I had to figure out a way to get the chain detached from my ankle. That would be my first chore. *I'm not going to just lie around crying and begging. I'll fight back in every way I can*, I thought, and suddenly had a new surge of energy.

When he returned, he had his arms full of garments and socks, with a hairbrush and a mirror on top. He brought it all to the sofa and put the items down carefully. He had a pair of light-blue slippers that he held up quickly.

"You were right about my mother's shoes. She had big feet for a woman. These are mine. They're big, too, but I'm sure you'll get around in them."

"What about my own shoes?"

"Got rid of all that. I don' t want you having memories of an unhappier time."

Unhappier time? How could he think this would be happier for me?

"I need shoes. What good are nice clothes if you don't have shoes, too?"

"Yeah, sure. I'll buy you new shoes and some boots. Yes, you'll need boots someday, and newer socks. You do what you said. You make a list. There's a pencil and some paper on the shelf there with the books. Let me put this mirror up," he said, showing me the small round mirror in an ivory frame. "I took it from my mother's bedroom." He went into the bathroom, and I approached the pile of clothes and began to separate the garments.

There were three more nightgowns, two skirts, two blouses, and a ruby-red dress with an embroidered bodice. All of it looked like it would float on me the way the nightgown I was wearing did. His mother must have been stout with a heavy bosom, I thought.

"Couldn't you at least have saved my own panties and bra?" I asked when he came out of the bathroom.

"You don't need that stuff now. Later," he said. "Rome wasn't built in a day." He was getting testy. Maybe I had pushed him a little too far, but I couldn't stop now. I had him doing things for me.

"How can I wear this?" I asked, holding up the dress. "It's so big."

"I'll fix it tomorrow. Do the best you can for now. There's a belt in that pile. Just tie it around your waist. You've got your hairbrush. Go do your hair and put on the dress," he ordered. "I've got to get back to our dinner. No more interruptions."

I saw how easily he grew impatient. That was my plan, to get him frustrated. It was dangerous, I knew, but if I could get him to be disgusted enough with me, perhaps he would say we weren't meant for each other and send me away. The trick, I thought, was not to whine and cry but to complain, complain, and complain without sounding too pathetic. He wouldn't believe it if I sounded like a spoiled young woman.

"There's not enough light in here," I said from the bathroom. "Can't you put in a stronger bulb?"

"No," he said, without looking back at me. "The fixture can't take a bigger bulb."

"Well, there's not enough light. Maybe you could get a bigger fixture."

"I'll look into it," he said, the irritation building.

I slipped off the nightgown, cowering behind the little wall space that would block me from view, and put on the ruby dress. It was ridiculous even when I tied the belt around my waist. His mother must have been very tall, too. The hem touched the floor. Mr. Moccasin came to the doorway and gazed at me.

"I look stupid, don't I, Mr. Moccasin?" I said.

Anthony turned around. "You don't look stupid. You can't look stupid in my mother's things."

"They're nice, but they don' t fit. It's not even close. Did you really throw away my clothes?" I asked. "Can't I have them back until you fix these or get me something new?"

"I threw them in the Salvation Army collection box near where I work. They're gone. Make do for now," he ordered. "Y ou're ruining the mood for our first romantic dinner with all these complaints."

"It's easier for a man," I said. "All you do is throw something on and brush your hair quickly."

He smiled. "My mother used ta say something like that. My father would just growl back at her . At least, that's what it sounded like to me, a growl. He was half pack dog. And he had a lot more hair on him than I do. Well, I do, but I shave it," he said. "He had as much hair on his back as most guys have on their heads. I get a barber to do my back. Maybe you'll do it for me now."

The expression on my face brought a smile to his.

"Don't worry. I won't ask you to do that. Girls have weak stomachs, I know. My mother wouldn't do his back, and he wouldn't let anyone else do it. So most of the time, he looked like an ape when he was naked.

"Hey," he said, waving a stirring fork at me, "don't fret. You look damn pretty, even in a dress too big. You got the hair. I know how proud you are of it, too. My bad. I shoulda brought down one of her hair ribbons. I'll remember next time. She had lots of that stuff. I buried it all in a carton in the closet in her bedroom."

He turned back to his stove. "You set the table," he ordered.

I walked slowly, afraid that I would trip over the hem of the dress. As I was carrying the dishes to the table, a salad plate slipped and shattered into small pieces as soon as it hit an uncovered part of the floor. I froze, staring down at it.

Trembling, I turned to him. He was glaring at me, all softness gone from his face.

"Those are my grandmother's dishes," he said slowly. "How could you be so damn clumsy? Don't you care about the value of older things, family treasures?"

My shoulders shook. *I can't do this*, I thought. *I can't pretend in order to make him happy and keep him from doing something terrible to me.*

It was making me too sick inside. Tears began to trickle down my cheeks.

How would Haylee handle this? I wondered. There wasn't anyone, including teachers, who could intimidate her. Where was the Haylee in me when I needed it the most?

"I'm sorry," I said. "I can't do this. I shouldn't have led you on to believe I could. It was immature of me to flirt with you. I'm not right for you. I really don't believe anything I said about us. You shouldn't want me here. I'll just disappoint you constantly."

He stared hard, his eyelids narrowing.

Then he broke into a wide smile. Was he going to let me go?

"It's just one dish," he said in a tone completely opposite to the one he had just used. "Don't make a federal case over it. The dishes are a bit brittle, old.

Maybe we should have a new set of dishes. Y eah. I'll buy new dishes for a new home, but until then, try not to break any more, okay? Go on, set the table. I'll clean up the mess. Go," he ordered, and returned to the food.

He really doesn't hear anything he doesn't want to hear, I thought, *or he just refuses to*. Ironically, Haylee could be like that, too. She was the one with the bag of excuses: *I didn't hear you. I didn't understand you*. And of course, to Mother, that had to mean both of us.

I continued to set the table. What else could I do?

"Get the music going," he said as he mixed our salad. "You know how to use them things better than me. I was thinking of getting you a pair of headphones, too. I might get tired of the music you like. But then I thought I shouldn' t do that. I shouldn't dislike anything you like. See? I'm will - ing to make changes for you. You should be willing to do the same for me. Go on. Get the music going. I'll light the candles."

Where was this leading? What would happen tonight? Obviously, he thought we were going to have a romantic dinner. He opened a bottle of wine at the table while I was getting the music going. When I looked at the CDs, I realized they were indeed singers and songs Haylee preferred, some of which I didn' t, some of which I actually hated.

Why would she put those on the list? There were even some that she hated almost as much as I did.

There was so much fear rising in my body as I envisioned where all of this was headed. What had I done by being so cooperative? Perhaps all I'd done was support his mad belief that I wanted to be here after all. I had trouble manipulating dials and switches. My fingers were trembling, but if he noticed, he didn' t say. In his mind, he was probably telling himself I was excited about everything.

The music started.

"Perfect, he said, and sat at the table after he had cleaned up the broken dish. He served our salads and poured the wine. "Yeah," he said. "This is sweet, like our first dinner should be. C'mon. Sit. Tell me more about that crazy mother of yours and how she drove your father nuts."

He sipped his wine and began to eat, looking around and nodding as if we were in some fancy restaurant and not in his hidden basement apartment.

"Well? Tell me."

"I forget what I told you."

"You said she wouldn' t let you decide a thing for yourself. What'd ya call her? An ogre. That's the way I often felt about my mother, too. I mean, she's your mother, but you can hate her, too, right?"

Haylee had told him that? Was she simply trying to make him feel comfortable about his own parents? She couldn't hate Mother that much, could she?

He nodded at my salad. I had yet to touch it. "It's all fresh stuff, crisp, and that salad dressing is made to perfection. I made it for my father and mother once, and my mother liked it. My father did, too, but he wouldn' t admit it. He wouldn' t admit that anything I did was done good. Stubborn bastard. I bet Death' s unhappy he met him," he added, and laughed. "He got a heart attack right out front of the house. I was down here playing with my dart game. Oh, I got that in a closet, and I'll bring it down for you. So," he said, chewing.

"How did you know, then?"

"Know what?"

"That your father had a heart attack?"

"I heard my mother screaming for me. Go on, eat," he said. "We don't waste food. My father used ta make me eat for breakfast what I didn't eat for dinner. He'd shove it in front of me and say , 'Eat this or starve.' "

I started to eat. It was good; it was fresh, and the dressing was not bad at all. My whole body wanted to revolt against liking anything, but I was hungry, and that overpowered my reluctance. *Keep him talking*, I thought. *Maybe he'll say something I could use to help me escape.* "What did you do when you heard her screaming?"

"I ran up the stairs and outside, and sure enough, there he was spread-eagle on the sidewalk he built out of slate. He looked like he was trying to fly or something. I swear, the first thing I did was laugh. You wanna see someone get mad, you shoulda seen my mother. 'Don't laugh, you idiot,' she said. 'Go see about him.' She pushed me forward. She had long fingernails. Did I tell you that? Thought it made her glamorous or something. My father didn't like it, but she wouldn't give in to that. Her finger-nails stung like a knife when she pushed me. I didn't know what to do. I never saw a dead man. I poked him and called to him and tried to turn his head, and then I just shrugged and said, 'Ma, he ain' t right.' 'How's that?' 'He ain't right.' Truth is, he was never right to me."

"Didn't anyone else come to help?"

"Who'd come? We don't exactly have neighbors close-by."

"No one driving by could see?"

"We're up from the road. It ain' t easy to see someone lying on his face."

"What happened next?"

"Ma ran to the phone and called the police, I think. Took a while for an ambulance to come. Maybe they knew him and didn' t want to come," he said. "I knew you'd like that salad."

"How far did they have to come?"

"Far enough."

It sounded like we were on some back road with so much undeveloped land around us.

"How's the wine?"

I sipped some. He was waiting for my response. "It's okay," I said.

"Just okay? That bottle was expensive. I wanted something extra special for our first romantic dinner."

"I don't know much about wine."

He thought a moment. "I coulda sworn . . . you said you did. You mentioned some wines I never heard of, said your father liked them. I'm sure this is one of them. I wrote it down when you said it. You even spelled it out for me. You said you wanted it for our first dinner together, just like you wanted the candlelight and the music. You ordered what we'd eat, too."

"I lied, just like I lied about everything else," I said. "That's why I'm sorry, but this won't work. I'm not old enough for you, Anthony." *I'll force him to listen*, I thought. "I'm too young to be any - one's wife. I don't even know how to cook anything. We had maids when we were young, and my mother did everything for us."

"Naw. In half the world, girls are married younger than you. You'll learn stuff. I'm a patient guy." He drank some more wine and then picked up our salad plates and returned to the stove.

"You should have someone older," I insisted.

"Someone who can make things easier for you and not harder."

He turned and looked at me. "When I look at you in Ma's dress there, you remind me a little of her when she was young. I seen her pictures. Y ou know, she was married just a year older than you are. But you knew that. Don' t be afraid to tell me when I'm repeating stuff," he said. "W e should be telling each other new stuff."

He brought our food to the table, serving me first and then himself.

"You know," he said when he had sat again, "after Ma called the police and the ambulance was coming, I went back out and took my father's watch off him. I bet they would have stole it, huh? I was going to pull off his wedding ring, but it was as good as soldered on his finger. Ma got it later and put it in a drawer." He held up his hand to show it to me. It was a simple silver band. "I put it on the night you arrived."

Then he reached into his pants pocket and took out another ring.

"Give me your hand," he said. I started to shake my head. "Go on, don't be shy, now, Kaylee. Your left hand," he commanded. "Do it!"

I held it out, and he slid the ring onto my finger as if he had known it would fit because he had sized it. I stared at it in disbelief. It was silver , too, but with very tiny diamonds embedded in it.

He held my hand. "Do you, Kaylee Alexander, take Anthony Cabot as your loving husband?"

"That's not my name," I said. "My name is Kaylee Fitzgerald." Haylee had given him a false name.

"It doesn't matter what your name was. Now your name will be Kaylee Cabot. Well?"

I tried to pull my fingers out of his hand, but he tightened his grip so hard that it hurt.

"Our food's getting cold," he said. "You're supposed to say 'I do.'"

He didn't loosen his grip. I started to cry again.

He smiled. "All brides cry a little on their wedding day and their wedding night. That' s perfect. So?"

Daddy, I thought. *Daddy, please come home and help me. Please.*

Anthony picked up his knife. "Y ou don't say 'I do,' we won't be married, and then you won' t need the ring or a finger for it."

He put the blade on my finger.

"I do," I said.

5

Haylee

They came early in the afternoon. I was still in my room, having told Daddy that I didn't want any lunch when he had stopped by to ask.

"I know what Dr. Bloom said, but I can't eat," I said. "My stomach is tied in knots. Maybe later"

He didn't know, but before, while he was in with Mother, I had gone down and gotten a banana and some cookies. When he knocked and entered this time, I was lying in bed in the fetal position. I'm sure my body looked as tight as a fist. He stood there looking at me so long that I opened my eyes.

"What is it? Any news?" I asked, sitting up quickly.

"The detectives are here, Haylee. They want to speak with you. Come downstairs."

"Is Mother downstairs?"

"I got her to eat some toast and jam, but she's better off not being part of this," he said. He sounded very tired.

"What? Why not? W on't she be angry if she' s not included?"

"Just come down," he said, and left.

I got off the bed slowly, actually feeling afraid for the first time since Kaylee hadn't returned to the movie theater . *Detectives*, I thought, and recalled the good-looking one, Simpson. I hoped he was here, too. Just in case, I changed into a light-turquoise sweater. Everyone thought that color was very attractive on me, which of course meant Kaylee as well, but she wasn' t as fond of it as I was. I changed my jeans, too, putting on a black pair, and slipped on a pair of low-top black sneakers with pink laces. When I glanced at myself in the mirror, I wondered if I might look a bit too cheerful. I really liked how I looked but thought twice and then quickly changed into a dull gray sweater and a pair of worn blue sneakers instead. I looked back at my turquoise sweater and those low-top sneakers mournfully as I stepped out of my room.

Soon, I told myself. *Soon you'll be able to come back to life.*

But not just yet.

I prepared myself for the interrogation I knew was coming and descended the stairway as if I were descending into a pit of gloom and doom. Daddy stepped out of the living room when he heard me.

"In here," he said.

I moved quickly and entered the room. The same two detectives were here, Lieutenant Cowan and Detective Simpson. Neither smiled. They were seated on the sofa looking glum, actually angry.

"Sit," Daddy ordered, nodding at the chair across from them. I did.

"What is it?" I asked. I clutched my hands together like someone who was expecting to hear terrible news. "Kaylee?" My eyes quickly teared up.

"Tell us again how you learned about what your sister was doing," Lieutenant Cowan began. They were looking at me like doctors searching for the symptoms of some Third World disease or something.

But I wasn't nervous. I certainly didn't want to look nervous. "What's happened to Kaylee?" I asked, instead of answering.

"Just tell them what they want to know, Haylee. Please," Daddy said, standing to the side, his arms folded across his chest.

"I can't remember the exact day, but one afternoon when we got home from school, she came into

my room very excited to tell me she had met someone she liked. I was surprised, of course. My sister
and I rarely did anything apart from each other and
if she had been with a boy from our school or even
from another school, there wasn't much chance I
wouldn't know anyway."

"She said 'met'?" Detective Simpson stressed.

I shrugged. "Yes, 'met.' Before I could ask her
anything, she started talking about him, how ma -
ture he was, how sensitive and sweet. I remember
she said he was polite and timid. Before he asked
her anything, he would say, 'May I ask you something personal?' Then she said she had been talking
to him for days, almost a week, I think. Y ou can
imagine how surprised I was to hear that."

"And all this was conducted on her computer?"
Lieutenant Cowan said.

"That's what she told me." I glanced at Daddy
and then looked back at them. "Of course, I warned
her about having contact with any stranger , especially a man, on her computer but she tossed off my
warnings as if I didn't know half of what she knew
and just kept talking about how mature he was and
how he would tell her very personal things about
himself."

"How personal?"

"She just said personal. Oh, like he had never
slept with a woman. He was a virgin, because he

believed relations between a man and a woman were something holy, just like we were taught. I told her that he was probably lying, but she wouldn't hear of it. How could I say such a thing without knowing him like she did? Then she told me that the relationship was her big secret, and if I ever revealed it, she would hate me to the bone. I remember her saying that, 'to the bone.' We shared secrets, of course. She knew things about me that I didn't want anyone to know, so I promised, but I kept trying to get her to stop." I looked at Daddy again.

"And you never saw her on her computer carrying on with him?" Detective Simpson asked.

"No, sir," I said. "She didn' t want me in her room when she talked with him. She wanted that to be her own thing. Privacy was not something we had enjoyed very much of, so when we finally had it, we respected each other's. For most of our lives, we were practically conjoined twins. My father can attest to that, right, Daddy?"

He looked at me and then turned to them. "They weren't allowed to have their own rooms until they were nearly thirteen," he said.

"Nor could one of us do something without the other. We were just used to it, but when we got older . . ."

"She never said she had any other contact with

him except through her computer?" Lieutenant Cowan asked. "You're absolutely certain of that?"

I shook my head. Of course I knew why, but I asked, "Why?"

"Nothing was found on her hard drive that would trace to anyone talking to her on any of the usual websites or private chat rooms. We have some very sharp computer geeks working for us," Lieutenant Cowan said. "Any one of them could work for the CIA. Her computer is clean."

"What does that mean?" I looked at Daddy and then at Detective Simpson. Were my eyes big enough?

"She didn't have contact with any man over the Internet using her computer," Detective Simpson replied. *Good*, I thought. I'd rather be talking to him.

"She lied about that?"

"She obviously met him somewhere, some - how," Detective Simpson said. "Can't you think of anything she might have done or a place she might have gone without you?"

I looked down just the way anyone trying to remember might. Then I looked up at Daddy guiltily.

"What?" he said. "This isn't the time to hold anything back, Haylee."

"I'm just so surprised that she lied to me, but maybe she was afraid I would say something, and you or Mother would have her computer taken and studied just the way the police did."

"So?" Daddy demanded. "T alk, Haylee! An - swer the question. Where else would she start a relationship with someone?"

"There were times we weren' t together after school," I said, in the tone of a confession. "If Mother would have found out, or even if she finds out now . . ."

"Tell them everything, Haylee. A lot of valuable time and energy has been wasted."

"Well, not because of me!" I wailed. "She lied!"

"Just make sure you tell the truth. All of it, and now," Daddy stressed.

I nodded, looking like *poor trapped me*. "There were weekends . . . we had Mother take us suppos- edly to a friend's house or to a movie matinee, and we'd split up. I was going with someone I didn't think Mother would like. Kaylee would go off on her own to give me time to spend with him."

"Where exactly?"

"Mostly at the mall." I brightened, acting as if a lightbulb had gone off above my head. "I sup- pose she might have met him at the mall and then used every opportunity to meet him elsewhere. She could never be with him that long, because we had to get back to where Mother had dropped us, just like she was supposed to do at the movie theater this time."

"So she might have called him on her cell phone?"
Lieutenant Cowan asked.

"I don't know. I never saw her talking to any -
one we didn't know."

"You said you left your cell phones home.
Where's your sister's?" Detective Simpson asked.

"It should be in her room in the drawer of the
nightstand by her bed. It' s where I keep mine," I
said. "Mother wanted us to keep our things in similar places. Our rooms are exactly the same, same
furniture, everything."

Detective Simpson smirked with skepticism.

"Go look for yourselves," I said.

"I'll go look for it," Daddy offered.

"I'm sorry, Daddy. I believed her; otherwise, I
would have told about my secret date. I'm not seeing him anymore, by the way," I added, looking at
Detective Simpson. "He told me he had broken up
with someone, but he really hadn' t. It's so hard to
know who you should trust."

Daddy hurried out.

"Is my sister's abduction in the news yet?" I
asked. "I haven' t turned on a radio or television.
I've been sleeping most of the day."

"We're getting ready to release it and circulate
her picture," Lieutenant Cowan said. "W e need a
list of her friends. One of them might know something."

"More than what I know? I doubt it. Normally

we'd never tell anyone else anything we didn' t tell each other."

He stared at me. They were both looking at me skeptically again.

"It's the way we were brought up," I said, more adamantly. "But I'll give you a list of names, even though we had the same friends."

"Only the same friends?" Detective Simpson asked.

"Mother wanted us to have the same friends. If one of us didn' t like someone, the other wouldn' t have him or her as a friend. Mother insisted."

They exchanged a look of amazement, and then Lieutenant Cowan handed me a pen and a small notepad. "Give us phone numbers if you can. Full names and addresses."

I began to write names. "I don' t know every-one's exact address, and I didn' t memorize all the phone numbers, but I can go up and get my cell phone," I said.

"Please do that," Lieutenant Cowan said.

"From what you're telling us, you should both have similar lists of contacts on your phones," Detective Simpson said.

"Very little is different, yes," I said. "There was that boy I knew for a while, but he turned out to be disrespectful and a liar. He thought *no* was a foreign word." I stood. "I'll go get my phone."

They sat back.

When I was on my way up the stairs, Daddy came to the top of the stairway and waited for me. "Her phone isn't there, Haylee," he said.

I stopped walking. "It has to be, Daddy I mean, I thought it was there."

"It isn't anywhere in her room from what I can see. I looked in drawers, in her closet . . ."

My face trembled.

"Haylee?"

"She lied to me so much!" I wailed. "She lied so much. It's like a nightmare that won' t end, that keeps stretching and stretching." I wobbled as the tears came. I'm sure I looked like I might topple down the steps.

He rushed to embrace me. "Take it easy. Think. Where else could the phone be? Someplace in the house?"

"I don't know now. Maybe, maybe she did have hers with her when we went to the movies and was going to use it to contact him. It was another secret from me," I said, now sounding angry . "I've got to get mine and copy down all my contacts for the police."

"Go on," he said. "Don't say anything to your mother if she hears you and gets up."

I nodded and went to my room. I found my phone and then hurried out but paused for a mo - ment and went to peer into Mother's bedroom. She was lying on her back. Her eyes were wide open, and she was staring at the ceiling. W as she thinking, or was she in some sort of daze? Did she blame herself for what was happening? Maybe she would lock herself in the pantry like she used to lock us in when we disobeyed her. I should feel sorrier for her, I thought, but right now, I couldn't.

I tiptoed away and then descended and entered the living room.

"You think your sister might have had her cell phone when she left the movie theater to meet this guy?" Lieutenant Cowan asked as soon as I stepped into the room.

"Maybe. I guess I can' t swear about anything she said or did when it came to him," I added. "If she didn't trust me, she didn' t trust anyone. I was always her best friend, and she was always mine. It's how my mother taught us to be."

I sat and began to copy out my friends' names and numbers. Daddy went through drawers and looked around in case Kaylee' s phone was some - where other than her room.

"Don't worry, Mr. Fitzgerald. We'll get into the phone records," Lieutenant Cowan told him when he returned empty-handed. The policemen stood.

"Call us if you think of something else or find anything that would help," Detective Simpson said after I handed my list to him.

"I don't want to leave the house," I said. "But if you'd like me along when you do another search . . ."

"Better just help your parents deal with it all," he told me. I thought he was going to smile, but he walked away before he could.

Daddy followed them to the front door . I sat and waited for him.

"I feel like I'm peeling an onion here," he said when he returned. "The last thing I suspected was that one of you would do anything so weird without your mother discovering it. Meeting boys secretly? In Kaylee's case, a man?"

"It's not Mother's fault. She was trying to have a new social life, Daddy," I said. "You know how that can take up so much of your time and attention that you hardly have any left for anyone else."

I thought I could see the sting in his eyes. Before he could say anything, I started to cry . He walked over and put his hand on my shoulder.

"Where is she? Where is she?" I moaned. "What is he doing to her?"

"Easy," Daddy said. He sat on the arm of the chair and put his arm around me, pulling me closer so I could lay my head against him. "Try not to think of the worst things. Stay hopeful. It will help us all if we stay hopeful."

"I'll try," I said, my voice cracking.

I felt him kiss the top of my head, and then I quieted and we just sat there together in a way we never had.

It occurred to me that for the first time, I really felt like almost everyone else in my school.

I believed I had a father.

6

Kaylee

After dinner, Anthony brought out the cake for our dessert. It was a large, round chocolate cake, and he'd had the baker write *Anthony and Kaylee Forever* in the center of a pink-framed heart in green letters. It reminded me eerily of Haylee' s and my last birthday cake. Mother had ordered the same cake, and it even had a heart on it, with our names and *Happy Birthday*.

"I told him it was an anniversary," he said when he placed it on the table. "I suppose anniversaries begin a minute after you say 'I do,' right? W e'll keep track of every minute, every hour, and every day. I love celebrating happy things. Yeah, I know you do, too. Don' t be surprised if I bring you something extra special and very expensive after only a month. I had nothing to spend my money on before. You can just imagine what I'll do after our first year together."

His face lit up like a little child's on Christmas Day. The way he spoke about how long we would be together made me feel like a condemned prisoner in front of a judge, hearing herself being given a life sentence without parole. Who would hear my appeal? I stared down at the cake as if it spelled *Doom* instead of his name and mine with the word *Forever*.

Somewhere deep down inside me, where hope still lived and tweeted like a baby bird, helpless and dependent, I thought that perhaps my name was being circulated in newspapers and on television, and perhaps the baker thought, *Kaylee . . . that's unusual.* Maybe he mentioned it to someone, who then said, "That's the name of the missing girl." I could imagine both of them going to the police and the baker describing Anthony , maybe even knowing enough about him to give them his ad - dress. Perhaps they were on their way here this very moment.

"Like it?" Anthony asked proudly.

I nodded, because I thought that I might like it way more than he realized. "Where did you get something so special?" I asked. I thought it better to keep him talking. I knew so little about where I was.

"It's not that difficult to get. You said you had cakes like this. What this is, is thoughtful," he said. "My father never did nothing like this for my mother, even on their twentieth anniversary. He'd say something stupid like 'I'd rather forget it. That's when my troubles began.' Or 'When I was single, my pockets did jingle.' How do you think that made her feel?"

"Not very good," I said. "But where did you get this? It looks extra special." I held my breath. Was I asking too much, trying too hard? Would he realize what could happen if my name was recognized, or would he realize I was fishing for information?

He shrugged. "I was on a work errand about fifty miles from here and just stopped at a super - market that had a bakery. This old lady behind the counter did it for me. She said she wished her husband was still alive so they could have some - thing like this. It would be their fortieth wedding anniversary. I told her we'd still be together for our fortieth."

He began to cut the cake.

"First piece goes to the lovely bride," he said, handing the dish to me. "Wait," he said. "I almost forgot."

He hurried back to the refrigerator and returned with two small bottles of champagne and two champagne glasses.

"These are called splits. Cake and champagne,"

he said, pouring my champagne into a glass and then pouring his own. "W e go deluxe. First, I'll make a toast. To my beautiful bride and the love of my life, Kaylee Cabot."

He nodded for me to raise my glass, and then he tapped it with his and began to drink. He was waiting for me, so I began to drink, too. What else could I do?

I wasn't trembling inside, but that wasn't because of the wine, the food, and the champagne. I realized I was numb all over because of constant fear. It was as if I had left my body. Maybe that was good. If I could ignore his every touch, not feel it, then it would be like it wasn't happening, wouldn't it?

"Happy?" he asked. "I'm so glad you are," he added quickly. What was he looking at? Did he imagine a smile on my face? Did he not only hear only what he wanted but also see only what he wanted?

"No," I dared to say. "I want to go home."

"You are home," he said, holding his smile. Only the glint in his eyes showed a little displeasure.

He finished his champagne and began eating his cake.

"Delicious. You'll like it," he said, pointing his fork at my piece. "Eat. You told me this was one of your favorite things, so I went out of my way to get it."

Chocolate cake *was* one of our favorite things. Haylee hadn't told him only lies.

I began to eat it.

How odd it was that something could still taste good to me. It was as if my own body was betraying me. I didn't want it to feel good about anything. My rationalization was the same as it had been with everything else he forced me to do, however . *Eat, drink, keep strong, or else you won't have the strength to escape when the chance comes* was my mantra.

"Tonight," he said. "You don't hafta do nothing. I'll clean up. A wife should be spoiled on special oe casions, don'tcha think?"

"I'm not a wife. Y ou have to be married by a clergyman or a judge," I said.

"This means more," he insisted. "We told ourselves we loved each other and wanted to be hus band and wife, without someone we don't know or care about telling us what to say and when to say it. A judge married my parents. Lot of difference that made. And what about your parents? They're divorced. They got married in a church, right? Might as well have been married in a whorehouse. That' s what a woman who marries a man she don't love is, a legalized whore."

"My mother once loved my father very much," I said. Why I cared what he thought was beyond me, but I felt I had to say it if only because Haylee might have told him something otherwise.

"Love ain't something you fall out of," he in

sisted. "Some people get on a train just to take a ride. They don't care where it goes. Don' t tell me what's love and what ain't."

He tightened his jaw. I thought he was going to get really angry now, but suddenly, he smiled.

"That's not us. W e're on a train to happiness forever. Tonight is just the official send-off. All aboard," he sang, and laughed.

He started to clear away the dishes. Mr. Moccasin followed him, waiting for him to drop a scrap of something. I looked at my unfinished champagne and then drank it quickly . After that, I turned to my unfinished wine. I thought of them both as anesthesia. *Get drunk. You won't feel anything*, I told myself.

"Hey," he said when he saw me pouring more wine into my glass. "Take it easy with that."

"It's good," I said. "And this is an anniversary." I gulped the remainder of the wine.

He looked a little confused. I could almost hear him wondering. Should he be happy or concerned about my behavior?

The food, the cake, the champagne, and the wine began to argue with themselves in my stomach. That was what Daddy used to say when he ate and drank too much. It made me laugh, remem - bering.

Anthony broke out into a wide smile. He was misreading everything.

"You're having a good time, huh?"

My head spun a little. It wouldn't take much to get me drunk, probably because I was so mentally and physically exhausted.

He stood there gaping at me with that clownish happy grin. I felt my insides stir.

"I'm having a good time? Sitting here with my leg attached to a chain, wearing a dress that belongs on a woman twice my size, locked in and kept from my family? You call this having a good time?"

I downed the rest of the wine in my glass. There was only a little left in the bottle, but I poured it in and drank that, too. The alcohol was giving me courage.

"I can't go outside. I can' t breathe fresh air . I have no one to talk to but a cat."

"You're where you wanted to be," he insisted, holding out his hands. "I followed your every wish, Kaylee."

"That wasn't me!" I screamed. "That was my sister! Her name is Haylee!"

He stood staring, his lips moving but with no words coming. It was a terrifying sight. He looked like he was boiling over and might charge forward and rip my head off my neck. A small cry of fear came from my lips like a tiny soap bubble. I started to rock in the chair and folded my arms across my stomach and moaned. His eyes widened with surprise.

Suddenly, what I had eaten and drunk came rushing back up my throat. I couldn' t stop it. I heaved onto the table. He jumped back as I heaved again and again. When I paused to catch my breath, he looked stunned, then angry again.

"That's your fault! You ruined our anniversary dinner. You don't know when to stop."

I moaned again and continued to clutch my stomach. The room was spinning faster and faster I gagged and dry-heaved and spit. He grabbed a dish towel from the sink and rushed to press it against my face.

"Stop!" he ordered. His fingers were like steel, squeezing my cheeks so hard that I thought my cheekbones would fracture. I squirmed and turned in the seat until he pulled away and I lost my bal - ance and fell off the chair. I lay there, sobbing and gasping.

"You go to bed," he said. "You go right to bed. You don't deserve to enjoy a celebration."

He reached down and grabbed my upper left arm, lifting me to my feet. His fingers felt like they were punching holes through my skin. Then he pulled and pushed me toward the bed. When we were there, he reached down and grasped the skirt of the dress. With one motion, he lifted it off me, leaving me totally naked. I tried to cover myself.

"You messed the dress. Y ou've messed my mother's dress," he said, and pushed me roughly onto the bed. He grasped me around the waist and lifted my body so he could pull the blanket down. He dropped me and tossed the blanket over me. "Don't you throw up in our bed. Don' t you do that," he warned. I held my breath and kept my eyes closed. My heart was turning like the wheels of a train on a track, thumping, stealing away my breath. I swallowed and gasped. I was too weak to cry or speak.

I could hear him moving about, continuing to clean up, and cursing under his breath.

"Ruined our anniversary dinner . Ruined it," he muttered. I kept my eyes closed. "Spoiled. Just spoiled."

This will be over, I thought. *This will be over soon. He's disgusted with me now. He won't want me. He might kill me, but it will be over.*

Soon.

I was still dizzy, and my stomach felt like it was churning, grinding up what was left inside it. The only mercy I enjoyed came with sleep, because then I couldn't think. I welcomed the darkness.

I awoke sometime during the night and heard him snoring beside me. My head began to pound so hard it brought tears to my eyes. I moaned, and he stirred, but he didn't wake up. I did feel his hand close to my thigh and gently moved away . I tried not to rattle the chain. When I turned to get onto my back, I saw that Mr . Moccasin was lying between us. The cat didn' t move away but raised his head and kept his gaze on me. In the darkness with just the small glow of a light over the stove, the cat's eyes looked like yellow diamonds.

I couldn't help wondering if Mr. Moccasin had any sense of the evil in the man who kept him. Jack the Ripper could have had a dog that loved him. Maybe that's what I would become, his pet. I was on a leash already. He fed me. He expected me to be loyal. The next thing he'd have for me could be a tag around my neck.

My dream of the baker realizing who I was and alerting the police shattered like broken glass. No one had come; no one was coming; no one would ever come. What was my solution? I had tried not talking to him, but that didn't work. My upset stomach provided another idea. I decided I wouldn't eat or drink a thing. If I was going to die here, I might as well choose how. Mr. Feldman's comments about choice and identity seemed the perfect fit for this situation. I was, after all, like someone caught in a current and unable to swim against it.

Anthony groaned and then turned. I held my breath. I didn't look at him, but I could feel him looking at me. His hand moved slowly   , crawling like a spider toward my body . I cringed as his fingers moved over my hip to the small of my stomach, where he opened his fingers and laid his palm flat against it. I could try to fight him off, but I knew I wouldn't win.

I suddenly recalled Haylee bringing up the subject of rape when we were alone in my room doing homework. A serial rapist had been captured in Philadelphia. He had killed three of his victims, and it clearly looked like they had put up as much of a battle as they could. They were brutally beaten, and two of them were around our age.

"Would you fight or just lie back and enjoy it?" Haylee had asked.

"Enjoy it? How could you enjoy it?"

"You just imagine the rapist is someone you like."

"That's disgusting."

"At least you'll live."

"I couldn't do that," I'd said.

She'd laughed. "I could," she had said. Then she had looked at me so seriously that it took my breath away. Gone was her impish little smile, a smile I knew Mother wasn't fond of seeing because I never had such a smile.

"You look like you have indigestion," she would tell her. "Stop that."

"You could do that?" I'd asked Haylee.

"Yes, Kaylee. You see, there are really big dif - ferences between us despite what Mother believes, deep differences."

"I agree," I had said, nodding. " *Vive la dif-férence*," I'd added.

Her impish smile had popped and disappeared like a soap bubble. "Yes, *vive la différence*."

Remembering that short but disturbing discussion about rape, I wondered if I could do it. Could I imagine that Anthony was someone I really liked?

My body tightened even more as his hand stirred again and moved up to my right breast. He cupped it, his thumb touching my nipple, and then, as if my breast had caught fire, he pulled his hand away and turned onto his back. I hadn' t breathed the whole time. Now I gasped and tried to swallow the scream that was stuck in my throat. He was moving his hand over his own body , moaning as though it was my hand.

"I love you," he whispered. "I really love you."

A shocking thought went racing through my mind: *Just as he hears what he wants me to say and sees what he wants me to do, he feels what he wants me to feel about him.* It was almost as if it really didn't matter if I was here or not, and to me, that was the most alarming realization of all, because in the end, he wouldn't see my pain or hear a cry. He might not even notice if I didn' t eat or drink. My death might come as a total surprise.

The tension in my body exhausted me. De - spite my determination to stay awake, I dozed on and off. Maybe I just didn' t want to hear him or see what he was doing. I did turn onto my side so my back would be to him. The morning light that penetrated through the gaps in the boards on the windows seemed to tiptoe its way through the dim basement apartment to the bed as if it was afraid of being discovered.

I heard him get up, but I didn' t turn. I cringed in anticipation, but he didn't touch me or speak to me. I could hear him putting some cat food into Mr. Moccasin's dish and giving him some water . He spoke to the cat, complimenting him on how well behaved he was. I think he said it loud so I would hear. After that, he went out and up the short stairway.

I sat up and quickly located the nightgown I had been wearing before he'd brought me his mother's clothes and put it on. Then, despite what I had planned, I got myself some water. My throat was painfully dry. How was I going to go on a hunger strike if I couldn't even begin? I felt utterly defeated. I returned to the bed and sat staring down at the floor. Minutes later, he returned. I heard him enter, but I didn't look at him.

"Well, you're up," he said. "I hope you're feel-ing better. Got to learn to control that happiness. Ma used ta say too much good time leads to bad times."

I still didn't look at him.

"However, since you were so excited about our

anniversary dinner and so happy to be here now , I decided you didn' t need that chain," he said. "I want you to really feel at home."

I turned in surprise as he approached me. He was stark naked. His skin looked sunburned red, and he had a good-size scar on the right side over his ribs. There was no embarrassment in him. I tried not to look. Haylee liked to show me pictures of naked men because she knew how it embar - rassed me.

"Get used to it," she had said. "Hopefully you'll see more than one."

Anthony was smiling and holding up the key to the cuff locked around my ankle. I didn' t say a word. He knelt down and unlocked it, taking the chain away and curling it up under the hook in the wall.

"That's better, huh?"

I nodded softly.

"So. Let me get dressed and make you some oat meal. I think your stomach will appreciate it. And some coffee, of course."

I didn't move.

"What a night," he said as he crossed to his side of the bed. I heard him dressing. "It takes time. Falling deeply in love takes time, but we're well on our way. You'll find me a patient man. We both know what we want, so it's not going to be hard."

"What do we want?" I asked, turning to him when he stood up to button his shirt.

He smiled. "Why, what else? A family," he said. "I'm just marching along to your orders. A baby in the first year. That's what you said."

I started to shake my head but stopped, turned away, and muttered to Mr. Moccasin, who was sitting and looking up at me, "Haylee, what have you done to me?"

7

Haylee

It took Simon Adams quite a while to get up the nerve to call and ask about Kaylee. He was probably still shaking all over from the events at the movie theater. I didn't think we'd ever hear from him again.

Daddy had looked in on me before he went downstairs in the morning to answer phone calls. I knew he was standing in my bedroom doorway, but I didn't turn or open my eyes. He closed my door softly, and then I turned onto my back and looked up, infatuated for the moment with the way the morning light sliced through the window curtains and shifted shadowy shapes over the pale pink ceiling. The part of my brain that had always been my Kaylee part tried to project her face, with her pleading eyes gazing down at me, but I washed my own face with my dry palms, and she quickly disappeared.

I hadn't had even one dream, not one nightmare, about her. When we were very little, she had often clung to me when she was frightened by something, and I'd hated that because it brought her fear into me. I'd have to practically tear her arms away from me, but only when Mother wasn' t looking. Then she'd cry, and I'd cry so Mother wouldn' t know what I had done.

Just like she wouldn' t know now. Of course, I wondered what Daddy really thought about all this. Thanks to the demands Mother was making on him in her hysterical state of mind, he hadn' t asked me too many detailed questions. I was sure that would come, but I'd be ready for it, and if he got too upset with me, I would turn the tables on him and blame it all on the way he had deserted us.

I wondered how his night had gone. I had fallen asleep the moment my head hit the pillow , and I hadn't heard any talk or movement outside my door. Right now, I didn't feel like facing all that was unraveling, but I did have to pee, so I got up.

When I came out of the bathroom, Daddy had just brought Mother her breakfast. I poked my head out to listen and heard him urging her to eat something. I didn't hear her voice, so I closed the door. He stopped by my room again. This time, I turned to look at him.

"How are you doing?" he asked.

"I didn't want to worry you, but I had one nightmare after another and hardly slept at all. You didn't hear me, but I got up in the middle of the night and went to look in Kaylee's room. I saw you asleep in her bed and hurried back here."

He nodded. "You don't need to be asleep to have a nightmare. This whole thing is a nightmare. I just brought your mother something to eat. Come down when you're ready."

"I heard the phone ring a few times this morn - ing. That's what actually woke me. Anything new?"

"Just my secretary and some people at my of - fice," he said. "They're releasing it all to the news media this morning. Hopefully , that will bring results. Good results," he added, and went down - stairs.

I didn't rush to follow him. Instead, I turned on my television, keeping the volume very low , and I saw Kaylee's picture on the news. The commenta - tor talked about the dangers of Internet relation - ships, especially for young girls, and some male detective out of Philadelphia discussed the problem in general. Once again, Kaylee's picture was shown, and police numbers were flashed to call. It gave me a funny feeling, because although I knew the difference between us, of course, I still imagined those who knew us saw the picture and were, for the moment at least, thinking it was me. Anyone who didn't know we were identical twins, strangers on the street, would look excitedly at me when they spotted me.

I imagined someone rushing over to me and asking, "Are you the girl who was kidnapped?" They would probably think they had found the missing girl.

"Oh, no," I would say with a terribly sad ex - pression, close to tears. "That' s my dear identical twin sister. She's still missing."

I decided to shut off the television and go downstairs. First, I looked in on Mother . She ap - peared to have fallen asleep again, with her tray on her lap and little, if any, of her food eaten. I was still in my pajamas. As I anticipated, my cell phone started ringing only minutes after Kaylee' s picture was posted on the morning news. I didn' t answer, of course. I returned to my room and switched the phone off, but then my landline began ringing. I turned off the ringer, and those calls went to voice mail, too.

Daddy had just hung up after speaking to some- one and turned to me when I entered the kitchen.

"Was that the police?"

"No. Melissa Clark."

Melissa was one of Mother's older friends. For a long time, Mother had had very little to do with any of the women in her group, especially after the divorce. She had started to see some of them again when she began dating, and now, with the breaking news about Kaylee on television and radio, they were all sure to be calling.

"I looked in on Mother, and she was asleep with the tray of food on her lap."

"I'll go back up soon."

He poured himself another cup of coffee and shook his head. The look on his face frightened me. Had he discovered something? What mistake had I made?

"We might have to get some temporary help," he said.

I released the air I had trapped in my lungs as if I was blowing out birthday candles. Anyone would think I was crazy, but I enjoyed the excitement this had brought into my life. It was as if the wide spotlight that had always been on the "mirror sisters" had been tightened and was now on only me.

"What kind of help?"

"Dr. Bloom suggested a private-duty nurse for a while, one with a psychiatric background. Just to help us out," he said, "especially when I'm not here, and to help you with your mother when you return to school."

"I thought you were moving back, Daddy."

"I'm here. I'll be here until . . . until she comes home, for sure, Haylee, but I'll have to go out to do some work now and then. I still have a business to run, with many people depending on me."

"It's all right. We don't need a nurse. I'll be here to do what has to be done. I'm not going to school until my sister comes home," I said. "I couldn' t possibly concentrate on anything else."

"We'll see," he said. "I don' t want you to miss too much, and it might be a while."

"The school will get my work to me. You'll let them know, okay?"

"We'll see," he said.

The phone rang again.

"I don't want to talk to anyone, Daddy," I said quickly.

He picked up the receiver.

"Who's Simon Adams?" he whispered, with his hand over the mouthpiece.

"Her latest," I said with a smirk. "She was out with him when we went to that movie theater and Kaylee disappeared."

"No," he told Simon, "there's nothing new yet. I'll tell her you called, yes. Thank you," he added, and hung up.

"He's pathetic," I muttered. "And he was more terrified than Mother and me."

Daddy almost smiled. He widened his eyes at my remark and then offered me some toast. I shook my head.

"Haylee . . ."

"Every time I eat something, it gets caught in my throat," I whined.

"Haylee, if you get sick on top of everything else . . ."

"Okay, okay. I'll force it down," I said.

"I could make us some eggs, too. I scrambled some for your mother."

"Mother's not eating. I told you. She fell asleep again with the food getting cold."

"She'll doze on and off, probably. She said she would eat and then she would get up and come down." He hesitated like someone who didn't want to say any more.

"Oh. So she's feeling strong enough? Why would you think we needed a psychiatric nurse, then?" He was still hesitating. "Daddy?"

"She asked me if you were both at breakfast already."

"Huh? You mean she forgot what's happened?"

"I don't know if I'd call it forgetting," he said. "That's why I was thinking you and I might need some help with her, but we all might need someone with experience in these sorts of things. The effects are deep and lasting." He shook his head at how pessimistic he was sounding and then started on some scrambled eggs.

Of course, Daddy was right, but I really didn't want some stranger poking her nose into our af - fairs, whether she was a trained psychiatric nurse or not. Maybe I was afraid she would look at me and tell my father that I wasn't acting right. It was enough that I had the detectives questioning me with skeptical eyes. By now, they surely had gone to most of the kids I had listed. I wondered if any of them would say anything to put doubt about me in their minds. I didn't trust some of Kaylee's friends, but I couldn't exactly leave them off the list. That would have brought more attention to me.

The eggs looked and smelled delicious, but I poked at them as if even the smallest nibble would upset my stomach. If you're suffering because your sister's been abducted, you don't have a hearty appetite.

I looked up when I felt Daddy's eyes on me.

"Have you thought harder about things, Haylee? Is there anything else, any detail that might help the police? Surely Kaylee said something that might be a lead," he said, and sat across from me. "You two were so close."

"A lot has changed since you left us, Daddy. We haven't been as close as we were. Every time I asked her something specific about her Internet friend and warned her that she was playing with fire, she told me it was her business, not mine."

"That seems so unlike her."

"You weren't here ninety percent of the time. You didn't see how she changed. Having something of her own, even this, was more important to Kaylee than it was to me, Daddy . And we both knew how Mother would react if she found out what she was doing."

"Why didn't you ever think to call me?"

I sat back and grinned in what I knew to be my condescending way. "That's almost a joke, Daddy. If I had ever gone to you instead of to her, we would have suffered ten times as severely , and whatever we had holding us together as a family after you had left would have shattered as easily as . . . as the bone china dinnerware you bought for one of your anniversaries."

"I didn't actually leave you," he muttered.

I tilted my head and held my smile.

He nodded and returned to his food. "Well, just keep raking your memory," he said. "Like the de - tectives said, the smallest, most insignificant detail to you could be important to them."

The phone rang again, and again it was one of Mother's friends.

"I can't imagine her answering one of these calls," he said after he hung up. "When I'm not around . . ."

"I'll just let it go to voice mail," I said. "I can' t talk to people about it, either . I shut off my cell phone. If I start to answer their questions, I'll just cry and cry."

"Okay, but we don' t want to miss the police should they come up with a question for you or for me. And of course, your grandmothers will call, as well as my brothers, I'm sure."

"Whenever I can, I'll look at the caller ID first," I said, "but I hate to have to tell our relatives any - thing. They'll only bring me tears."

"There's no way to make this easier , Haylee. The two of us have to stay as strong as we can now And most of all, we should keep positive. Kaylee will be coming home."

"Of course she will," I said. Did I sound posi - tive enough for him?

"You always think of things like this happening to other people. If anyone had ever told me that someday one of you . . ."

We both looked up when Mother entered, car - rying her tray. Neither of us had heard her coming down the stairs. She was walking like a zombie. Her hair wasn't brushed, and she wore no makeup, but what amazed me more was that she was wear - ing the same dress she had worn to go out with Simon Adams. She was even wearing the same shoes. She would never wear the same clothes she had worn a day or two before, often not even a week before.

"Keri, you didn't eat enough," Daddy told her when he saw her tray.

She looked at him as if she had forgotten he was here. When she saw me, she turned angry . I took a deep breath. *Here we go again*, I thought. *Why didn't I tell her what Kaylee was doing?* But she surprised me.

"Why did you come down to breakfast without your sister?" she asked. "You're always supposed to wake each other. You're each other's alarm clock."

As insane as it sounded, believe it or not, that brought relief. I guessed Daddy was right about her mental state. Maybe she was still in a state of shock. Maybe she would never get out of it. *How will this end?* I wondered. *Will I end up living with Daddy?*

There was no doubt which of them was easier to get around.

I turned to him. I didn' t want to say anything wrong and make matters worse.

He stood quickly and gently took the tray from her. "You should rest, Keri," he said. "You've been on heavy medication. Kaylee is still not here," he added softly.

Her lips began to tremble, and then her shoul - ders shook as if she was crying inside and unable to shed a tear.

"Haylee!" he shouted, and I jumped up to take the tray from him so he could embrace Mother and keep her from sinking to the floor. He practically lifted her to guide her out of the kitchen and into the living room. I heard her tell him she didn't want to go back to bed.

"Just lie on the sofa, then," he said. "I'll get you a pillow and a blanket."

I dumped the cold eggs and the piece of toast into the garbage. Then I washed off her dish and coffee cup. She hadn't touched her juice. I shrugged and drank it. I heard Daddy go up to get her the pillow and blanket, and then I finished my own eggs and gobbled down my toast and jam. The phone rang again. I imagined Daddy had answered upstairs, because it rang only once. There was no doubt that as the day went on, more of Mother' s friends would start to call, as well as Daddy's. They might start coming to the house, too. If they did, they'd find me still in my pajamas no matter what time of day they arrived. They would see that I wasn't thinking of anything or anyone else but Kaylee.

Actually, that really was what I was doing. I couldn't help wondering exactly what had hap - pened and how. It was intriguing, like watching a soap opera or something. What would happen tomorrow and the day after that? W ould he ever realize she wasn't me? I was sure she was denying it like crazy. More important, would he care? To him, the girl he had was the girl he had seen.

I tried to feel sorry for her. I really did. But all I could think was that I would never have to share anything again. Whenever she escaped or he let her go, she would be so different that no one, de - spite our physical resemblance, would ever think of us as the same. Even Mother would have to get used to that. Of course, Kaylee would blame me, but in the end, it would be my word against hers, wouldn't it? I'd simply say she was trying to get out of being blamed for being so reckless and stupid. I'd cry about how she had often tried to blame me for things she had done. She'd often gotten away with it, hadn't she? Mother would be confused, of course, and Daddy, well, Daddy would just be happy it was all off his shoulders.

Kaylee would hate me for a while, but eventually, she probably would forgive me. She was always like that, eager to stop us from being angry at each other. She couldn't even stay angry at me when I had tricked her first real boyfriend into making love with me thinking I was her.

Of course, there was always the possibility that she would never return. So many abducted girls or girls who ran away were never found. Maybe if I began to tell the police how difficult our lives had been living under Mother's rules for us, they would conclude that she really had run away. Many times, I'd almost done so myself. They'd tell each other that this girl didn't want to be found. Why waste any more time on the case?

I had no doubt that Daddy would eventually accept that Kaylee was gone.

Meanwhile, I thought, the atmosphere here now was really not very different from what it would be after a funeral. The weather had changed since I had gotten up. More clouds had come sliding in on the edges of a coastal storm. The morning seemed

especially to drape our house in a dismal gray , as
if nature knew this was the place on which to rain
depression. I practically tiptoed about the house.

The lights weren' t turned on in most of the
rooms downstairs. The dining room looked dreary
even with the curtains pulled wide open. Just as
at a wake, we were all speaking very softly . Only
the constant ringing of the phone broke the heavy
silence. I shuffled back to the stairway. Daddy was
sitting on the sofa at Mother' s feet now. She was
under the blanket and still looked stunned. He
glanced at me and shook his head. She was always
too much for him, now more than ever . I pulled
in my lips and fought back tears. He didn't know
whom to feel more sorry for, Mother or me.

As I walked up the stairs, I wondered how
long I could be maudlin. It was one of the most
difficult things for me to do deliberately , especially looking at myself in a mirror and seeing
how tired I appeared, even a little pale. I looked
hungrily at my lipstick and couldn' t help run -
ning my brush through my hair a little. I was so
tempted to turn my cell phone on. I knew what I
would eventually say, but it was too early for that,
so I resisted.

I did brush my teeth, of course, and splashed
my face with cold water. I thought about taking a
shower and putting on some clothes, but I decided
to wait, maybe for the whole day . When I heard

Daddy coming up the stairs, I hurriedly went back to my bed and hugged the pillow, just the way Kaylee and I had hugged sometimes when we were little girls. Everyone had thought that was so cute. How devoted we were to each other , how inseparable, just the way Mother wanted us to be.

We were hugging different pillows now, I thought.

Daddy knocked and entered. "She's not making any sense, Haylee. She's blocking it all out of her mind. I'm going to look into the private nurse, but in the meantime, Dr. Bloom has recommended a psychiatric nurse who can help all of us."

"Why all of us?"

"You don't realize yet what a deep impact this is having on you. I know you're putting on as brave a face as you can, but something like this has long-term effects, Haylee. We'll all need some help."

"I'm upset, but I'm not crazy, Daddy."

"This person is more of a counselor than a psychiatrist. It's recommended for families in this sort of a crisis. Besides, anything that will help us right now is welcome, don't you think?"

I reluctantly nodded, but then I looked up at him quickly. "Maybe we should have done this long ago, Daddy."

"Long ago?"

"Don't tell me you didn' t believe that Mother was a bit of a kook, especially when it came to Kaylee and me. In a way , she drove Kaylee to do something like this. She was desperate to be her own person. You saw it all. You were overwhelmed, too."

He stood there looking at me and thinking.

I was ready to add, *and you didn't do anything to stop it, you ran away instead,* but I didn't have to say it. I could see he was thinking it and feeling guilty.

"It's not going to serve any good purpose now to blame anyone for anything," he said.

I hoped he didn't see the smile I was unable to keep from pushing its way around my lips. "No, I guess not. I guess we shouldn' t blame each other for anything," I said. "I hope this counselor or whatever he or she is doesn't make us say things we will regret."

"It's a woman, Dr . Ross. I'm sure she knows enough not to do that."

"Good. Every once in a while, I feel like screaming. I do scream, but into my pillow." I turned and buried my face in it. I heard him come farther in and felt his hand on my shoulder.

"You've got to hold together , Haylee. I'm de - pending on you."

I turned, the tears so well behaved on my cheeks, and reached up for him. He leaned down and hugged me, cherished me like he never had, and then kissed the top of my head before letting go and leaving my room.

He closed the door softly, as softly as an apology.

It will be easy to change when it's the right time to change from the devastated, sorrowful sister to the daughter who has to be strong for her parents, especially her poor mother.

I leaped off my bed and threw open my closet to consider what I would wear when it was time to look stunning. I sifted through some things and for a few minutes didn't realize I was humming one of my favorite new songs.

I slapped myself in the face. "Not yet, Haylee Blossom Fitzgerald. You're still the devoted identical twin. And remember, what Kaylee suffers, you feel, too."

For a moment, I paused to think about it. What if I really did feel her suffering? What if Mother had always been right about us?

Naw, I told myself.

But I'd be lying if I said I wasn't just a little afraid.

8

Kaylee

I ate the oatmeal Anthony had made and drank some more water and a little coffee. Starving and dehydrating myself seemed pointless. Despite all my resistance, he continued to be exuberant about our life together, rattling off different things he was going to do to make our apartment cozier and more beautiful, like repaint, lay new carpet, bring in new furniture, and build some himself, especially a closet for my new clothes and shoes. He said he had seen a dresser that would match our bed and fit perfectly in the corner. He claimed that everything he mentioned had been agreed on between us on the Internet and that actually I was the one who had given him the ideas. I had no doubt that he was telling the truth about that, about what Haylee had said to encourage him.

Even though I was unchained from the wall, I was still trapped in his fantasy . If I charged at the door, could I get up the stairs and out of his house before he grabbed me? Probably not, and then what would he do to me? Surely he would chain me up again. If I was going to escape, I had to be far cleverer about it than simply trying to run away from him when he left the door unlocked while he was down here or when he turned his back on me. He didn't leave the key in the lock, either, so I couldn't rush out, close the door, and lock it behind me. He wore the key on a ring on his belt, along with the keys he used at work. No, my only hope was to go back to the idea of swimming along with the cur - rent, only swimming faster.

"Wait a minute," I said, and then sat back as if I was giving everything he had rattled off serious thought. "Why are you doing so much for this place? Why don't we just live upstairs in your house? I know, from how my mother did it, how to fix up rooms, change curtains, rugs, decorate. I could change it all to fit our taste and needs."

For a moment, I thought he was going to agree. It looked like the idea had never occurred to him, but then his eyes widened and he clenched his teeth. He brought his fist down so hard on the table that all the dishes, cups, silverware, and glasses jumped.

I flinched and quickly wrapped my arms around myself.

"What are you talking about? Upstairs isn't our house. This is our house. We talked about it all the time, how we were going to make it our home. This is where I lived. Upstairs still smells like my parents' house. I have barely touched anything of theirs, just the things I brought to you and things we need down here. I haven' t thrown any of my parents' clothing out or given any away. My father's shaving stuff is still in his bathroom. What are you talking about? You're going back on everything we planned."

"I just thought . . . we'd have more room, that's all." I looked around. "I didn' t realize how small this place was until you brought me here."

"You saw it. I showed you every part of it."

"I know. But things are always different when you're actually there, right?"

He continued to stare angrily at me. He was opening and closing his hands, and his eyes were twitching. Any moment, he could leap over the table and choke me to death, I thought. I fought back my fear, shoving it down and under the sur - face of the pool of terror I was in. *Keep talking*, I thought. *Keep talking.*

"It's so gloomy down here with our only two windows boarded up. Y ou never said I would be

waking up to mornings without any hope of sun -
shine. You never said that," I emphasized, hoping
it was true. "It makes me feel like I'm living in a
closet. Surely you don't want that."

I hoped I was at least confusing him, but the
anger in his face looked cemented.

"What good are new things if they look gloomy?
You'll be unhappy, too."

My voice was weakening under the unflinch-
ing intensity of his furious glare. Perhaps he hadn't
heard a word after I had said the things that infuri-
ated him. His hands were still opening and closing,
as if he wanted to make fists to beat me with one
moment and then changed his mind the next. I was
tiptoeing over thin ice with every word I said, every
look on my face, and every move I made. I saw
myself as someone given the task to disarm a bomb.
Tremble too much or make the wrong choice, and
you would instantly become dust.

"But if you think this is better, you know better
than I do," I continued. It was too late to stop now
"I mean, you know the upstairs, and I don' t, so
you're probably right."

I looked back at my food, sipped some now-
cold coffee, and tried to act as casual as I could,
undisturbed. I should be more excited for us, I
thought. I had to get him to think I was all aboard
his ship, sailing to his dream life.

"When I woke up this morning, I was thinking

about some curtains for the windows. Curtains are really important when you want to give your home some warmth. My mother taught us that. I bet your mother thought the same way. Windows without them look naked, right? Just look at them. I'm surprised you never had any down here. Can you get some pictures of curtains? I'll pick the best ones. And I like your idea about building a shelf for a television over there," I said, nodding toward where he had said he planned to put it.

He turned and looked at the area again. His body softened, and he took a deep breath and nod-ded, but his breath was nowhere near as deep as mine. He nodded, and when he looked at me now I saw that his face had relaxed, the ice in his eyes had melted, the muscles in his jaw had calmed. It gave me the eerie feeling that he could put on and take off masks in a second.

"Right, right," he said. "You're right about the windows. I'll take off those boards. W e need the sunshine. We'll do all of it like we planned together. I know how to lay carpet, and I'll show you what to do to help. I'll even get you a pair of coveralls. We'll work side by side, just as I imagined we would."

"You'd better show me choices for the carpet," I said, "before we get too far . Men don't know as much about these things when it comes to color coordination."

He smiled. "Yeah. Sure. My mother told my father he was color-blind. I'll bring some catalogues back."

"Can you get them today?" I said, trying to show even more excitement.

"Today?"

"It will be something fun to do. Together," I said. "I'd like to get started as soon as we can. You're busy during the week. We'll only have weekends and whatever time we have in the evening."

He nodded. "Yeah, today. I have to do some shopping anyway."

"You don't want me to go, too, just to help choose things?"

"No," he said sharply. He saw the look on my face and added, "Not yet."

At least he believed there would be a time when he would let me out, I thought. I had to work for that.

"Tell me more about the farm," I said. "You didn't tell me enough about the outside."

"I told you plenty."

"I wasn't concentrating on it. I was thinking too much about having my own home. You saw how excited I was about it, right?"

"Yeah. There's not much to tell. It's not really a farm anymore. I grow some vegetables, and we have two great apple trees in the back."

"What was there? Cows, horses, chickens?"

"Years and years ago, all three. We had chickens when I was little, but one night my father butchered them all in a rage."

"Why?"

"Drunk and unhappy about something at work. He didn't like the mess and noise they made. I don't remember him doing it. I was asleep, but I remember all the blood and feathers when I woke up and went outside to get some eggs for breakfast. My mother sulked in a corner in the living room all day and later she made him clean it all up. But I don't want to think about that. That's why I don't talk about the farm."

"But you have acres, right?"

"Ten. Almost all overgrown. I'm no farmer, and my father certainly wasn't. But we don't think about what this place was. It's what we're going to make it now," he said, rushing back excitedly to his vision. "We're like Adam and Eve, aren't we? Creating our own Garden of Eden, just like you said once. I liked that. You know what?" he said, an idea sparked in his head. "I'll make a sign and put it on the house: *Garden of Eden*."

"Who would see it?" I asked, as innocently as I could. "You said we were far from the road and there were no close neighbors."

"Who cares? I'll see it. We don't do things for strangers or neighbors."

"Will I see it, too?"

"I'll bring it to you before I put it on the house,"
he said. He nodded at the childish pictures on the
wall. "As you can tell, I have a knack for art."

I looked at the pictures and nodded. "When did
you do them?"

"Oh, now and then," he said. "My father
thought they were stupid, but my mother liked
them." He stood up. "All right. You clean up, orga-
nize things, while I'm out doing some shopping and
getting those catalogues."

"I need clothes," I said.

"You got clothes."

"Things that fit better. I don't look as good as I
can. You want me to look good, don't you?"

"You look good enough," he insisted.

I was hoping he would go to a department store
and attract attention by buying clothes for a teen -
age girl.

"Maybe later," he said. "I don't have time now.
You women can nag." He seemed to be taking on
what he had said was his father' s attitude and de -
meanor. Then he smiled. "But I like it. Makes me
feel . . . like I got me a woman who cares. So nag,
nag, nag."

He laughed and started for the door . Then he
stopped and turned to come back to me.

"You always give your man a kiss when he
leaves," he said. He stood there waiting.

What do I do now? I thought. *Do I continue to*

behave as though I agree with it all, or do I whine and cry and threaten? His moods changed as quickly as the snap of a finger. It took everything I had to do it, but I stood up obediently and offered him my lips. He leaned in closely , his eyes wide open, watching me suspiciously, so I put my hands on his shoulders, closed my eyes, and kissed him.

My stomach churned. I thought I would heave up what I had eaten, but Ilowered my head quickly and turned away.

"I'll make the bed," I said.

I could feel him still standing there watching me. Surely he was wondering if I was sincere or not. Then I heard him slap his hands together "I'm off," he said. "This is going to be better than either of us imagined."

"Wait!" I cried, and he paused. "Please take the boards off the windows like you said you would. I'd like to have some sunshine today."

He looked at the windows hesitantly . If there was no one close by , why would he be afraid? Someone must come here, I thought, maybe the gas man or the electric man to check a meter or perhaps a mailman did come to the house occasionally.

"I don't know if I like the idea of your face in that window, looking out as if you wanted to get away," he said, thinking aloud.

"Oh, I wouldn't put my face in a window. That would be silly."

"Maybe later," he said.

He might be mad, have some mental illness, but he wasn't stupid when it came to keeping me trapped. It was so frustrating and discouraging. Was I smart enough to defeat him? Of course, nothing I had done in my life was as challenging as this, my battle to survive. How silly and insignificant to me now were all the little intrigues Haylee and I had gotten into when we entered public school and began to socialize. Even placating and confusing Mother so we could get our way didn' t begin to compare.

And besides, Haylee was far better at these sorts of things than I was. She knew just how to slip past a rule, fly under the radar, whether it came to something Mother wanted or something the school enforced. She always made sure to grab my hand and drag me along with her. Mother was more re-luctant to punish us for something if we both did it, especially when we were older.

She had tried her best to ensure that Haylee and I would always be alike. She wanted us to cherish our similarities, cling to them more than we clung to anything. Both of us began to rebel against that, Haylee far more determinedly than I, but in so many ways, I tried not to follow her , tried to avoid making the same choices. I wanted to be free to own my own smiles, my own tears, my own thoughts. I didn' t want to be as cynical and selfish. She was stingy when it came to spending her sympathy. When someone in our school got hurt or was in trouble or had family misfortune, she would sneer at those who showed compassion and look for ways to blame the victims. They were stupid or clumsy or certainly wouldn't "shed a tear over you."

Could I be as cynical and selfish now? Could I be hard enough to endure whatever Anthony did to me, imposed on me, so that I could eventually fight back? Haylee put me here. Now could I in every sense, even ironically the way he insisted, become Haylee after all? I hated her for what she had done, but I envied her for what she could suffer and yet still grow stronger. I needed her confidence, her ego, her narcissism. If she were the one here, no matter what Anthony did, she would overcome.

All right, then, Mother, I'll see if what you wanted, what you predicted and dreamed for us, will come true, will be true. I'll harden my heart. I'll smother my tears. I'll dig a hole in a corner and bury my self-pity. I'll become my sister and survive.

What was Haylee doing now? Was she becoming more like me in order to keep Mother happy? Even if she was, I was sure it would be short-lived. We would have switched places. She would be the one shedding tears, suffering openly , draped in mourning, refusing to smile or laugh, curling herself up in a ball, and inviting the sympathy she so disdained and hated to spend on someone else. How many hugs and kisses would she welcome in my name?

"I want my sister!" she would cry out, and stop everyone from talking. Dozens of hands and arms would reach out to her. She'd bathe in their com - fort, and then, one day she'd turn to someone offer ing condolences in school and say, "She was stupid to be so trusting. I can't cry over her anymore. I've got to go on with my life and do what I can for my mother and father."

And she would leave it at that, the memory of me swept out onto the doorstep to blow away in the wind.

All these thoughts raced through my mind as I watched Anthony go to the door. *Forget to lock it*, I prayed. *Be too excited for us, and don't pause to insert the key in the lock.* I waited anxiously when he closed the door, but my heart sank. I heard the lock click into place. He didn't trust me after all. I didn't have him convinced, but I understood that wouldn't matter to him anyway. He wouldn't mind my pretending as long as I was pretending what he wanted. I was at a crossroads. I didn't know which way to go, whether to fight him in subtle ways the way Haylee probably would or be submissive and hope that soon he would be satisfied and convinced and let down his guard.

For now, I had to do the latter . Despite how

much I wanted to be like my sister and confront him as hard as she would, I saw his temper . He could kill me in an instant or punish me severely . I had to strengthen myself with the belief that no matter what Haylee had said or done, everyone was involved in trying to find me, even the FBI. I'd be rescued soon. How could I not be? I told myself, and somehow heard Haylee laughing at my hope.

I went to work on the basement apartment, cleaning up, making the bed, and taking another shower and brushing my hair . I had to feel like I was alive, or else I wouldn't fight to survive. I even chose another one of his mother's dresses, tan with a frilly collar. I tied a belt around it to keep the hem up and wore his slippers. When I saw myself in the mirror, I thought I looked like a madwoman who had wandered off the grounds of a mental clinic.

What if I do become someone else? I thought. *What if I'm here so long that in order to survive, I lose track of myself and take on all the characteristics of the woman he is inventing?* Years and years from now, when I finally escaped, would I even want to go home? People wouldn't recognize me. Old friends would shy away. Even Mother would look at me like she would look at some stranger . Part of that reaction would be because I was so strange, but they might also be afraid of me, afraid that I had become truly mad, even dangerous in some way. I'd be lonelier than ever.

And while all this was happening, what was happening to Haylee? Would she even bother to look in at my empty room, or would she close the door and walk by as if it had been walled up? How long would it take her to forget me? Would she ever have a night of terrible regret and cry? Oh, she would pretend, but would whatever of me was in her pop to the surface occasionally and fill her with remorse?

How was my father going to react to all this? In so many ways, he had become like a stranger. We had seen him less and less, especially when he was living with another woman and her child. I had heard similar stories from others whose parents had divorced, with one or the other becoming so distant that the children were never sure again that there was any deep love for them. Daddy had missed so much about our growing up, especially these past few years. He was almost always unable to attend any school functions or meetings about us. He even missed one of our birthdays and had his secretary send over gifts—two of each, of course.

Was he even involved in the search for me, or was he on some business trip? If he was there in our home now, was he comforting Haylee? Despite how hard Mother was surely taking all this, outsiders would certainly direct a great deal of attention to Haylee. Surely something like this had to be more devastating for an identical twin. The image of her hugging Daddy or crying on his shoulder sickened me. After all, a weight had been lifted from her shoulders.

She didn't have to worry about me agreeing to do the things she wanted to do. She didn' t have to think about people comparing us. Once she had said, "Sometimes I feel like I'm competing with myself, thanks to you," like it was my fault that we were identical. Wasn't it simply logical that people would wonder who was smarter, who was the better athlete, who would have more friends, and, of course, who was nicer to be with?

All these thoughts were like needles pricking me around my temples. I slapped my hands over them and stamped my feet, as if they had fallen out of my brain and were crawling at my feet on the floor.

"I can't stand this! I can' t stand this!" I cried, and rushed over to the sink to get a butter knife. Then I went to the door and explored the tooth of the lock. Perhaps I could pry it back and pull the door open. Of course, the upstairs door might be locked, but maybe I could do the same thing. He was surely going to be away long enough.

I could barely see what looked like the tooth of the lock, but I inserted the butter knife and tried to move it while pulling on the door handle. Suddenly a piece of the doorframe where I was working splintered. *Oh, no*, I thought. He was sure to see it and know what I was trying to do. I didn't want

that chain hooked to my ankle again. I studied the
little piece of splintered wood and then went to the
cabinet by the sink and looked for anything that
might be sticky. I was lucky; I found some chew -
ing gum. Returning to the door with a piece I had
chewed to soften it, I used it like putty and neatly
got the splintered wood back onto the frame. That
should work.

The butter knife looked all right. I put it back
and sat for a while, frustrated. Then I went to the
window and boosted myself onto a chair to peek
out between the boards. It looked sunny . I would
never take a beautiful day for granted again, I
thought. I would probably take deep breaths of
fresh air every hour on the hour when I was free.
I'd never be bored simply taking a walk. I imagined
myself lying on a blanket on the lawn, the way we
used to when we were little, staring up at the clouds
imagining how they looked like an animal or a boat
or a face. Sometimes Haylee and I would argue
about it until Mother was nearby and could hear
us. Then one of us would point to a cloud and tell
her what it was. The other would not object. Argu-
ments, even about clouds, were very dangerous and
unsisterly.

And then there would be the nights, of course,
and the moon and stars. Did I ever—did any of us
ever—think that we'd miss seeing them? People
who live in cities with all their lights don't see many

stars, but when they do, they notice, at least once in a while.

I remembered how my first real boyfriend, Matt Tesler, was into stargazing and knew the constellations. Haylee had ruined my budding relationship with him. It wasn't long after that he and his family had moved away, but first loves are always there in your memory, like a stain that won't wash out with time or new loves. Of course, your best love will be lasting and true. That's what Mother told us and believed even after she and Daddy divorced. He just wasn't really her best love, she had said. "Mine is still waiting to be discovered. And so is yours, both of yours."

Would I live to make that discovery?

Would I live to graduate from high school, go to college, meet my love, and get married?

Would I have children?

Would the distance between where I was sitting and the door to this hellhole in which I was trapped be the last and only distance I would ever travel? Every prisoner, every other kidnapped person, surely wondered the same things. Could I outlive the frustration and fear?

I had a new one. Suppose something happened to Anthony. How long would it take before someone came to this house? He seemed to have no one. Eventually, someone would come, of course, but would it be too late for me? W ould the food run

out? New nightmares were pounding on the door,
trying to get in.

Just as I was about to turn away from the win -
dow, I caught the shadow of something moving. I
strained to look to the right, and then I saw a shadow
again, and I began to scream. I screamed as loudly
and as hard as I could. Then I waited, hoping. Sud -
denly, something furry appeared, and a rabbit looked
in at the window. I could see its nose twitching as it
sniffed. The disappointment weighed so heavily on
my heart that I sank quickly onto the chair and then
stepped off and put it back where it was.

Mr. Moccasin sat by his bowl watching me.

"Stop looking at me!" I screamed at him, and
then I stepped threateningly toward him. I didn' t
want to hate him, but I hated everything about this
place and everything connected to Anthony. "How
can you like him?" I shouted. The cat walked
slowly and arrogantly along the wall and found a
new place to sit. We stared at each other, and then I
threw myself onto the bed and closed my eyes.

I didn't sleep because I was tired.

I slept to escape.

9

Haylee

The psychiatric nurse came in the afternoon. I didn't know Daddy had definitely decided to go ahead and hire her. I was still in my light-pink pa-jamas, barefoot, bored to death since I was still not returning phone calls or answering the phone. Ex-cept for the ringing of the phones downstairs, the house was as quiet as a class taking a test.

I was never fond of self-imposed silence. When Mother would put me or both of us in the pantry to punish us for something, I was always crying and screaming inside myself. She'd listen at the door to be sure we weren't talking to each other, and if we did, we'd get more time in the "box."

Every hour, at least half a dozen people called, many of them students in our school, girls we knew, girls I hung out with, and some boys. I could tell by looking at the phone and seeing the caller ID. It was hard to resist answering, but I did.

One time, I had to go to the phone because it was my grandmother Clara Beth, who insisted that Daddy let her speak with me. W e hadn't seen her in nearly two years. I always felt that for a grand - mother, she was way too formal with us, sometimes reminding me of a mean grade-school teacher like Mrs. Cabin, who could burn you with her furious glare. At least, that was how I felt. Sometimes when she reprimanded me, I'd walk out of her room rub bing my face.

Nana Clara Beth had a voice as sharp as Mrs. Cabin's. She talked to Mother in a similar way   , and Mother was just as cold in return. When I was younger, I found it odd that my mother and her mother were so distant. It was the first time I wondered if a mother could dislike her own child or vice versa.

"How are you handling this situation?" she asked me as soon as I said hello.

I wanted to say *with kid gloves* or something equally stupid, but instead, I simply said, "The best I can, Nana. It's not easy to lose your sister , especially if she's a twin."

Most of my friends and Kaylee' s called their grandmothers warmer things, like Granny, Nanny, or Nana. Some even had loving nicknames for them, like Kelly Graham, who called her grandmother Dolly, which had nothing to do with her grand - mother's real name. She said she had called her that since she was a very little girl and had never changed it, whereas I wished I could get away with calling her Clara Beth instead of Nana. I never really felt she was a Nana.

"Well, I'm sure your mother is worthless when it comes to helping the authorities or you and your father with this," she said. "When she would get a splinter in her finger, she would cry and scream so hard that her father would want to take her to the emergency room. So?"

"She's very upset, yes," I said. I thought it was a little bit too harsh to say *worthless* or to compare Kaylee's abduction to getting a splinter in your finger. At least I wouldn't say it, even though it was probably true, and I especially wouldn' t have expected a mother to say it about her daughter . Maybe Mother defended us and bragged about us so much because her mother had not done so when it came to her. After all, what if it had been me?

"It all sounds like a mess, a terrible mess. When things like this happen, Haylee, you have to become far more mature overnight. Y ou don't want your father or anyone having to worry about you now , too," she warned. "Be sure to help out at the house."

"I will," I said, wanting only to get off the phone.

"We'll think about coming there," she added,

but it sounded weak, as good as saying *Someday we'll see you*, which she had often said.

"Okay, Nana Clara Beth." I think it annoyed her for me to say her full name like that, so I was sure always to do it.

"Is your father still close by?"

"No. He went upstairs to see about Mother," I said, even though I had no idea where he was at the moment.

"Tell him I'll call again soon."

"I will. Thanks for calling. Good-bye, Nana Clara Beth."

She didn't say good-bye. She simply hung up. I smiled to myself, imagining her look of irritation.

I realized that Daddy wasn't upstairs. He was in what had been his office when he lived with us, and he was on the phone with people from his business. I wondered if I should go in and complain about him doing anything except sitting with me and being worried sick. But maybe that was too much, I thought, and returned to the living room. I had just flopped onto the sofa when I heard the doorbell. I waited, hoping Daddy would come out to answer it, but he didn't. The doorbell rang again. I heard him shout, "Get that, please, Haylee. I'm on the phone."

I half hoped it was one of my friends or Kay - lee's. I knew just how I would act and look. I'd make sure that they'd be sorry they had come. Of course, it could be the police with some important news. I looked out the window first and saw an ordinary late-model white Honda in our driveway. The detectives had a four-door black Ford.

I opened the door to find an African-American woman who looked like she was in her sixties. Her short hair was neatly trimmed and almost completely gray, a dull sort of dirty gray because of the way the black strands resisted in places. She was an inch or so taller than I was but heavy, with very manly shoulders and dark-brown eyes that looked too small for her face because of her heavy cheeks and wide forehead. She was not in any sort of nurse's uniform, so I had no idea that she was the nurse Daddy had hired.

For a moment, I considered that she might be a Jehovah's Witness, but she had nothing in her hands to give away, no pamphlets or cards. She wore a dark-blue jacket over a cream-colored blouse and a pair of black slacks, with what looked to be specially designed gray walking shoes and the ugliest thick white socks that rippled around her ankles. She wore no makeup, not even lipstick, and didn' t even have on a pair of earrings. Her watch had a big face and looked like a man's watch.

I was going to say *We don't want any* before she spoke, but she said, "I'm Mrs. Lofter."

That gave me no clue, of course. She could just as easily have said, "I'm Miss America."

"Are you with the police?" I asked. I had no idea why any other stranger would come here if not to sell something.

"No. Dr. Bloom called me, and your father called this morning. I mean, I think he' s your father."

"Me, too," I said dryly. Then it hit me. "Are you a nurse?" I still hadn't backed away to let her in.

"Yes, of course," she said.

"Daddy!" I screamed, standing there and still looking at her. He'd have to get off the phone now.

Mrs. Lofter's face exploded with surprise, her eyes bulging. I stepped back.

"He didn't tell me about you," I said, as an ex-cuse for my hard reception. "Daddy!"

He hurried to the entryway . "Coming." I imagined he thought it was the police at first. "Oh. Sorry. I was on the phone. Mrs. Lofter?"

"Yes," she said.

"I'm Mason Fitzgerald, and this is my daughter Haylee," he said, offering her his hand.

I didn't move.

She looked at me as if we hadn' t met in the doorway or she still didn' t believe I was really his daughter.

I had to practice that look of devastation, I thought.

"So it's your sister," she said, not needing to fin-ish the sentence.

"Yes, my identical twin sister ." I didn't think I ever told any stranger that Kaylee was my twin sister without adding *identical*. That was Mother's influence. I decided I would start dropping the *identical* part now . No matter what happened, we would no longer be so exactly alike. I might even reduce it to just *sister*. Kaylee was sure to be changed if and when she returned.

Of course, if she did return, I had all sorts of good answers and excuses rehearsed for what had happened.

"How do we go about this?" Daddy asked. "I assume you've been made fully aware of the situ - ation?"

"Yes. We want to take care of our basic needs first," she began, with the tone of someone who had been part of our family for years, if not always. There was strength and authority in her voice, but she didn't sound as condescending as some of my teachers and my grandmother Clara Beth. However, she directed herself more to me than to my father

"The two of you have to remain as strong as you can and go about your daily lives as best you can. I'm here to help make sure you can do that. It will have a great influence on your mother's condition."

"Our daily lives," I said, as sourly as I could. We weren't supposed to have daily lives right now, not with the whole world watching to see how things would turn out.

"The more you work at keeping yourselves strong, the better results we'll have keeping your mother well enough to go on," she said, beginning her explanation. "Now is the time to give her moral support. There is nothing more devastating to a mother or a father than their child being in grave danger. It's indescribable emotional pain."

"It hurts me, too," I protested, my arms twisted together under my breasts. "It's my twin sister, my identical twin sister. We've been together from the moment we were conceived. Sometimes I feel like I can't breathe thinking about her."

"Haylee," Daddy said, softly chiding.

"Well, it's true, Daddy." I turned back to Mrs. Lofter. "I know what you're going to say . You're going to say a mother feels it more because her daughter was literally part of her body once. Kaylee and I were as much a part of each other as any mother and daughter. We shared every part of our DNA. No one could tell who either of us was by simply testing our DNA."

My outburst didn't even cause a wrinkle in her smooth face or make her step back. She looked as if she could seize hold of wherever she was and plant herself as tightly and firmly as an oak tree. "Nevertheless," she began in a very calm and controlled voice, "I know you want what' s best for your mother in this circumstance. Don't you? In the end, that will be helpful to all of you."

I hated the way teachers and doctors and now someone like Mrs. Lofter could play on your sense of guilt to get you to do what they wanted you to do. They made you feel like murder was less of a sin than selfishness.

"Yes," I said. "Of course."

"Then please help me to help you and your father and your mother."

"What do you want me to do?"

She looked at me so critically that I felt like a little girl again and wanted to step behind my father to hide from her eyes.

"For one thing, get dressed. Look and act as strong as you can. Your mother and your father," she added, looking at Daddy , "are hanging on a thread of hope. From what I've been told, your mother is seriously disturbed. She's more than just as terrified as any mother would be. We want to surround her now with a sense of normalcy so she can remain optimistic, so you all can."

"You want me to get dressed and act like everything's normal?"

"I'm not telling you to look like you're at a party, but for your mother's sake, do what you can to give her a sense of stability," she said. "If she sees that you're in great difficulty, that will wear on her, too. I'm not saying you should behave that way with anyone outside this house. Right now, all she can do is think of terrible things and cry . We can't keep her on tranquilizers forever, and we want her to keep up her strength. I'll be spending all my time with her, but I can't do it alone."

"We understand," Daddy said, looking sternly at me. "Thank you, Mrs. Lofter."

"Please take me to her now , Mr. Fitzgerald. We'll look after my things after I spend a little time with her and decide whether I can be of any help," she told him.

She glanced at me again. She had yet to offer an expression of sympathy or even a soft, compassionate smile. Perhaps it was because I had come on too strong and she didn' t think I was really as upset as I claimed to be. I vowed I'd make her see that I was suffering, too. She and Daddy went to the stairway. I went to the kitchen and grabbed a chocolate-covered cookie and went up after them to my room. In a way, I was glad she had come and demanded that we behave normally for Mother' s sake. I would take a shower, wash my hair, and put on some lipstick now. I might even start answering my phone calls. If anyone was critical or surprised that I was so put together , I could easily say that our special psychiatric nurse had ordered me to be so for my mother's sake.

When I had come out of the shower and finished blow-drying my hair, I heard a knock on my door and tightened the bath towel around myself.

"Yes," I called, wondering if it was Mrs. Lofter

with a list of things she had forgotten to demand from me.

It was Daddy. "She's very good," he said im mediately. "I watched her with your mother. She's already gotten her to eat something, and she' s talking her into taking a shower and changing into other clothes."

"Where has she worked?" I asked.

"She did most of her nursing in a mental clinic, and then she semiretired to do private-duty jobs. We lucked out there."

"Mental clinic?"

"That's good. She' s really what is called a mental-health nurse practitioner, Haylee. They do many of the same things a psychiatrist does, like diagnosing and prescribing medication, and from what Dr. Bloom tells me, she's had experience with people suffering what we're suffering."

I grimaced and nodded. "Y ou're right, Daddy. I suppose we all need help dealing with it," I said. Then I looked at myself in the mirror and consid ered what I would wear. People would be stopping by. I had now decided to greet them and tear their hearts apart with my deeply felt sorrow.

Daddy was still there, watching me.

"You always thought Mother was nuts, didn' t you, Daddy?" I asked, without looking at him.

"Don't say such a thing, Haylee, especially not now."

I spun on him. "Kaylee wouldn't have been so intense about being different, and it wouldn't have driven her to carry on with some older man on the Internet, if she wasn't so insane about us being exact sisters. You shouldn't have left us." I hammered at him. "You should have stayed here and helped us."

He flinched as much as he would have if I had slapped him across the face. "It won't do anyone any good to rake up all of that now . We have to concentrate on doing what we can to help your mother and the police."

"Whatever," I said. "I'm doing what Dr. Nurse says. I'm getting dressed so I look presentable. Is she going to stay here all day and all night, too?"

"Yes. She'll take the guest room. I've brought in her suitcase. I've got to run out for a while, a few hours. Call me on the cell phone if you need me or you hear something," he said. "Maybe I'll pick up something for dinner. What would you like?"

I hesitated. Despite what our psychiatric nurse advised, I still thought it was better if I didnt show too much enthusiasm too soon. "I don't care," I said. "Food is the least important thing." I really wanted Chinese.

"Okay. I'll think of something."

"Did you call the police to see what's happening?"

"Can't keep calling them too often, Haylee.

Best to let them do their work. They'll call us the moment they get a lead or something."

"I doubt that she did, but maybe Kaylee said something to one of our friends that will give them some sort of clue when they interview them," I told him. "I might invite someone over to see what others out there know."

"I don't think that's wise just yet," he said. "Let's wait until we get your mother settled down a bit more, okay?"

"Okay. I'll just talk to them on the phone."

He left.

As if it had heard me speak, my phone lit up. I had forgotten that I had turned off the ringer . From the caller ID, I saw that it was Sarah Morgan, a girl whose family had moved here just three months ago. This was her first change of school and the first time she had to find new friends. The principal had assigned Kaylee to be her "big sister" and show her around, introduce her to other girls in the class, and help her adjust. Mother had been planning to complain about that, to call the prin - cipal and ask her why she didn't assign both of us to be Sarah's big sisters, but I had talked her out of it because I really didn' t want to be burdened with being big sister to anyone. To get Mother to calm down about it, I had told her it didn't matter. Whatever Kaylee did with her , I would be doing anyway.

"It would be impossible, after all, to hang out with one of us and not the other, right?" I'd said.

Mother had accepted that. Nevertheless, Kaylee did most of the big-sister nonsense.

Actually, I thought they were made for each other. Sarah was a meek, doll-like girl with light-brown eyes that might as well be exclamation points. She was always shocked by anything I said, especially if it was about any of the boys in our school. Although she said her family wasn't particularly religious, her parents had sent her and her younger brother, Ruben, to a private school outside of Pittsburgh called Sacred Hills. She had to wear a school uniform there. Apparently, our school had a good enough reputation for her parents not to seek out another private one.

When I had first met her, I'd felt a little like Satan in the Garden of Eden. I couldn' t believe how innocent and naive she was, and I had enjoyed destroying that. Kaylee had tried to shield her from being "corrupted" too quickly, as she told me, but it wasn't long before I had her dressing sexier, wearing some makeup, and cursing in the girls' room with the rest of us. Her previous boyfriends at her old school sounded more like cut-out dolls.

"Stop teasing her," Kaylee would tell me, or , "No, Chuck Benson is not the right boyfriend for her. Don't encourage him or her."

However, I had gotten her to go on a date with Chuck to a party at Marsha Bowman's house. It had been her first experience with real drinking. Kaylee had had a hard time getting her sobered up enough to go home and blamed it all on me, of course, and not Chuck, because, she'd said, "He doesn't know any better, but you do!"

My goody-goody sister, always lecturing me. How goody-goody was she right now? I wondered as I picked up the receiver.

In as dead a voice as I could create, I said, "Haylee Fitzgerald."

"Oh, Haylee," Sarah began. "I've been praying for Kaylee all day."

"Pray for us all," I said.

"I have, I have. How are you? I'm so sorry . How are you? Your mother must be so sick with worry. My parents wanted me to tell you how sorry they are, too."

"No one can even begin to understand what we're going through unless they've lived through something similar themselves," I said. I remem - bered that line from a movie I had seen recently . I felt like a dairy farmer . *Milk it*, I thought. *Every little bit helps.*

"I know. Any news about her?"

"No," I said. "I'm sorry . I just can't talk any - more without crying. Tell everyone thanks."

I heard her start to cry.

"Good-bye, good-bye," I said, and hung up. For a moment, I actually did feel bad. I heard a knock on my partially opened door . Was Daddy back?

"Sorry to bother you," Mrs. Lofter said, keep - ing her gaze down. I was still wrapped in a towel. "But your mother's asking for you."

"For me? She asked for me specifically?"

Mrs. Lofter looked so surprised that it was nearly comical. "Why is that so unusual?"

"Isn't she still quite mixed up? I mean, she did forget that Kaylee's been abducted, you know. That was part of why my father called you, wasn't it? I thought she would be asking for us both."

"She goes in and out for now," she said. "It's the mind's defense mechanism to deny the painful real- ity. Eventually, it will pass." There was that hateful word again, *eventually*.

"Are you sure?"

"Yes."

"I guess you know . You're the psychiatric nurse," I said. "I'll be right there as soon as I dress."

She nodded and backed out, closing the door . Could this woman be that effective already? How good was she when it came to understanding what her patients were thinking and, more important, what the patient's relatives were thinking?

I struggled over what to wear. It couldn't be too

flashy, too sexy, and yet I didn't want to look drab, either. Maybe Detective Simpson would stop by . Some of the clothes Mother had bought us were so dull and uninteresting that criminals would feel safe wearing them in an identification lineup. I settled on an older blouse that looked a bit faded. It was a pink gauze long-sleeved shirt I usually would roll up to my elbows once we were out of the house. Right now, I kept it buttoned at the wrist and put on a pair of new blue jeans and blue Cleatskins. Re alizing that my first stop was going to be Mother's room, I checked my lipstick once more to be sure I didn't look too radiant. Normally, she would jump all over that, so she might very well do it now , I thought, and then went to her room.

She was sitting up in the upholstered wing chair that matched the bedroom set. Mrs. Lofter was brushing her hair when I entered. She would never let one of us brush her hair; otherwise, she'd have to mess it up again and let the other sister do it. Mrs. Lofter paused in her brushing and nodded at me. I stepped forward slowly. Mother was focused as closely on me as ever, just the way she would be when she suspected one of us had done something wrong.

"Tell me why," she said. "Tell me why she would put herself in such danger."

I shrugged, relieved that it wasn' t me she was accusing of anything. "I told you, Mother."

Mrs. Lofter stepped back but didn' t leave. She stood there watching me, waiting to hear me elaborate.

"It was exciting to her, I guess. She was finally doing something only she wanted to do. She knew I didn't want to do it, but she did it anyway."

Mother shook her head. "She never hid any - thing from me like this."

"That's why she did it," I said. "She wanted to do something dangerous, I suppose. I told her many times to stop. She thought I was jealous." I looked at Mrs. Lofter. She was making me nervous with her staring. Did she realize I was lying? "My sister and I always checked with each other first before we did any social things. It was the way we were brought up," I told her.

She said nothing.

"You're helping them find her for us, aren't you, Haylee?" Mother asked. "You're doing everything you can?"

"I told them all I knew, Mother. I offered to go out and look, too, but Daddy didn't want me to. All I can do is wait to hear from the police. I made Daddy some breakfast and had something to eat myself. I'm glad you're eating," I added, nodding at the dish and the empty cup. "We've got to stay strong so we can be here for Kaylee."

"How sweet. See how sweet my daughters are?" she asked Mrs. Lofter, who smiled. Mother shook her head. "But I see," she continued. "Y ou're so lost, aren't you? It's like you've been taken away as well, isn't it?"

I nodded, but this time, when I looked at Mrs. Lofter, I thought she looked skeptical, even suspi cious. She shouldn't be here when I spoke person ally with my mother, I thought. I intended to tell Daddy.

"I'm trying to be strong for all of us, Mother ," I repeated, more for Mrs. Lofter than for Mother . "I'm helping Daddy in every way I can, too. We've got to keep hoping they'll find her."

"Yes, that's a good girl. My girls are good girls," she said. She finally smiled and looked at Mrs. Lofter.

"Of course, Mrs. Fitzgerald," she said. "That' s why things will turn out just fine."

"Where is your father?" Mother asked.

"He's out doing things he has to do."

"What sort of things?"

"Things. I don' t know. He'll be home soon. Nana Clara Beth called," I said, remembering.

"What did she say?"

"She said she would think about coming to see us."

Mother was silent.

"Is there something I can do for you, Mother?"

She sat back, her eyes glazing over. "It's hard to look at one without the other," she muttered. "It's so painful. It's like looking directly at the sun." She put her hand over her heart.

"You should get up and about, Mrs. Fitzgerald. Best to find ways to keep yourself busy," Mrs. Lofter said.

Mother shook her head. She seemed to be dwindling right before my eyes, shrinking into herself. "It's hard," she muttered again. "One without the other . . ."

I heard the phone ringing and then the doorbell.

"I'd better go see about that," I told Mrs. Lofter "It might be important."

She nodded.

Mother raised her head quickly, her eyes widening with hope. "She's back? Kaylee's back?"

"Haylee is going to see and come back to you," Mrs. Lofter said.

I turned and fled rather than just leave the room. Mother was making me feel terrible. I didn't pick up the phone. It went to voice mail. I could hear that it was Daddy's brother calling from Hawaii. Instead, I went to the door.

This time, it was the two detectives, Cowan and Simpson.

"Have you found her?" I asked the moment I set eyes on them.

"Not yet, Haylee," Lieutenant Cowan said. They came in. I didn't like the way they were looking at me. Lieutenant Cowan opened a small notepad. "Your sister's friend Sarah Morgan," he began, and paused.

"Yes?"

"Close friend of hers?"

"She's closer to Kaylee than to me. Kaylee is more generous when it comes to spending time with losers," I said. "She felt sorry for her, so I put up with her to please my sister. Why? Does she know something that will help?"

"She says Kaylee was very upset these past few days. She wouldn't tell her exactly why, but she says she had never seen her so agitated. She says your sister promised to tell her why soon."

I looked at Detective Simpson and wondered if he had a girlfriend. He wasn' t wearing a wedding ring.

I shrugged. Was that all they had gotten from her? "No mystery about that. I threatened to tell Mother and Daddy about her Internet romance, so she became nervous. I was going to do it, too, but she talked me out of it by saying that when she met him, if he wasn' t what she thought he was, she'd stop, but I think she was playing me."

"Playing you?" Detective Simpson asked.

"To get me to go along with her plan about the movie and all."

"And you thought she might think of running away with him if she did like him?" Lieutenant Cowan asked.

I nodded. "She also threatened to do that if I so much as hinted at what she was doing on the Internet. I never saw her so determined about anything, and I didn't doubt her."

"Sarah says she's your sister's best friend," Detective Simpson said. "She says that if Kaylee were even thinking of running away , she would know . She would have told her. They were that close."

"Like, no," I said. "She wishes. She never went out with us. She didn' t even go to the parties we went to, and lately , Kaylee didn' t even invite her here. I wouldn't depend on anything she says."

"Did you and your sister fight over a boy named Matt T esler?" Lieutenant Cowan asked quickly, like an attorney trying to break a witness in a court trial.

"What's the point? Why does that matter now?"

"We're trying to understand everything, Hay - lee, so we can figure out what Kaylee's done and why," Detective Simpson said.

I shrugged. "That happened a while back. W e don't even talk about it anymore. She's long over it. Sarah Morgan is pathetic," I said. "Kaylee wouldn't go looking for a romance with an older man to spite me or something, if that's what she's telling you."

"We want to be sure you and your sister con - fide in each other as closely as you say," Lieutenant Cowan said. "Maybe there are things you don' t know."

He was beginning to annoy me. "Of course there are things I don't know. I don't know where she is or if she deliberately is staying away or what."

"Okay," Lieutenant Cowan said. "You keep thinking about it all. Check everything. Maybe there's something, some clue, in her things."

"I will," I said. "Right now, we have a big problem with my mother. There's a psychiatric nurse here taking care of her. I have to go back upstairs to see what she needs."

"Where's your father?" Detective Simpson asked.

"He had some work-related things to do. I'll tell him you were here. He should be home very soon."

Neither policeman spoke. Lieutenant Cowan reached for the doorknob.

Just before they stepped out, Detective Simpson turned back to me. "You left that name off the list," he said.

"What name?"

"Matt Tesler."

"Oh. He doesn't live here anymore."

"Where did he go?"

"I don't know. He wasn't the love of my life or anything. I guess the school can tell you about him and his family, but I don't see how it helps us now."

He nodded and closed the door behind him. I stood there fuming. That wicked little nobody, Sarah Morgan. She never liked me. She'd want to cause trouble. *I'll fix her*, I thought. *I'll tell whoever calls me all about her, how she almost sent the police on a wild goose chase while my sister suffers.*

I turned and hurried back up the stairs, think - ing and planning with every step I took. I thought I would tell Mother and Mrs. Lofter that the police were just here to tell us how hard they were work- ing to find Kaylee. I'd sound as hopeful and opti- mistic as I could. Mrs. Lofter would like that. Later, with Mother not around, I would show her how devastated I felt. I smiled, thinking maybe Mrs. Lofter would start brushing my hair, too, not that I'd want her to. She'd never do it right.

The moment I walked in, they looked at me, but before I could get a word out, Mother spoke and shocked me.

"Kaylee," she said. "Thank God, you're home."

10

Kaylee

I heard what sounded like more than one person going up and down the stairs just outside the locked basement apartment door. Then I heard the key turning in the lock and sat up, hoping it was my rescuers.

I had fallen asleep and dreamed vividly about this. In my dream, my sister, Haylee, had broken down in front of Daddy and Mother and confessed all she had done to get me into this situation. She had thought she could handle any guilt she might experience, but my empty room, my books un - opened on my desk, and me not being in my chair at breakfast and dinner had torn away her shield of indifference and left her crying so hysterically that our doctor had to give her something to calm her. She'd been shaking like someone who was freezing.

It was then that she had told the police exactly where to go. I envisioned them capturing Anthony right outside this house and then hurrying down the stairs to find me. There was even an ambulance waiting in case it was needed, and of course, Mother and Daddy were right there, waiting just outside. Haylee was in the rear of a police car , looking ashamed.

The door opened. I held my breath. W as my dream a premonition?

There was someone there, but it wasn' t any-one who'd come to rescue me; it was Anthony , wearing a broad smile on his face when he looked at me, or I should say right through me, for he didn't see a look of disappointment. He saw the girl of his dreams overjoyed at his homecoming. I thought that even if my disappointment and my fear stopped my heart from beating, he would keep me in a chair or on the bed, talking to me as if noth ing unusual had occurred. I wondered which need was stronger, his need to have someone to love who would love him or my need to escape and go home. Which would win out in the end?

In a strange and eerie way , he reminded me of Mother. No matter what Daddy said, what our grandparents said, or what our teachers and other people told her, she refused to see Haylee and me as two separate girls. She either ignored or explained away any differences we exhibited. She planned our lives as if one of us was the shadow of the other . When we were very young, neither Haylee nor I knew how to oppose her . I never denied that we needed to be our own persons, but I was never as defiant and determined as Haylee was when we'd grown older and should have been bolder. Was that wrong? Did she hate me for being so tolerant? Did that make things harder for her? W as this her way of getting revenge?

Anthony hugged large catalogues. He put them on the dining table and then returned to the door - way to pick up the bags of groceries he had brought as well. There had been no sirens. There were no policemen behind him. No one had found me. I felt like I was sinking into the bed. My rescue had been only a dream, wishful thinking.

"Got you your homework," he said, nodding at the catalogues as he brought the groceries to the counter by the sink. I hadn't moved. He started to unpack. He looked back at me, surprised. "Go on. Don't wait for me. Give it a look-see. I know you can't wait. If there's one thing women love to do, it's buying things to dress up a home. My father kept my mother on a leash, but I ain't him."

He waited to see my reaction. I'd better look and act enthusiastic, I thought, and rose quickly to go to the table. There were three thick catalogues

of carpets with samples and two catalogues of curtains. I remembered when Mother was redoing the
living room and Haylee and I had sat at the table
with her as she examined the possibilities. I recalled
some of the reasons she had preferred one type over
another. At least I knew what to say so it would
look like I really was interested.

"You can't claim you ain' t got enough choice
there," he said. "So," he said, rubbing his hands
together. "What'll we have for lunch? You want
turkey and cheese? I've got these delicious rolls."
He held one up. It looked soft, the kind both Haylee and I enjoyed. My stomach actually churned in
anticipation.

"Yes, thank you," I said.

"You don't thank me. I thank you," he said,
smiling. "You're making me feel alive. I ain't felt
as alive since . . . since I don' t know when." He
laughed. "Maybe I never did. Star -crossed lov-
ers really complete each other , you know. That's
what we are, two people who found each other in
space, only it's called cyberspace, right?" I could
see he thought that was clever. He waited for my
reaction.

"Right," I said, with as much of a smile as I
could force.

I sat and opened a catalogue. Just looking at all
this reinforced my sense of dread. It strengthened
my fear that I would be here for a very long time,

so long, in fact, that after a while, even people who loved me would have trouble worrying about me or even thinking about me. Their lives would demand that they put me aside for most of their day , and eventually, I'd be gone so long that I would be as good as dead to them.

What else could happen? They couldn' t spend their lives waiting by the phone, waiting for the police to bring them good news, or any news, for that matter. Maybe every week they'd go on a search party themselves, until they decided that it did no good. Maybe Mother would make Daddy put my picture on billboards or take out ads in newspapers, even pay for radio and television pleas, but eventually, even the news people would go on to other stories. Everyone had to continue with their lives, didn't they? The hardest things to hold back were the hands of a clock.

Of course, I wondered how fast Haylee would get used to my not being at her side. I wanted to think it would take her much longer than she had hoped. I wanted to hate her and wish great pain and suffering on her, but I couldn't do it. I could imagine her sitting in a dark pool of regret, and as hard as it would be for anyone to believe, I felt sorrier for her than I did for myself. In the end, no matter what she did, I always felt sorrier for her She hated that. Maybe deep down, that was why I did it.

"Don't you dare pity me," she would say. "I'm

not a bit weaker than you are, Kaylee. If anything, it's the other way around."

I saw her even now , my proud, self-centered identical twin sister , pouting at the living-room window, gazing out at the world she dreamed was hers, a world far different from the one we were in.

"You know what, Kaylee?" she had once said to me when I'd asked her why she was staring so hard out the window . "I prefer looking through win - dows rather than looking into mirrors. That way, I don't have to see you, too."

It was so shocking a thing to hear that it sent not only a chill down my spine but a sharp pain into my heart. Brothers and sisters could love each other more than anyone else could ever love them, but they could hate each other more, too. The rup- ture in family ties was more painful because it went so much deeper. It went right through your blood and ripped apart your heritage. Nothing left you more alone. It was the very definition of homeless- ness. You could see it clearly in the faces of those discarded and left on some unfriendly street to slowly drift into invisibility . Even the memories of them cast off shattered like glass stars and fell into the gutter to be swept into some sewer of the forgotten.

The sewer of the forgotten was where I could end up, too. It was only a matter of time, time that pressed against my face and pushed me further and further away from those who knew and loved me, even Mother. She was sure to drift into some fog where, confused and defeated, she would wither years before her time and become as silent and useless as a bell that was never rung. I was crying inside for everyone but myself. How could I change it? How could someone who had never been very selfish suddenly become ruthlessly so?

I flipped through some more pages and then looked at Anthony working so diligently on my sandwich. He was measuring out the ingredients as though a tenth of an inch mattered. He cut the sandwich into four perfectly equal pieces and then framed some lettuce and tomato around them with great care. When he was finished, he gazed at it for a moment, like someone who had just made a beautiful work of art for someone he loved. He turned to me, smiled, put a napkin over his arm, and brought me the sandwich just the way a waiter in a very expensive restaurant would.

"Madam." He put it before me and stepped back. "How's that? See? I'm really an artist. Oh, I got your favorite soda, too, root beer ," he said, and returned to the refrigerator to take out a bottle, open it, and pour the soda into a glass.

That was Haylee's favorite soda, not mine. Had he taken notes about everything she had men - tioned? What hadn't she told him about herself and the things she preferred? Actually, it didn't surprise me. She was always eager to tell everyone else what was the best this or that. I wasn't very fond of root beer, but I never refused it when she asked Mother for it. Drinking and eating things she liked and I didn't particularly care for was so much a part of my life that doing this now seemed perfectly normal.

On the other hand, if I liked something and she didn't, she would eat it when I asked for it the first time, but later she would warn me never to ask for it again, or she would find things I really didn't like and deliberately ask for them. I could have argued and stamped my foot like she often did, but it was easier simply to do what she wanted. Now , ironically, it was easier to do what Anthony wanted. In some ways, if I closed my eyes, I was home again.

"Go on," he said. "Start eating. Don' t wait for me. I know you're hungry."

He returned to make his own sandwich, and I did begin eating. I hadn' t been here that long, al - though every passing minute was more like an hour to me, and the passing of a day, despite how hard I tried to fight it, was like the pounding of another nail into my coffin. Any hope I had was changing from merely dripping away to leaking heavily out of my heart. I wanted to resist, even hate, every kindness he directed toward me, but my body con- tinued to defy my will.

I was hungry. I was thirsty. I could tell myself I

needed to eat in order to have the strength to fight, but I knew I would accept the food and drink no matter what, and I was upset with myself for it. The more I consented to whatever he offered, the more discouraged I felt. I was surrendering in little ways, especially by keeping myself as clean as I could and as healthy as I could. I knew he was pleased, and I did think that now, seeing how he simply would refuse to believe my resistance, it was futile to continue to defy him openly. I really despised myself for my next thought, because it was as if I was finding ways to justify my compliance by forgiving him, but I considered him emotionally desperate, someone to pity.

From what he had told me, he had no family, and from what I could see, he had no friends. Yes, he had abducted me and chained me to the wall, but he was capable of being merciful and even considerate. How could I really fight such a person? Would I have the will and the strength to stab him with the bread knife and, if not kill him, wound him seriously enough to enable me to escape, especially when he was asleep beside me? I'd have the opportunity, but could I do it?

He returned to the table and sat. "How's the sandwich?" He needed compliments, but it wasn't difficult to sound honest about this one.

"It's very good," I said.

"Fresh stuff. Can't beat it," he said, and began

to eat. He had poured himself a beer   . "When I moved down here, mostly to get out of my father's hair, if you want to know, Ma would bring me dinner. One day, my father got so mad about her doing that, probably one drunken day, that he made her give me leftovers from the night before, even two nights before. 'Course, I didn' t realize it at first. She still dressed it up good, but I eventually found out. 'You can always come upstairs to eat with us, Anthony,' she told me when I complained.

"I knew what my father wanted. He wanted me to give in, tell him I was sorry or something, and beg him to forgive me and let me move back upstairs, see, but I didn't do it. I ate the leftovers. Except for holidays and stuff. He thought that was okay."

"Why did your father dislike you so much?" I asked.

He paused. I could see he was debating whether to tell me. "Truth is, he never believed I was really his son," he said.

"Why not?"

"I didn't look that much like him. Different hair color, different eyes. I was better-looking. You know what he believed?"

Of course, I thought that his father believed his mother had an affair with someone, but I didn' t want to suggest anything bad about his mother, so I shook my head.

"He thought I was switched in the maternity ward and my mother didn' t notice. He said I was the child of some teenage girl who got pregnant and was going to give me away anyway. He claimed he knew one was there at the time."

"But who would make the switch, and why?"

"He said there was a nurse who didn't like him. Stupid, I know . . . like where was the real me, then, right?"

"Right," I said. I couldn't imagine having someone like that for a father , someone who despised your very existence.

"So even when I was little, if I did something he didn't like, he'd say I was the stupid kid from the stupid girl and not his. His kid wouldn' t be so dumb."

I shook my head. I had finished my sandwich and my drink. And then I thought of something he'd like to hear. "Maybe he was right. It sounds like it's the other way around, though. He wasn' t your father."

"What?"

"He was too dumb to be your father. You were so much smarter than he was."

He stared at me, and I held my breath. I could see he wasn't sure whether he liked what I had said. I realized that I was also saying his mother was too stupid to know she didn't bring home her own child, which I couldn't imagine any mother doing.

However, his face broke into a wide smile, and he leaned back and laughed. Then he slapped the table.

"I shoulda known enough to tell him that. That's a good zinger. Damn. I shoulda had you here long ago."

"I'd have been too young," I said. I was too young now, but I didn' t add that. Instead, I rose and took my dish and his to the sink.

He sat there finishing his beer and mumbling about the good zinger . He wished his father was still alive so he could stick it to him. "Y ou and I would be some team," he said. "We'd show him."

My gaze went to the door. I was almost positive that he hadn't locked it this time. Could I rush to it now and get up the stairs and out before he caught me? I felt stronger, having rested and eaten, but I would have to do it barefoot, taking off his slip - pers and running, maybe over gravel or rocks. I'd endure any pain to get away.

My heart was pounding so hard that I feared I might faint before I reached the door . I turned off the water and picked up the dish towel, keeping my eyes on the door. It wasn't locked. In fact, it looked slightly open. I felt sure I could leap up the stairs, maybe even before he reached the door himself. I was worried again that I could get lost upstairs, not having seen any of it when he had brought me here, but the chances were good that I'd spot the front door quickly. Perhaps one of the infrequent cars would be going by on the road below . Someone would see me running frantically and stop to help me. I'd be saved.

I put the plate down, and then, just as I was about to lunge at the door, he put his arms around my waist and drew me back against his chest so he could kiss me on the top of my head. I hadn't heard him get up. I had been too lost in my own thoughts, but now I realized that he surely would have caught me trying to escape if I had lunged for the door

His hand opened and rose toward my face. In his palm was a woman's watch. "This," he said, "was my mother's, and now it's yours." He ges - tured for me to take it, so I did. Then he plucked it from my fingers and put it on my wrist. "That's a real tiny diamond over the twelve, you know. This watch is about thirty years old, rose gold. See how well she kept it? My father once tried to hock it, but she stopped him. She threatened him with a meat knife, and he knew she meant business, so he gave it back to her, and from then on, she kept it hidden. Besides her, only I knew where it was. She showed me in case something happened to her. She said, 'You give it to the woman you marry.' "

He stepped back.

"So what do you think?" he asked.

"It's beautiful. Thank you."

"Consider my mother gave it to you, not me. Take good care of it," he warned. "To me, it's priceless."

I nodded.

"Well," he said, slapping his hands together "I'll clear off the rest of the table, and we'll go over the catalogues now, okay?"

"Yes," I said, and returned to the table, my gaze returning to the partially open door as I sat. I should have moved faster. Now it was too late.

The watch read 1:34. Maybe I was better off not knowing the time, I thought. That way, I wouldn't be looking at the minutes and hours and wishing they'd move faster. I couldn't stop believing that my rescue was coming. If I did, I might as well be dead, I thought.

I opened one of the carpet catalogues and began slowly to peruse the samples.

"A tightly woven rug might work better down here," I said, running my fingers over a sample. "It'll be easier to keep clean. Mr . Moccasin sheds hair. We'll need to vacuum all the time, and if the padding is thick, it will feel soft enough."

He nodded, looking a little impressed.

"We won't choose curtains until we choose the carpet color, of course," I said. "Everything should coordinate. We might want to paint where there's no paneling and rethink the colors in the bathroom."

His eyes widened even more. "Right, right. Good. I didn't think of that."

"Of course, I don't know anything about doing this yourself. Nobody in my family is handy that way."

"Oh, I do. I've done it for many people." He looked around. "The room is a good size, twenty-five by seventy. I know just how many square feet we'll need. I've got all the tools. I even have knee pads for us both. W e'll work side by side. W e'll clean the subfloor first, see, to make it smooth, and then we'll install tackless strips and the carpet pad, a good thick one like you say. I'll do the trimming and notch the corners. I'll glue the seams, stretch the carpet using something called a binder bar, and then do the finishing touches."

"You do know a lot about it. Is that what you do for a living?" I asked.

"I'm an all-around tradesman. I do electrical work, too, got a license and all. And plumbing. I've even done some roofing lately. Didn't think you had such a smart guy, huh?" he said, leaning back proudly.

"Do you work for a company?"

"I did, a few, but now I work for myself—or, I mean, for us," he said.

"How do people find out about you? Do you advertise in newspapers, on the radio?"

"Naw. Word of mouth's enough. Don't worry about it. I can get as much work as I want."

I nodded and turned another page.

I had hoped to find out something more specific about him, but then I thought, what good would it do me? I couldn't get a message out to anyone. A part of me, however, was truly curious about him. Maybe I would learn something that could help me fashion an escape. He didn't seem to mind my questions. In fact, he thought it meant I was more accepting.

"Did you learn all this from your father?"

"Hell, no. He had no patience for me, and besides, as soon as I was old enough, I left school and went to work and got to know more than he ever knew. My mother would usually ask me to fix things around the house."

"I bet he didn't like that."

"You're smart. He hated it. Sometimes I think he'd go and break something I fixed just so he could say I didn't do it right."

"Do you have carpet upstairs?"

"In every room but the kitchen," he said. "I laid the tile for the kitchen floor, too."

"Maybe you want a color similar to what's upstairs, then."

"No," he said emphatically. "This is our place. It's got to be different. I'll tell you if we can do the color you pick out."

It took until we reached the middle of the third catalogue before he approved the color, a medium-green cut pile.

"I knew you'd make the right choice for us," he said. "I can get this pretty quick."

"Why don't we start on the floor today? I need exercise," I said. What I really wanted was for him to leave again and maybe, just maybe, forget to lock the door behind him.

His smile widened. "Start today?" He thought a moment. "Yeah, good. We'll start by preparing the floor. I'll go up and get the equipment and the vacuum cleaner and all."

"Don't you have to go buy things?"

"No, not for step one. I told you, I do this for a living. I got all we need here."

He stood and leaned down to kiss me.

"My own little homemaker," he said. "We'll make this place cozy and beautiful together. Then it will mean more. To both of us."

I watched him carefully as he left. This was possibly still very good. He hadn't locked the door behind him, and I was sure he had to have his tools somewhere other than in the house, perhaps in a shed or in the garage. *I might not get as good a chance as I have now*, I thought. I took some deep breaths and went to the door.

Mr. Moccasin followed me, as usual. I tried to wave him back. He didn't retreat.

"You want out as much as I do, don' t you?" I said, and then I opened the door, keeping my body between the cat and the opening. I listened for a moment. The stairway, as short as it was, loomed before me, looking formidable. What if I was only halfway up and he opened the door above? The very thought gave me shivers. I listened. *I've got to try*, I thought when I heard nothing. *I've got to risk it.* I slipped out of his too-big-for -me slippers, closed the door behind me, and started up the stairs. When I reached the top, I realized that I had held my breath so long that I might faint and topple back down. I steadied myself by gripping the banister.

As quietly as I could, I opened the upstairs door. Again, I paused to listen for him. Hearing nothing, I opened the door a little more and saw that I was in a short, narrow hallway. It was lighter on my right, so I imagined that was the way out. Directly across from me and the basement door was a bedroom, its door wide open. I stepped out and turned to the right, but something caught my eye in the bedroom. I paused to look, and this time, I really did come close to fainting.

I did not enter the bedroom. I stood just outside the doorway and gazed in amazement. A coffin had been placed right on top of the bed, which had a rosewood headboard. The coffin was made from the same wood but had an unfinished look to it. It took up most of the bed, which had a cream-colored top sheet with rosebuds and two large matching pillows. There was a small, working grandfather clock on the right nightstand. On the opposite side was a vase with what looked like freshly cut roses. The light-blue shag carpet appeared recently vacu - umed. The darker-blue curtains were fully opened. Looking through those windows, I could see a thick wooded area. Between the house and that was a browned, spotty lawn with a rusted table and two rusted chairs.

Whose coffin was it? Was it meant to be mine? Was that why it was unfinished? Why had it been put on a bed? I was trembling so hard that I didn't think I could continue, but I walked down the short hallway and saw the front door. It was open, but there was a screen door , too. The sight of a sunny sky with only a patch of clouds restored my determination.

Carefully, I approached the screen door . The front porch had only a few wooden steps. I saw Anthony's van parked on the right. The gravel driveway did go down a small incline. I'd have to step out to see the road, but I was sure the best escape was to run down the driveway and take any direction once I reached the road.

I started to open the screen door . The hinges weren't rusted, but they needed some oil, because they began to groan the moment I pushed out.

I had the door more than halfway open and had taken a step out when I heard what sounded like a door slamming and looked to my left. Anthony was pushing a wheelbarrow loaded with equipment toward the house. I knew he would see me the moment I started down those porch steps. I could run only so fast barefoot on gravel. He'd catch me for sure.

I backed up, closing the screen door as softly as I could, but I wasn' t disheartened. There was still a good chance, I thought. I would stay out of his view, and as soon as he started down the stairs to the basement apartment, I could run out and down the driveway. I might even be able to hide some - where off the road until a car came along.

So I turned and went first into the small kitchen and then into the living room, where I knelt behind a large brown sofa to wait and listen.

11

Haylee

Never, from the moment I could realize anything until now, had I ever seen or heard Mother confuse one of us for the other. Although I sensed it never bothered Kaylee as much as it did me whenever anyone confused us, especially when we were younger, one of us was often quick to correct the person. I did notice that sometimes Kaylee didn't seem to care at all. It was barely worth a shrug. When I complained, she said, "Oh, they'll eventually realize who's who." That was never good enough for me. I grew to hate the word *eventually* anyway. So many things were *eventually* in our house. Mother would use it to justify everything she believed about us.

"Eventually, the two of you will think more

and more alike. . . . Eventually, you'll want the same things. . . . Eventually, you'll appreciate how I brought you up. . . . Eventually, people will see how perfectly alike you are."

If I asked when I could have something on my own, something just mine and not duplicated for Kaylee, whether it was clothes or shoes, anything, Mother might simply say "Eventually" and leave it at that.

Who didn't confuse us sometimes? T eachers, Mother and Daddy's friends, relatives, our grand - parents, even other students often would call me Kaylee or call her Haylee. Most of the time, they corrected themselves quickly when they saw the re- action on my face. Those who were trying to be my close friends got to the point where if they were mo mentarily unsure, they would keep their traps shut.

But Mother never confused us, at least never until now.

Right now, she had the same look on her face that she'd had when she came down and asked where Kaylee was. Only a little while ago, she was asking how Kaylee could have done all this. Thoughts were bouncing around in her head like ping-pong balls.

I looked at Mrs. Lofter, who closed and opened her eyes to signal that I should be gentle, under- standing. Then, perhaps afraid that I didn' t appreciate what she was subtly suggesting, she shook her head emphatically to tell me not to contradict Mother.

She must have seen the displeasure in my face and how close I was to correcting Mother. I had to remind myself that Mrs. Lofter was trained in how to read people' s faces and sense their emo - tions. Of course, I didn't know exactly what she expected me to say. Should I contradict her with a little amazement? *Oh, no, Mother, I'm Haylee.* Or should I pretend I hadn' t heard her? Mother was the only genuine nutcase I knew. I didn't have the experience.

"Yes, I'm home," I decided to say . At least I didn't say I was Kaylee. All I said was that I was home.

Anger slipped in beside Mother' s gleeful sur - prise. I didn't need psychological training to realize that; I had seen it too often. "We're going to have a good old-fashioned mother-daughter talk about all this, young lady," Mother said. "You go get your sister and meet me in the living room in two min- utes. And I mean two minutes. I don't want to have to go looking for either of you."

"Looking for us?"

"Exactly."

This ought to be amusing, I thought. Go get my sister? What did she think was happening here? Who did she think Mrs. Lofter was? Why was this stranger in her room? Was this emotional or psychological breakdown she was having going to get worse? Had it gotten seriously worse in a matter of minutes? I looked to Mrs. Lofter for instructions.

She didn't look pleased with the way I had re-acted and ignored me. "Perhaps you should rest a bit now first, Mrs. Fitzgerald," she said. "You've been through quite an emotional shock." She smiled at Mother. "Most of the time, we are simply unaware of how much of a toll our emotional tur-moil takes on us. You want to be strong for your girls, don't you?"

Mother looked up at her, blinked rapidly, like someone with dust in her eyes, and nodded.

Mrs. Lofter moved forcefully to get Mother to return to bed, seizing her arm and guiding her out of the chair. "We have a little something that will help you rest," she said, and handed Mother a glass of water and a pill after she had her lying down. "There'll be lots of time to address the things you want to address."

I was amazed at how Mother did what she asked without any resistance. Mrs. Lofter fixed her blanket and her pillow, and Mother closed her eyes. I thought she was going back to sleep, but then her eyes opened quickly and she started to sit up.

Mrs. Lofter kept her hand on Mother's shoulder and stopped her. "Now, now, just give it some time, Mrs. Fitzgerald. You have to be strong for every - one, just as we agreed, and you can' t be strong if you're not well rested."

Mother looked at her suspiciously for a mo - ment and then relented and lay back again. I had never seen her so firmly manipulated. I couldn't recall her ever doing anything she didn' t want to do, especially if Daddy had asked her or even her own mother. I seriously considered learning the things Mrs. Lofter had learned, perhaps making it my career, too. I'd have loved to have the sort of power that let her control and influence others. I knew I was simply too impatient and definitely too intolerant with people. I often snapped my sarcasm at some of the girls and most of the boys in school, like a verbal whip. It didn' t help make me Miss Popularity.

Kaylee had always criticized me for being clumsy and overbearing when it came to making and keeping friends or speaking with teachers and other adults. "You get more with honey than you do with vinegar ," she'd say , mimicking Grand - mother Fitzgerald. Especially when we were both younger, Kaylee liked to lecture me. She'd take on Mother's or one of our grandmothers' posture and tone of voice and pace back and forth, tossing out these tidbits of wisdom and instructions the way we tossed peanuts to monkeys at the zoo.

Now, when Mother appeared settled, Mrs. Lofter turned to me and nodded toward the door - way. We practically tiptoed out. She didn' t speak until we reached the stairway.

"Let's talk a bit downstairs," she said.

"Did I do something wrong?"

"Let's have a chat," she insisted.

Here it goes, I thought, *my psychoanalysis*. I led her into the living room and purposefully took Dad- dy's favorite chair. It helped me hold on to my sense of superiority. I sat back, with my arms on the arms of the chair, looking, I was sure, like some sort of princess holding court. This was, after all, my king - dom and not hers. She sat on the sofa across from me.

"I know that what you see happening to your mother is quite disturbing for you," she began.

I pounced. "My mother never confused us. She never called me Kaylee or called her Haylee. Never! And she wouldn't permit anyone else to get away with it, either, even my father."

"I understand, but you have to realize, Hay - lee, that your mother is in a state of shock. At this point, it will only do more damage to force her to accept Kaylee's disappearance when she blocks it out. It's better if we go along with it as best we can when that occurs."

"How can we do that? Kaylee's not here! If you

didn't drug my mother again just now , she would have come down here to lecture the two of us and would have remembered that Kaylee is gone," I snapped back. "Then what? W e pretend Kaylee's in another room or in the bathroom until you give Mother another pill?"

She closed and opened her eyes, projecting that tolerance I hated on the faces of my teachers and especially on Kaylee's face. It had the effect of forcing your words to echo back at you and turn - ing your anger into regret. "For now , we have to humor her, pretend that Kaylee is here when she forgets or blocks out that she isn' t. We can try to get her to change her train of thought, which was what I was doing. I'm afraid she' s going to move in and out of this state of mind, I hope for only a while. Sometimes she'll remember Kaylee' s gone, and sometimes she won't."

"Hopefully for only a while?"

"Yes, hopefully for only a while."

"What are you saying? Y ou mean she might not? She might never believe Kaylee's gone?"

"I've had patients like that, yes. The situation would need more drastic approaches. Look, the mind is incredibly stronger than we often imagine. It will do what it can to protect her from realizing something so painful. Eventually , facing Kaylee's disappearance, if the disappearance continues, of course, will be quite devastating."

"Eventually? It looks to me like it is devastating right now."

"It can and might get a lot worse," she said, as firmly as Mother had ever said anything.

"How can you tell all this so fast? You haven't been here one full day?" I asked, more like de - manded. Her superior self-confidence was annoy- ing me. And I certainly didn' t want to hear that Mother might never believe that Kaylee was gone. Nothing would change if that was true.

Concerned, however, that Mrs. Lofter might read something more into my irritation, I tried to hide it, stuff it under a look of sadness. But it re - fused to be kept silent.

"That would be terrible, horrible. It would be like living with a ghost in the house."

"Yes, it would. I've been involved in many simi- lar situations, I'm afraid. Many of them involved an only child, which, as you can imagine, shatters par- ents, perhaps mothers more than fathers. Your fam- ily situation is complex, even without this event."

I stared at her a moment. She seemed to know a lot more about us, about Mother. "Complex?"

"There's a divorce. There are other issues," she added softly.

"What other issues? How do you know about our issues?"

She was silent.

I leaned forward. "You and my father met be-

fore you came here, didn't you?" I asked, my suspicion rising like mercury in a thermometer.

"Why do you say that?" she countered, but
weakly.

I looked away. I could recognize guilt in someone's face. As Kaylee used to tell me, "It takes one
to know one." Mrs. Lofter's response was a yes, I
was sure.

I turned back to her, no longer intimidated by
her. "Why did my father pretend to be meeting you
for the first time here? What's going on? I won't be
treated like a child."

"No one wants to treat you like a child."

"Well, then, why be dishonest?"

She looked trapped.

She might have the education and the experi -
ence, but I had the instincts. I'd knock her down a
peg or two.

"We didn't want to frighten you more than you
already would be," she confessed. "No one was trying to fool you or do something behind your back,
Haylee."

"Which was what you did," I said dryly "I suppose the three of you met—you, Daddy , and the
doctor—and discussed me as well as Mother?"

"It was all to make sure I could do the best possible job for you all," she said. "I don't simply walk
into a new assignment cold."

I smiled. "Yes, I'm sure you don't," I said. "Well,

maybe you don't know it all. Y ou said when this sort of thing happens to people who have an only child, it's especially devastating to the mother."

"In my experience, yes," she said.

"This did happen to people who have an only child."

"Excuse me?"

"My mother never saw us as anything but two halves of one daughter. Kaylee and I once had an argument over how she used the word *you* when she referred to us or either one of us. Y ou know, *you* is one of those words that can refer to many or just one. Well, when Mother used it, she meant only one, us, Haylee and Kaylee. She's missing half of each child," I said bitterly.

"Do you feel you've lost half of yourself, too?"

Oh, so here's where the psychoanalysis comes in. Careful, I thought. *Don't get too far ahead, and don't be too smart for yourself.*

I pressed my lips together hard, which always helped me make my eyes teary when I wanted them to be, especially when a teacher was reprimanding me.

"Yes," I said in a little girl's voice.

"Nothing is confirmed yet, Haylee," she said, her voice far more compassionate. "Y ou mustn't lose hope. I know how difficult it must be for you, but if you can keep up a confident appearance for her, your mother will get stronger and maybe help herself more, which will only make things easier for both you and your father. It's a great deal to put on your shoulders, I know."

"I told you, I'm not a child. I can handle it." I was talking again without thinking. I forced my face to tremble. "In front of her, I mean," I added. "Everyone's going to blame me, you know ," I blurted. Now I was really crying. "I should have spoken up sooner. I shouldn't have gone along with her crazy plan. She's not here, so I'm the one they can blame. It won't be the first time we were both punished for something only one of us did."

"No one should blame you for loving your sister and wanting to keep her loyalty and faith in you. Those were good motives. In the end, we've all got to face the fact that we're responsible for ourselves. Your sister's mistake was her mistake. She brought this on herself. But let's not rush into more tragedy, Haylee."

"That's not completely true. Parents are responsible for their children," I said. "It's not fair to put the blame entirely on Kaylee. Mother made us the way we are, and my father fled instead of changing things."

"I see. You're very angry with your father , aren't you?"

Here we go, I thought. *The psychological X-ray.*

"We both are . . . were," I said. "W e seem to have everything any girl our age would want except a happy family life. It' s not fair. Parents shouldn't have children if they're going to care more about their own happiness and desert them."

She stared a moment too long for my comfort. I could almost read her thoughts now . Her suspicions were expanding. She was weaving them in her mind the way a spider weaves its web.

"What?" I asked. "Why are you looking at me like that?"

"If this is something you both planned in order to punish your parents, especially your father , it will not go well for either of you, Haylee. Its best if you tell me now."

"What?"

I almost started to laugh when it suddenly oc - curred to me that Mrs. Lofter might also be work - ing with the police. Perhaps she would report to them about me, about how I was really reacting to my sister's disappearance, or maybe she would start asking me more detailed questions to see if there were any contradictions. She wasn't here simply to help us with Mother and to help Mother deal with Kaylee's disappearance; she was here to spy on me, too. I was sure of it.

"Okay. You might as well know everything," I said, as if I was exhausted from the burden of heavy secrets.

"Oh?" She leaned forward.

Looking for a confession? I thought. *Look again, Mrs. Lofter. You're the last person to whom I would confess.*

"You're not entirely wrong with your suspi - cions," I said.

"I see. Please explain."

"I don't like talking about Kaylee like this."

"It's for her own good."

"We never betrayed each other's confidences."

"I understand, but this is a different situation now. It's grown far more serious. I'm sure you realize it."

I took a deep breath. Oh, how painful I made it look. Were they standing off to the side with my Oscar? "My sister was more frustrated than I was with how our mother insisted on and enforced our similarities," I began.

Mrs. Lofter sat up straighter. "Go on."

"She often talked about running away, but like that sort of talk was for me, I thought it was just wishful thinking for her. Maybe there was no In - ternet romance. Maybe she lied to me. She wasn' t herself these past weeks. There was a time when we would tell each other our most intimate thoughts, down to how we felt when a certain boy touched us in places boys want to touch you. W e hid nothing from each other."

I paused again to take a deep breath and wipe an

errant tear from the crest of my cheek. *Good touch*, I thought. Sometimes I was so good at this that I convinced myself I was telling the truth.

"I don't know what to say, Mrs. Lofter. I don't mean to give the police or anyone false information, but I feel terrible revealing these intimate things about Kaylee. It's like . . . revealing things about yourself, don't you see? It's so hard, so hard to explain." I had the police wondering about this already, so I didn't think I was doing anything damaging to myself. *Keep it all consistent*, I told myself.

"If she did indeed run away of her own accord, where would she go?" Mrs. Lofter asked.

I smiled to myself, thinking she wasn't so clever after all, even with all that education and experi - ence. She was so obvious. Why would she care about any of this if she was here to be a nurse and not a detective's assistant?

I shrugged. "She saved money. We both did. She used to talk about going to California and becom - ing an actress or a model. Either of us could do that. Mother herself often told us so, and so did many other people, including some teachers. T o us, it wasn't such a far-fetched dream, although I would say Kaylee believed it more than I did."

"Maybe you should discuss this more with the police," Mrs. Lofter said.

"I've told them as much."

"But if you have any more details . . ."

"I don't," I said.

She looked skeptical. That was fine. I was keeping them all off balance. And wasn't that what she was really doing to Mother, keeping her a little confused, a little foggy, so she wouldn't suffer so much? Everyone was lying to everyone else in one way or another.

The truth was, in this world, we couldn't exist without lies. Mother had been lying about Kaylee and me all these years, telling people we were exactly alike, even in our thoughts. Daddy had lied his way out of here. My grandmother Clara Beth certainly lied all the time. I could see the lies teachers spun when they tried to convince one of their students to work harder, claiming they could do so much more. Lies were gray and dark, like angry clouds swirling madly above and around us, always threatening to rain the truth on us and make us do what Mrs. Lofter did not want Mother to do: face cold reality head-on. The truth was too strong.

Some believed that suicide had become an epidemic among depressed teenagers and wounded war veterans. If Kaylee never came home, Mother might just do that. If she did, how would I feel? I didn't know. Maybe, just before she killed herself, I would confess to save her, or maybe I'd do what Mrs. Lofter believed people did and block out reality to keep myself from suffering at all.

The phone rang. I looked at it as if I had just realized we had one.

"You should start talking to people, especially your close friends," Mrs. Lofter said, rising. "It's at times like this that we need our friends. Don't drive them away. I'm going to look after my things and settle in."

Sure, I thought. *What you're really going to do is call the detectives on your cell phone and report everything I told you, I bet.* I nodded at her.

The phone rang again as she walked away. "Haylee Fitzgerald," I said after I had picked up the receiver.

"Hey," Daddy said. "I was afraid you wouldn't answer. How's it going?"

"Not good. She gave Mother a pill, even though she told us she wasn't going to keep her on pills. Maybe this is all too much for her to handle now that she sees what's happening. I mean, she didn't know much about us before she came here," I said, to see if Daddy would reveal that he and Dr Bloom had met with her. "It's very complex."

"No, no, she knows what to do and when to do it, Haylee. She's trained for such things. But did anything else occur to upset your mother? Some - one call or . . ."

"Nothing to upset her, but something occurred to upset *me*."

"What do you mean?"

"Mother called me Kaylee," I said, and started to cry, sucking in sobs. "When she saw me, she thought I was Kaylee, who had come home."

"Well, under the circumstances . . ." I knew he didn't think that was anything to lose sleep over , even before all this.

"No. You don't understand. She's never mixed us up, Daddy. She really didn't know who I was. It hurt. A lot."

"Okay, okay. She's not herself. You can't take any of it to heart."

"I know," I said in my little-girl voice. "Mrs. Lofter explained it all, but it still hurts."

"Stay strong, Haylee. We've all got to stay strong."

"I'm trying."

"Good. I spoke with Lieutenant Cowan a little while ago."

"And?"

"They found someone who lives on that street where another witness thought he might have seen your sister. She's an elderly woman but apparently quite healthy, alert. She gave them a description of a white van that she says she'd never seen parked there. It's not much, but it' s something. They're showing her pictures of vans to see if they can isolate the make, model, and perhaps year. They're really trying."

"I hope so," I said.

"Anyway, I thought I'd stop at the Lotus House on the way home and pick up some Chinese food for us. How's that sound?"

"Okay," I said. "I don't even remember if I ate any lunch."

"Hang in there, sweetheart," he said. I loved hearing him say that only to me. "You might be the strongest of all of us."

"I'll try," I said. He didn' t know it, but I had always believed that I was.

After we hung up, the phone rang again. It was Mrs. Letterman, one of Mother's hens, as I called them. I didn' t give her a chance to hide behind any empty expressions of hope. I went on and on about how difficult it was for the police and how we had to have the psychiatric nurse for Mother , who was on the brink of a terrible nervous break-down.

"We have to keep her sedated," I said, as if I was as much in charge as anyone. "For her own good. I'm so frightened for her."

"Oh, dear, dear. You always think things like this happen to someone else."

"I'm sorry. I've got to go. I think I'm going to throw up, Mrs. Letterman. Thanks for calling," I said, and hung up before she could utter another word.

The phone rang again, but this time, I let it

go to voice mail and went upstairs instead. I was surprised at how mentally exhausted I was. Mov - ing from one emotion to another quickly, however cleverly I was doing it, put more of a strain on me than I had anticipated. I looked forward to when this would all be over, when they'd find Kaylee, or she'd escape and come home, or when it would be clear she never would. But I was always impatient, so it didn't astonish me that I had this attitude. Ironically, it was my sister who always kept me centered. I wished I had that part of her here.

As I lay on my bed, I wondered if after ev - erything, even now, I would discover that I really did miss her. What if, years from now , I did just what Mrs. Lofter feared Mother would do, losing my mental defenses and then suffering regret and remorse? Could I have a nervous breakdown, too?

I laughed, imagining it. Maybe Mrs. Lofter would be called in to help with me. *Too much thinking*, I told myself, and I rose and went to Kaylee's room. The detectives had asked me to do this, hadn't they? I reasoned, and went directly to her dresser. She always kept her things neater than I did, something that annoyed Mother more than me, of course. I reached into the drawers and began toss - ing out her panties and bras, her socks and scarves, just flinging them willy-nilly onto her bed until all the drawers were emptied. *What do you know?*

I thought. *I didn't find anything that might help the police.*

I went to her closet and ripped everything off the hangers, turning pockets in coats and jeans in - side out, flinging it all onto the floor. I even turned shoes and sneakers upside down in case a secret note had been placed inside one. When I was done with that, I attacked her vanity table, emptying the drawers onto the floor. I dumped out the contents of her jewelry box and then tore off her comforter and pulled up the sheets, bundling everything at the foot of the bed. I stripped the pillows, too. Exhausted, I plopped down among all the clothes and stuff.

That was where I was when Daddy came home and came looking for me. He stood in the doorway astounded. "What . . . what's going on in here?"

"The detectives asked me to go through her things to look for a clue!" I cried. "I got frantic and frustrated. Sorry, Daddy." I shook my head and shouted, "I didn't find anything! She didn't leave a single clue!"

When I began to sob, my shoulders shaking, Daddy rushed in and lifted me off the floor as if I was a little baby. He kissed my cheeks and held me tightly as he carried me out and back to my room.

Mrs. Lofter, hearing all the commotion, came running up the stairs.

"The police asked her to search her sister's room

for some sort of clue," Daddy told her . I had my face buried against his chest. "She didn' t find anything that would help us. Her heart is broken."

"Oh, dear me," Mrs. Lofter said. "Perhaps I was a bit too hard on her today. I'm sorry."

Neither of them could see me smile, and even if they could, they wouldn' t be sure that it wasn' t a sobbing face.

12

Kaylee

His arms were loaded with tools when he came
into the house, but I thought he might have to
make more than one trip. If he did, I hoped he
would drop these things off at the door and head
back out before going down and discovering that
I wasn't there. That would give me a better chance
to sneak away and a better head start after he went
out again to his tool shed. If I could get down to the
road before he returned to the house, I'd have all
the time it would take him to carry down the tools
and materials, see I wasn't there, and come rushing
back upstairs. He might waste time searching the
house first. I might even be able to reach his closest
neighbor.

I saw the look of eagerness on his face when he

was in the entryway. He was whistling, too, sounding as happy as I imagined he could. In his mind, everything he had planned and imagined with Haylee was coming true. He was building a new home here for his fantasy family. But I knew that the moment he realized I was gone, his happiness so high up would come crashing down hard, and I feared how he would be if he caught me. I trembled envisioning that but kept very quiet, holding my breath.

He did pause for a moment and look in my direction. Had I touched something, left some sort of evidence of my escape from the basement? One of the tools he carried looked sharp enough to cut off my head. Terror was almost at a boiling point inside me. I was sure I had uttered a small sob of alarm, as if there was truly a second me inside myself, a me I couldn't control.

Had he heard it?

He did stop whistling.

I cringed and waited, squeezing my eyes closed and pressing my hands so tightly against my breasts that they hurt. After a long and frightening moment, I heard him start whistling again and continue down the hallway. I stepped out and listened harder, hoping to hear the basement door opening. He appeared to have stopped again, probably right at the doorway to the bedroom that had a coffin on the bed. It seemed like minutes passing rather than

seconds, because he wasn' t moving, and I didn' t
hear the basement door opening. Was he unloading
his tools and coming back to get more things as I
had suspected? I waited, but I didnt hear anything.
I continued inching forward until I could see him
in the hallway, just staring into the bedroom. I
thought he was whispering.

I remained back, holding my breath. Finally, I
heard him open the basement door and start down
the stairs, carrying what he had. There would be
less time than I had hoped. I moved quickly but as
quietly as I could to the screen door and opened
it just enough to slip out, closing it softly behind
me. The house was higher up from the road than I
had envisioned and there was no lawn in front, just
patches of weeds, rocks, and gravel. I hurried down
the steps and, holding up the skirt of the oversized
dress, began to run to my right and down the slope.
The stones poked and cut the bottoms of my feet,
and some weeds scratched the bottoms of my legs,
but I did the best I could to ignore the pain. I had
to make it to the road below . I was nearly there
when I heard the screen door slam, sounding like
a gunshot.

He was coming.

Screaming for help at the top of my lungs, I
turned onto the macadam road. I didn't look back,
but I could hear him screaming, too, sounding like
a wild animal in pain. I looked down the road, hop

ing and praying for the sight of an automobile or a
nearby house, but there was nothing on the road
and nothing but wild brush, fields of hay, and thick
wooded areas. My feet felt as if the soles were on
fire because this was more or less a dirt and gravel
road. How far was I from the city?

I kept running. Vaguely, I imagined myself as
something of a comical sight. I was sure I looked
like I was tiptoeing over hot coals, keeping the skirt
pulled up to my knees as I charged forward. A thick
black snake slithered into the ditch and bushes. The
road was surrounded by trees and bushes, and as far
as I could see, there was no other house, no neighbor within reach.

Suddenly, the sound of an engine gave me hope.
If I could just stay ahead of him and keep going,
maybe he would realize someone was coming and
stop chasing me. A pickup truck was soon visible
in the distance. It was coming my way. I raised my
arms to wave frantically, hoping the driver would
see me, but the moment I let goof the skirt, the hem
fell just below my feet because the oversize dress
had slipped down off my shoulders. I struggled to
keep it up and then I stepped on the material, trip-
ping myself and sailing forward and to my right. I
hit the ditch hard with the right side of my head and
my shoulder. The pain shot instantly through my
back and took away my breath.

Before I could get back to my feet and continue

running toward the truck, I heard him shout. He dove and slammed down over my body, pressing my face to the dank earth. I gagged, and he quickly held my arms so I couldn' t lift them to wave at the driver of the oncoming truck. I squirmed and twisted, but he was too heavy for me to break free. The sound of the truck drawing closer gave me some hope, but when I went to scream, he shoved his hand hard into my mouth until I gagged and choked again. The truck went by, the driver apparently not noticing anything, because I didn' t hear the vehicle stop. Anthony waited until it was gone and then slowly retreated, lifting himself off me. I didn't move. I coughed and spit, keeping my eyes closed, my body frozen.

What would he do to me now? It seemed like a full minute had passed, but I dared not turn or try to get up and run. I was too frightened even to cry.

"Look at you," he finally said. "Ain't you embarrassed acting like that? Suppose somebody had seen you . . . and me chasing after you. Huh? What would they have thought? Damn. Y ou can't walk on those feet."

I still didn' t move. The scent of damp earth rushed up my nose. I saw some worms uncurl and start to slither away.

"Luckily," he said, "the one thing my father did teach me was the fireman's carry."

I didn't open my eyes, but I sensed he was cir -
cling around to stand in front of me.

"He didn't actually teach it to me. He liked to
do it to me, just come over to me while I was playing or doing something and whip me up, frighten -
ing the hell out of me. I'd scream, and my mother
would yell at him, but he'd just laugh and do it
again and again. Watch. I'll show you how it works.
Go on. Open your eyes. Open them!"

I did and looked at his feet as he squatted.

"First, facing you, I'm hooking my elbows
under your arms, and then I'm lifting you to your
feet," he said.

I closed my eyes again because my head was
spinning. His face was inches from mine. He leaned
forward and wiped some mud from my cheek with
his tongue. Then he spit it out.

"What a mess. Okay. Now I'm putting my right
leg between your legs, see, and I'm squatting down
and hooking my right arm around your right leg,
and then up you go." He lifted me and threw me
over his shoulder with ease. He held on to my right
wrist and turned, stepping out of the ditch and
starting back to the driveway.

My feet still felt on fire, my shoulder ached, and
I realized I must have scraped my face along the
right temple and cheek. He was walking steadily ,
easily, like I was a sack of cotton dresses. We started
up the driveway. I opened my eyes and looked

down the road to my left, hoping to see that truck
or maybe another vehicle, but there was nothing.

"I'm disappointed in you, Kaylee, but I understand. Young women are often nervous when they
first set up a new home. You should have just told
me how nervous you was. Running off like that is
not good for you or me. People misunderstand.
Who knows what anyone woulda thought if they
had seen you looking so frantic, huh?" he said.
"They'd never guess we was husband and wife and
about to set up a new home."

The fact that he sounded more reasonable than
angry actually frightened me more. A tornado of
madness swirled around us. Black was white, tall
was short, and thin was thick. Nothing in his mind
was what he didn't want it to be. I wasn't trying to
get away from him. Oh, no. I was just an insecure
young married woman afraid of disappointing my
new husband.

I bounced against his body as he walked up the
driveway and onto the porch. When I heard him
open the screen door, I felt my whole body give
up, every muscle that had tightened with some
resistance softening. I was back in the madhouse.
My moments of hope seemed cruel now , teasing
me. Did I dare to permit myself to think that the
driver of that truck had seen me, seen Anthony
fall over me, but he was too frightened himself to
stop? Would he report it to the police? Should I

live with that hope, any hope? Optimism had be - come a form of torture. I'd never even dream of a rescue now.

Anthony marched us down the hallway. He paused at the bedroom.

"You were right," he said. I turned my head. Whom was he talking to? "Not good to rush things."

He opened the basement door, and we started down the stairs.

"Hey, Mr. Moccasin," he said joyfully when we reentered the basement apartment, "look who's back. You were worrying she was gone for good."

He brought me to the bed and unloaded me gently. Then he stood back and looked down at me, shaking his head.

"What have you done to yourself? You don't want to look at your beautiful face. And these feet. You'd get nauseous if you could see them," he said, lifting them to look at my soles. "You're going to have a tough time walking for a while. Uggies, like my mother used to say. I'll get a warm washcloth and the disinfection stuff and some bandages. You made quite a mess of your dress, too. You ripped it at the shoulder, you know. I told you that was one of my mother's nicest dresses."

He seized my left wrist and looked at the watch he had given me.

"Lucky it's not scratched," he said, but he

unfastened it and put it in his pocket. "You don't deserve any of her good things yet."

He pulled the dress up roughly over my arms, leaving me stark naked. I covered my breasts with my arms and crossed my legs.

"Wow, look at that bruise on your right leg. What a mess," he said. "You're going to be achin' for days." He tossed the dress to the floor and went into the bathroom.

I was crying so softly that I didn't realize it until some of my salty tears reached the scraped parts of my right cheek and burned. I turned onto my side. He was back with the washcloth and grabbed my shoulder to turn me onto my back again.

"Just lay still," he ordered. He knelt and began to wash off my feet first, mumbling under his breath. "I did something like this to myself once," I heard him say. "I was running away from my father. My mother let me play in the little inflated pool she had bought me, and I was running the hose. He came home and screamed about wasting the water. We got a submersible pump here, ya see, and he was always complaining about wasting water. So he rips the hose out of my hand and smacks me one good one across my right arm and my back with it.

"Shit, that hurt something awful, but it fright - ened me more than anything else. I got up and out of the inflated pool and started running away. I didn't know where I was going. I just wanted like

hell to get away from him. I ran over the gravel
drive, too. My mother scooped me up before Iwent
too far, but I did damage and had to have her do for
me what I'm doing for you now.

"She tore into my father , of course, but her
curses and complaints were water off a duck's back
to him. He took out a knife and cut the hell out of
my inflated pool. I was too frightened to cry, but
I was hurting and cried when no one was looking.
Took days to get me to walk anywhere near normal.
Be the same for you, if not longer. This is a helluva
lot worse."

He smeared the disinfectant over the cuts and
scrapes and wrapped a gauze bandage around my
feet. He taped it and then started on my right arm
and shoulder. I tried not to look at him, but he kept
seizing my chin and turning me toward him.

"You're lucky I know what I'm doing here. I
took one of them courses in first aid. I was going to
join a volunteer ambulance squad once but decided
not to. Too many big shots were already in it."

He put some smaller Band-Aids on me, cover -
ing some of the other scrapes and cuts, and then
returned everything to the cabinet in the bathroom.
I lay there with my eyes closed, trying to deal with
the pain and aches that seemed now to be coming
from all sides of my body. I opened my eyes at the
sound of the chain.

Oh, no, I thought. "No, please!" I cried.

"Yes," he said. "We gotta go back to this, unfortunately. You ain't as ready as I thought."

He fastened the cuff around my ankle. I was hugging myself tightly. He stood back and looked at me.

"Even now, you look pretty to me," he said, smiling and shaking his head. Then he turned angry again. "We'll have to put off all the work on the floor and curtains and stuff. You're not going to be much help, and I want this to be something we do together. This is a big disappointment, Kaylee. I don't like setbacks. What you got to say for yourself now, huh?"

"I want to go home!" I wailed. "Let me go home."

He shook his head slowly. "Why would you say such a thing? I told you, you are home. Now , get yourself under the blanket. You're going without dinner tonight. You sleep and start healing, see? Move," he ordered.

I sat up and, because of the pains shooting up my legs and down my right side, gingerly turned on the bed so he could pull the blanket out and then toss it over me. I closed my eyes and turned onto my left side. He walked away and began putting his tools and equipment in a corner , mumbling to himself. I could hear him arguing with himself. He slammed things and cursed. His anger appeared to be growing. At one point, I thought he punched the wall. Every sound made me wince. Suddenly , he returned to the foot of the bed. I cringed in anticipation of his doing something worse to me.

"I'm going out for a while," he said. "Right now, I can't stand the sight of you. The disappointment's making me sick to my stomach."

I didn't open my eyes until I heard him leave. With the chain back on me, it didn' t matter if he remembered to lock the door behind him or not. I could feel Mr . Moccasin hop onto the bed and sprawl out beside me.

"We're trapped, you and I," I said. "Forever"

He began to purr. I wished I was a cat, too, and unaware of how miserable I was. Despite the pain, I felt exhaustion climb up and over my body, seeping into every pore and through every muscle. I had bounced hard between different emotions. That and my physical effort sapped the energy from me. Sleep was very welcome. Right now, it was my only means of escape. The oncoming night shut down what little light came through the boarded win   - dows. Darkness enveloped me. I drifted slowly into something that resembled unconsciousness more than sleep and didn' t wake again until I heard the door being opened roughly and Anthony cursing. He turned on the light by the kitchen sink.

I didn't move or open my eyes again. I heard him banging things around, and then it grew quiet, so quiet and for so long that I wondered if he had

left again. I was too curious to pretend to be asleep,
so I turned and saw him looking down at me at the
foot of the bed. He was stark naked. His mouth
was open dumbly. He looked surprised to see me.
It was as if in that insane mind of his, he had forgot
ten that I had run away or even that I was here. The
chill that went through my body overwhelmed the
pain. He stumbled around to his side and pulled
up the blanket. I could smell the beer. He reeked as
if he had taken a bath in it. It soured my stomach.
Whatever he said was garbled.

I cowered in anticipation. It took a while, but I
finally felt him reach for me under the blanket. He
seized me by the wrist and held on to me tightly. I
was waiting for him to do more. I thought he was
surely going to punish me with sex, but he didn' t
move. Minutes went by, and then his grip softened.
His hand moved up my arm and settled on my
shoulder. He stroked me surprisingly softly, affec-
tionately, but I still cringed.

"We need a baby. Once we have a baby, you'll
never want to leave me," he said. He patted me as
if he wanted to reassure me. "But we can' t make a
baby when you're in pain. I know that. My mother
told me that. A woman in any kind of pain won' t
give birth to a happy baby , she said. A baby re -
members its mother's pain. You'll get better. When
you're healed enough, we'll make our baby."

Why would his mother tell him such a thing?

Had he beaten some other girl? Was it possible that I wasn't the first one imprisoned down here? Was his mother as insane as he was? Could she have known? The possibility that I wasn't the first made what was happening to me even more terrifying.

He drew his hand away , and moments later, I heard his breathing, heavy and regular . Not long after, he snored and choked. He woke up many times during the night, and every time, he would reach for me as if to assure himself that I was still there. With that and with my pain, I didn' t sleep much. He woke in the morning with such a shudder that the bed trembled. I had my back to him, but I knew he had sat up. He pulled the blanket off me and gazed at me. I didn't speak. I didn't move.

"You look like hell," he said. "There are black-and-blues where I didn't expect."

He put the blanket back and rose, coughing. He hacked like someone with poisoned lungs. Maybe he was getting sick. Maybe he had lung cancer . Maybe he would die with me down here, and then what? If he died and I was still chained to the wall, what could I do? Ironically , I had to wish that he remained healthy. I saw him go into the bathroom and heard him peeing.

When he came out again, he stood for a while looking around and then at me. Suddenly, he opened the door and went out and up the stairs. I stood up and, although it was painful, dragging that

horrible chain along with me, I walked to the bathroom. When I came out, he had returned and was
standing with a faded blue robe in his hands.

"Put this on," he said. "It was my father'   s.
That's all you'll wear for a while. I'm not giving you
any more of my mother' s nice dresses and other
things until I think you'll have respect for them and
for me."

He tossed the robe at me. It smelled sour and
was stained with old food and drink, but I put it on
quickly and stood looking away.

"I'll make you   some breakfast," he said.   "I
shouldn't. I should keep you on bread and water
for a while to teach you a lesson, but the faster you
get better, the faster we can think about having our
baby. I know how mothers are. They never ever
think of leaving their babies. You'll be able to think
of someone besides yourself and me. Goon. Get off
your feet," he ordered.

Nearly tiptoeing to keep my weight off some
of the scrapes and cuts on my feet, I returned to
the bed. He started to make some coffee and eggs.
Either it didn't bother him that he was stark naked,
or he was doing that to intimidate me. It didn'   t
matter. I was intimidated and kept my gaze on the
floor.

"You stay in that bed for now," he said. "For a
while, I want you to keep off your feet except to go
to the bathroom. Those bandages got to be changed

every other day, even if I forget. We don't want no infections and fevers and all the other crap that goes along with it. But even if that happens, don't worry. I have pills. I have lots of pills."

Obediently, I got back under the blanket.

"Put my pillow behind yours, too, and sit up," he ordered. He continued to prepare a tray. "I'll be your servant for now, but once you're better, you'll be doing everything for us. You're too spoiled. All you rich girls are too spoiled. Rich bitches turn to witches if you don't use some switches," he recited, and laughed.

"I'm not a rich girl," I said. I was amazed myself that I cared enough to say anything. How could I care what he thought or what anyone thought about me now? I didn't feel human.

"Sure you are. You ever work? Well? Did you?"

"No."

"Then you're a rich girl. Ma warned me about rich girls, but you can be cured."

"Cured? What's that mean?" Did his ugly little rhyme mean something . . . *if you don't use some switches?* What else did he have planned for me?

I could see he was thinking. Then he turned when the right word had come to him. "T rained is what I mean. People can be trained just like animals. If my mother was here and saw you, she would say you ain't been housebroken yet. That's why you went and did this damn dumb thing. She was always saying that about my father. 'Course, he never was, and never could be, housebroken. When he was really drunk, he might pee in the kitchen sink and set her into some tirade. I seen her hit him with a frying pan once."

To my surprise, those memories seemed to cheer him up. He started to whistle as he finished making breakfast. He was happy again, mumbling about our future, the things he was planning to do for our family, behaving as though nothing had hap - pened. He simply refused to accept my rejection, even now, even after I had made such a dramatic and desperate attempt to escape. I watched him and thought how crazy he was, and yet he obviously could get by in the world without anyone realizing it or caring. Without friends and, apparently, without contact with relatives, who would know how he lived and what he did in his own home? How many weird people lived alone like he did and went about their daily lives unnoticed until they hurt someone or themselves? Yes, I thought, it was very possible that there had been another young girl kept down here, very possible that there had even been more than one.

Because he didn't work at a company and with the same people every day, his insanity was surely even less noticeable. If he was telling the truth about the quality of his work, he was possibly able to present himself as being normal enough

to work for people. There were probably people
who might have praised the work he had done
and, as he had suggested to me, recommended him
to others. Someday, if what he was doing to me
and with me was ever revealed, these same people
would shake their heads and say something like
"Anthony Cabot? Who would have ever imagined
that a nice, efficient working man like that would
do such things? He was always talking about his
mother. He must have loved her very much, a de -
voted son."

The thought reminded me of what I had seen.

"Whose coffin is in that room upstairs?" I asked.

He paused as he began to pour coffee into a
cup. "That's my mother," he said. "You went in
there," he added, as if someone had just whispered
in his ear.

"Why is her coffin on a bed in that room?"

"It's her room." He finished pouring the coffee
and put the eggs and some toast on the dish. Then
he placed it all on a tray and brought it to me. Care
fully, he put the tray on my lap. "Eat," he ordered.

I began. It wasn't until I had started to chew
that I realized my jaw was sore, too. When I had
fallen into that ditch, I had really smashed my face
into the hard soil.

"But why put her coffin in her room? Why isn't
it in a cemetery?" I asked as I ate.

"I wasn't going to bury her beside my father .

She didn't want that. The day she knew she was going to die, she made me promise."

"But you could put her in a grave that wasn't near his, couldn't you?"

"No. Stop asking questions about her. You ain't earned the right yet."

The right? He talked about his mother as if she was some sort of divine being. I was so tired, de - feated, and bruised that I didn't care.

However, a new thought came to me, one that was perhaps even more frightening.

"When did she die?"

He didn't answer. He continued to stare at me like he might, however.

"Recently? No one else knows she died? Is that it? You built that coffin, didn't you?" I said. "You've kept her death a secret."

"I told you to stop talking about my mother"

"You can't leave it like this. Didn't she have any friends? Don't people ask after her? Doesn't she have any relatives, a sister or a brother?"

"I told you, my mother didn't have any brothers or sisters. She was like your mother . Her mother died a while back, and her father left them when she was only ten. W e ain't heard from him ever ." He smiled. "That's why we're so alike, Kaylee. We don't spend time with relatives, remember? You don't like your grandparents, and you don't see your uncles or cousins much."

"That was my sister who told you that," I said. "You were talking to my sister, never to me."

His face hardened again, and he nodded. "Okay," he said. "We'll play it like that if you want. It'll be like the very first day you came here."

"I didn't come here. You brought me here against my will."

"We'll start all over," he said, not listening. "It will just take a little longer than I hoped. It's your fault. I'm sure you're sorry, or you will be."

He took away the tray even though I wasn't finished and brought it to the sink. I watched him dump the food into a garbage bag and put the dishes and silverware in the sink. Then he turned, walked halfway to the bed, and paused.

"What you need is a little solitary," he said. "What you got to understand is what it's like to live alone with no one to love you and care for you. Maybe then you'll appreciate me. You won't starve. There's food, nothing special, nothing like what we would have together or what you're used to having, and you got water. You take care of your own scrapes and bruises, too. The fixin's are in the bathroom. Change those bandages every other day yourself. There's no tender loving care now. I'm starting a new job. I wasn't going to take it, but now I will. It's not close by, so I won't be home till late. You'll get so you can't wait for the sound of my footsteps upstairs. I know how that feels. You won't hear nothing else but the house creaking. After a while, you won't even like the sound of your own voice. You won't even want to think.

"You want to know how I know about all this? My father kept me down here like that for almost two weeks when I was just ten. I didn't have as much to eat as you do, and I didn' t have anything much to do. My mother was in the hospital. She had a heart thing and had to have an operation. He never told her about what he did to me and never brought me to see her . I didn' t cry while I was down here, at least not loud enough for him to hear He didn't let me out until a day before my mother came home, and he warned me not to tell her , or else. He said it would make her sick and she'd die, so I never told."

He looked at the cat, who was sitting quietly and looking up at him as if he could understand every word. Then he reached down and picked him up.

"Mr. Moccasin won't even be here for you to talk to. He goes upstairs until I say you're ready and fit for family."

He turned and walked out of the basement apartment. I heard the lock click into place.

If someone was mistakenly thought to be dead and woke up just as the coffin was closed over her, the sound would have been exactly the same.

13

Haylee

I fell asleep for quite a while. It was dark outside when I awoke, but the days were shorter now , so I knew it wasn't that late. My bedroom door had been left partially open, the narrow slice of light from the chandelier in the hallway reaching my vanity-table mirror and reflecting eerie shadows on the wall, shapes that resembled fingers pressed against a glass pane. Kaylee might be looking out from some prison window and dreaming of rescue, I thought. A surge of regret washed over me, but I shook it off quickly.

Then I sat up and listened to see if anything new was happening. My stomach grumbled, reminding me that I hadn't eaten much today and now I was very hungry, so I got up, turned on the light to wipe the shadows off the wall, washed my face, and ran a brush through my hair. I could see the light blink - ing on my phone and checked it. There were seven messages. I imagined that the longer this went on, the more courageous our classmates would become. Most were probably afraid to hear bad news or had heard how upset I was and were afraid to talk to me.

Maybe their parents were telling them that they should be calling and offering to do whatever they could for me. That was fine. Later I would have a group of them trailing behind me and doing my bidding so they could think they were helping me cope with the terrible grief.

However, I wasn't going to return to school for as long as I could avoid it, and I really didnt expect too many visitors. I was afraid that, at least in the beginning when I did return, I would be treated like someone with a disease, the disease of sorrow. No one would want to invite me to parties or be funny in front of me. Over the next few days, teachers would send work home for me, but I really didn' t care. I was sure I would get away with procrastinat- ing, and if I did do an assignment and did it poorly, they would still give me a passing grade. It would be cruel to do otherwise.

Milk the cow of compassion, I told myself. *Enjoy it while you can.*

When I started down the stairs, I could smell

the aroma of reheated Chinese food. It was only
a little past five. When the days were shorter, we
ate earlier. The aromas heightened my hunger even
more. I didn't even bother to look in on Mother. To
my surprise, she was already sitting at the dining-
room table with Mrs. Lofter beside her , hovering
over her. She was wearing one of her more colorful
blouse-and-skirt outfits, and her hair was neatly
pinned back. She wore her favorite ruby earrings
and matching necklace, too. She had taken the time
to do her makeup. No one who saw her sitting
there would think anything even vaguely resem -
bling sadness had entered this house. It was enough
to make me pause for a moment and think that
maybe it had all been a dream.

"Hey," I heard.

Daddy appeared in the kitchen doorway . He
was wearing an apron and looked quite ridiculous.
Was this, too, part of some therapy, his doing do -
mestic work? I could count on the fingers of one
hand how many times he had done anything in our
kitchen before he had left us. He was never home in
time to help and had claimed he was so bad in the
kitchen that he would burn water when making tea.

"Hungry?" he asked. "Everyone else was starving, so I got things under way early ." He spoke
loudly so his voice would carry into the dining
room.

Everyone? I thought. *Who's everyone?*

"Yes," I said, and looked again at Mother.

Despite how nice she looked, she was staring ahead with a vacant expression, her eyes avoiding me. Mrs. Lofter was encouraging her to have some wonton soup.

"I fell asleep," I said, sliding into my usual seat.

Mother finally looked at me and smiled. "So did Kaylee," she said.

"What?"

I grimaced when I saw a place setting at Kaylee's seat. *If they put food on her dish, I'll go absolutely bonkers myself,* I thought. Maybe Mrs. Lofter could hear my thoughts. She focused those eyes of warning on me.

Mother turned to her, a broad smile settling on her face. It looked like tiny flashlights had been turned on behind her eyes, too. "Ever since they were born, they took naps at exactly the same time," she told Mrs. Lofter, "and woke up at the same time, even when they were in different rooms."

"Remarkable," Mrs. Lofter said.

"Yes, it is. They are," Mother said. She ate some soup.

Couldn't she see that Kaylee wasn't here?

Daddy began to bring in the food. "It's a feast," he said. "I got that sweet-and-sour shrimp dish you like and egg rolls and steamed rice. There's chicken with snow peas, beef with broccoli, and some egg foo young, pot stickers, lettuce wraps . . ."

"So much?"

"Tomorrow we'll eat for lunch whatever we don't eat tonight." He put a cup of Coke on the table beside me and whispered, "Coca-Cola." Mother never wanted us to drink soda because of the sugar, but he knew that I, more than Kaylee, loved it, especially Classic Coke. "Well, now," he declared, slapping his hands together . "Let's get down to some serious eating."

This was so weird to me. It was as if nothing had happened to Kaylee, and Mother and Daddy hadn't ever divorced. Daddy sat where he always had sat.

Mrs. Lofter began to serve herself. "It all looks so delicious," she said, and smiled at me.

I looked from Mother to Daddy , shook my head slightly, and began to eat.

The phone rang, and we all paused—all except Mother, who didn't appear to have heard it. Per - haps she was hearing conversations from years ago, I thought. She wore a familiar soft smile, like the smile she would have whenever Kaylee and I had done or said something that pleased her, especially if we had done or said it in front of other people at a dinner here or in a restaurant.

Daddy went to the phone. Mrs. Lofter and I paused to listen, but Mother went on eating, look - ing as relaxed and casual as I had ever seen her

"Thank you," Daddy said after a good minute or so. "We appreciate your keeping us informed."

He looked at Mother and Mrs. Lofter and then returned to the table and began to eat as if there had never been a phone call.

"Tell you later," he whispered, gazing at Mother, who had finished her soup and reached for an egg roll.

"My girls have perfect table manners. That was part of their homeschooling, you know ," she told Mrs. Lofter, who smiled and nodded.

"Very unusual these days," Mrs. Lofter said. "Most *parents* don't have good table manners."

"Oh, I know. I remember the first time we took them for Chinese food," Mother said. "Y ou ordered four different dishes, remember , Mason? There was so much food then, too."

"Yes, Keri."

She turned back to Mrs. Lofter . Who did she think Mrs. Lofter was, and why did she think she was here? I wondered.

"It was their first time at a Chinese restaurant. We wanted to see what they liked or didn' t like. Neither of them liked fried rice, and both hated peanut sauce. Remember, Mason?"

"I do," he said. "We took a lot home for the next day, most of which you and I ate."

I remembered that dinner. I loved peanut sauce, but I had to pretend that I hated it because Kaylee did. However, the next time we went to a Chinese restaurant, I made her eat the corn soup. I wasn't terribly fond of it, but I knew she didn't like it at all.

Tit for tat. It was always tit for tat.

I looked at Kaylee's empty seat and then at Mother. She was gazing at it, too, but her expression hadn't changed. Did she really see her there? Did she hear her? Would she see her everywhere? How long would this go on? I was actually losing my appetite, which was probably something anyone, especially Mrs. Lofter, might anticipate. After all, how could I have an appetite with all this tragedy happening? It made me angry. I had come downstairs with a ravishing appetite, hoping to get a little relief from the gloom and doom. I expected to find only Daddy here, with Mother and Mrs. Lofter up in her room, where Mother would be crying herself inside out.

However, to my surprise, Mother was eating as well as ever, obviously enjoying every bite. I looked at Mrs. Lofter, who now wore a look of satisfaction. What was there to be satisfied about? Keeping Mother in denial? Maybe she was just as crazy, I thought. Maybe a patient from the mental clinic was impersonating a nurse. I looked at Daddy. He seemed perfectly satisfied, too.

"That would be nice," Mother suddenly said, even though neither I nor Daddy had said anything. "Wouldn't it, Mason?"

Daddy looked up from his food. "Oh, sure," he said.

"What would be nice?" I asked. I couldn't help it.

"After we're finished, before dessert, you can play something on the pianos for our guest," Mother replied.

She looked from me to Kaylee's empty seat. I couldn't help the way my mouth fell open. I even choked on a noodle.

But Mrs. Lofter nodded and smiled. "That would be so nice," she said.

"Yes," Daddy said. "You'll be very pleased. They play so well."

I suddenly felt like my food would come rush- ing back up my throat and surge out of my mouth. I covered my face and looked away.

"Easy," Daddy whispered, sensing that I wanted to get up and race back to my room. "She's totter- ing."

Tottering? I looked at Mother . She looked as happy and as satisfied as ever. It was as if we had fallen back years and years, certainly to before the trouble between our parents had grown to the point of their thinking about divorce. This wasn't exactly how I envisioned it would be. How long was I ex- pected to pretend nothing had happened?

I tried to eat some more and then finally pushed my plate away. All I wanted to do was get out of there. Kaylee and I usually would clear the table and help Mother with the dishes. It wouldn't look good if I didn't make an effort to do it now, I thought. Why did we have to have Mrs. Lofter living with us? I had to put on a continuous act for her . How long would I need to perform? It felt like mice were chewing on the inside of my stomach.

Reluctantly, I stood and began to clear the table.

"Hey, don't worry about that tonight," Daddy said, reaching for my hand. "I'll help. You go to the piano."

"What?"

Did he really want me to play without Kaylee? I was sure he saw the shock on my face.

He nodded at Mother, who was looking very pleased. I glanced at Mrs. Lofter, who was gazing at me intently, almost defying me to refuse. How should I play this scene? I wondered. Shouldn' t I be too upset to do it? Why couldn' t I be selfish with my suffering, too? On the other hand, wasn't I worried about my mother? Wasn't it more important to protect and help her and follow the psychiatric nurse's directions? If I didn' t, I would attract new suspicions.

I almost felt like saying, *C'mon, Kaylee. Let's play for Mother and Daddy's guest.*

I did look back at Kaylee's empty seat, and then I went to the living room and sat at my piano. I sifted through some of the pieces we often played together. I settled on Brahms' s *Hungarian Dance*

No. 5. It was one I liked more than Kaylee did,
but Mother never knew which pieces either of us
preferred. Kaylee was good at keeping her opinions
disguised. For the piano recitals, at least, we took
turns compromising with each other.

Mrs. Lofter entered, holding Mother' s arm,
and they sat on the smaller settee. Mother had her
hands in her lap and her face frozen in a proud
smile, which right now looked more like a mask.
Daddy appeared in the doorway and nodded at me
to begin. I looked across at Kaylee's piano and her
empty piano bench. *I can't get rid of her*, I thought.
At least, not now. I would do what I usually did
when we played: lower my head so I didn't have to
look at her and begin. Ironically , I think I played
better than I ever had. When I finished and looked
at Daddy, I saw how pleased he was. Mrs. Lofter
appeared quite impressed, too, and Mother looked
more delighted than ever.

I thought I might go out the back door and
scream as loudly as I could. Instead, I rose and ex -
cused myself, looking directly at Mother and claiming to have homework.

"They're so diligent," she told Mrs. Lofter   .
"Top of their class, both of them."

I started out, but Mother raised her arms for me
to come to her and give her a kiss. Nothing drove
home her insanity more than that. Where was Kay-

lee's kiss? It was always right after mine, or mine was right after hers. I kissed her anyway and didn't look back. I didn't want to see her raising her arms again and turning her cheek for Kaylee's lips.

Daddy followed me to the hallway . "You're doing great, Haylee," he said.

"It's nuts, Daddy."

"I know. It's difficult. For now, it's what has to be done."

I started away but stopped. "What did the po - lice tell you on the phone, Daddy?"

"Because of the television and newspaper re - ports and Kaylee's picture being well circulated, they have received dozens of possible leads and are following through. They've put some other officers on the leads. They're going full out now."

"When will we know anything?"

"We'll know as soon as they hit something concrete. They assured me, Haylee. Right now, no news is good news." It was a dark thing to say, and he knew it the moment he uttered it. "I mean . . . let's keep hopeful."

"Okay," I said.

He moved forward and hugged me. "This is so hard for you, so hard. Y ou're my little cham - pion." He kissed me on the forehead. I held on to him a moment longer and then turned and went upstairs.

This was too dreary, I thought. I had to get back into the swing of things earlier than I had planned. I hadn't realized how boring it could be. I was never as strong as Kaylee when it came to being alone. That was why I dreaded Mother locking us away in the pantry when I did something she thought was wrong. Kaylee could amuse herself, whereas I felt like ants were crawling in circles inside my stomach.

I started to sift through the phone messages and decided to call Ryan Lockhart first. Just before Kaylee's convenient disappearance, I had been toying with him enough to annoy her. He was Rachel Benton's boyfriend, and Rachel was one of Kaylee's good friends. She had called and left a message, too, but I ignored her. She was crying through most of it anyway, a bit over the top, I thought.

It was just this year that Ryan had become more attractive. At six foot three, he was on the basket - ball team and wore his light-brown hair as long as the coach would permit. T o me, R yan seemed to have filled out overnight. He had stunning blue-green eyes, an impishly flirtatious smile, and a body some ancient Greek sculptor would have loved to use as a model.

I wondered how a girl like Rachel could win his interest. She was pretty, I guessed, but not very sexy. I had told Kaylee so and pointed out that Rachel didn't wear clothes that would accent her figure and she definitely needed a remedial class in eye makeup. Unlike Kaylee, I hadn't been afraid to tell Rachel so to her face, either.

"She's what I would call a convenient girl - friend," I had told Kaylee. "Too reliable."

"What? What's that mean?"

"He doesn't have to worry about her being there. She's like a pet poodle. And let me tell you, boys don't really like that. They act like they do because everyone expects them to, but what they really want is someone with more excitement, more challenge. He's always looking my way."

"Stop it," Kaylee had ordered. "Just stop it. Don't mess with every other girl's boyfriend, Haylee. You'll have everyone hating us."

"Hating me, you mean," I said.

And then I had started to flirt with him, especially because she had told me I shouldn't. Kaylee always believed in her heart of hearts that she car - ried enough conscience for us both.

Ryan answered his cell phone on the first ring because, I was sure, he saw my number on the caller ID. At the moment, there wasn't anyone else in our school who was more important for him to talk to, besides the fact that I knew he was already a little more than attracted to me. And contrary to what my mother or anyone else thought, when a boy was attracted to me, it didn' t mean he'd be automati - cally attracted to Kaylee. Anyone who looked at us for more than one second would see the difference. I was proud that I was sexier and more dangerous. *Sweet Kaylee but Hot Haylee*, that was my motto. I was even thinking of getting a T -shirt with that written across my breasts.

"Don't tell me how sorry you are," I said as soon as Ryan said hello. "It will only make me cry"

"Oh, well, can I ask you if you need anything?"

"Yes. I need lots. I need to get off this floor of dynamite. My parents are on the verge of mental crack-ups. We have a special nurse here to help with my mother. I'm afraid to leave the house in case there' s news about Kaylee. We're all on pins and needles."

"Yikes."

"Yikes? Who says 'yikes'?" I finally felt like laughing.

"My father," he said. "He grew up on a farm in upstate New York, and that was practically the only curse word my grandparents allowed."

"I bet that changed when he left for college."

"Not really. Dad's a . . . bit of a . . ."

"Puritan?" I was going to suggest a few other choice descriptions but thought I'd better not.

"Yeah, right."

"Are you planning to do anything tonight?" I asked. It was still early.

"Tonight? Oh, I was just about to leave the house to take Rachel to the new Bradley Cooper movie. She likes him."

"So do I. I wish I could go, but instead I'll watch the clock and shudder whenever the phone rings. That's my excitement."

"I'm . . ."

"Don't say it. You're sorry." After a pregnant pause, I asked, "Do you have to go to the movies?"

"Have to? I dunno, why?"

"I haven't asked anyone over. It's cruel to bring someone into this, I suppose."

"Oh. No, I don' t think that's cruel. Someone should be there with you. What about Rachel? I'm sure she'd want to spend time with you. I can drop her off at your house instead of taking her to the movie."

"She's more Kaylee's friend than mine. She'd be depressing," I said.

He was quiet.

"Well, enjoy the movie," I said.

"Wait," he said before I could hang up. "Let me see about it. I think I could take her to the movie another night."

"Don't disappoint her because of me."

"She'll understand, or she should," he said firmly. "How about I come over now?"

"That would be very nice. We'll hang out in my room. I'll wait for you by the front door and take you right up so you don' t have to see my parents, especially my mother. You sure you want to do this?"

"Yeah. Don't worry. Give me fifteen."

"Okay. Thanks," I said. "It's sweet of you."

I hung up. Anyone who saw the smile on my face would think I had won the lottery or some - thing. *Now to explain it to Daddy*, I thought.

Mrs. Lofter had taken Mother back to her room, and he was finishing up in the kitchen. He was still wearing that silly apron. For a moment, I simply stood watching him. I wondered if he had a new girlfriend and wished he could be with her instead of playing good daddy and ex-husband here. He hadn't lost his good looks since the divorce. If anything, whenever I saw him afterward, I thought he looked younger and more relaxed. He turned when he realized I was standing there.

"Hey," he said, holding a dish.

"I should have helped you."

"It's okay. I haven't had KP duty since my college days. You all right?"

"No. I can't stop the trembling inside me," I said, and ran to him. I threw my arms around him and pressed the side of my face against his chest.

He put the plate down and held me. "When bad things happen to people we love, we suffer almost as much ourselves," he said.

"I feel like I've been abducted, too. Whatever happened to Kaylee happened to me. It was always that way, and vice versa."

"I know." He kissed my forehead.

"I can't read. I can't watch television. I don't like talking to friends on the phone as much as Kaylee does."

"I understand."

I stepped back, wiping my eyes and taking deep breaths. "I have one friend. He's not really a boy-friend. He's just a nice boy, a good friend," I said. "His name is Ryan Lockhart. He just called, and I broke down talking to him. He insisted on stopping by for a while, and I said it was all right. Is it?"

He thought a moment and then nodded. "Yeah, sure, Haylee. It's too much to expect you just to sit around and wait for news. I know how nerve-racking it is. Probably be good for you to have a little distraction while we wait. Just don't bring him around your mother. It's not something he would understand, and . . ."

"I understand, Daddy. I'll take him right to my room, and we'll just stay there until he leaves."

"Okay," he said.

The phone rang, and he went to answer it. It was another of Mother's friends. While he talked, I slipped out and waited by the front door. I could see anyone pull into our driveway through the multipane window. Not more than five minutes later, Ryan drove up. As soon as he got out of his car, I opened the front door and stood there waiting for him.

"Hey," he said.

The moment he stepped up, I threw my arms around him. He felt awkward for a moment and then embraced me.

"This is terrible," he said. "My mother can' t stop talking about it."

I took a deep breath and pulled back, but I held on to his right hand. "Come in," I said. "Just follow me up the stairs."

Daddy didn't step out of the kitchen. I hurried Ryan through the entryway to the stairs and prac - tically dragged him up and into my room before anyone could appear. Then I closed the door.

He shrugged. "I was expecting to see police or the FBI or something."

"They come and go. No one is anticipating a demand for ransom. This is something worse," I said, and plopped onto my bed.

He stood gazing down at me. His awkward in- decision about what to do amused me. I turned over and pushed myself up to my pillows.

"It's all right," I said, patting the bed. "Take off your shoes and just lie beside me."

He glanced at the door, shrugged, and did as I had asked. "So no one's called yet, huh?" he asked.

"Just the police from time to time. How did Rachel take your not going to the movies but com- ing here instead?"

"I didn't tell her," he said. "If I did, she would have wanted to come, too."

"Very smart. There's no room for her on my bed," I added, and turned toward him.

His eyes widened as that sweet, flirtatious smile of his appeared. "Very funny."

"It's not meant to be funny ," I said, fixing my serious, intent sexual gaze on him. "I need to think of other things, or I'll go mad. Even the psychiatric nurse said that to me. Y ou can't dwell on sadness and worry all day and night."

"No, I guess not."

"It doesn't mean you don't love someone who's in trouble. It does them no good for you to get sick and weak, too."

"Right," he said.

"Can you take my mind off things?" I asked, running my left forefinger up from his chest to the tip of his chin.

He didn't move until I brought my lips to his. Then he put his arm around me and kissed me harder and longer . I could hear his breathing quicken. *Oh, how easy this is*, I thought, *and look at the excuse I have for whatever I do, no matter how I behave.* I sat up and pulled my blouse over my head. Before he could react to that, I undid my bra and dropped it off the side of the bed. When I turned back to him, he was trembling with excite - ment.

"Boys like it fast, don't they?" I whispered as I brought my lips to his cheek.

He looked at the closed door.

"I locked it when I closed it," I said.

"Why me?" he asked.

"Why not you?"

He started to undress. I rushed to pull back the blanket. He slipped in beside me, naked. We kissed, and my body, which had been under such dull depression too long, was electrified. He kissed his way down my neck, to my shoulders, over my breasts, and to the small of my stomach. Then he reached over the side of the bed, fumbled with his pants for a moment, and came up with a contraceptive.

"You answered the question," I said.

"What question?"

"Why you?" I said, and we began to make love.

I was more passionate and demanding than I had ever been with any boy . Every rush travel - ing up the insides of my thighs or down from my breasts in waves through my body was stronger than any I had ever felt. He was holding on to me as if I were a bull he was riding. I could see that the one fear in his eyes was that he would reach an orgasm before I was completely satisfied. He moaned almost with disappointment when it happened.

"It's all right," I said. "You were wonderful, just what I needed."

He fell back and caught his breath as he gazed up in wonder at the ceiling. "I feel good," he said, "but guilty, too."

"Because of Rachel?"

"A little, but more because I never dreamed this would happen now. I mean, with what's going on here."

"That's part of the reason, but only part of it," I added quickly. "I've always fantasized about you being here in my room with me."

"Really?"

"I think Rachel knows it, too."

"Oh. Maybe," he said. "What difference does it make now?" He turned to me, smiling.

"None that I can think of," I said.

A half hour later, we made love again, and then I thought it was best that I sneak him out of the house.

"Let me check first," I told him. I certainly didn't want my mother or Mrs. Lofter to see him. Daddy was in his office on the phone, so I was able to show Ryan out undetected.

I walked him to his car , and we kissed good night. "I'll call you tomorrow," he promised.

"No. Wait for me to call you," I said. "I don' t know what will be going on here tomorrow."

"Sure. I hope it all works out well."

"It will," I said.

He smiled at my optimism.

I wanted to add, *It already has*, but I just kissed him one more time and went back into the house.

It was quiet, but as I started up the stairway , Mrs. Lofter was coming down. "Y our mother is finally asleep," she said. "Come get me if she wakes up too soon."

"Of course," I said. I watched her descend. "Of course I will," I whispered.

On my way back to my room, I paused at Kaylee's door. Something made me want to open it and look in. Maybe I needed to remind myself that she was gone.

When I opened the door, I was in shock myself. *Move over, Mother*, I thought.

Someone, probably Mother, had put everything back exactly how it had been before I had torn Kaylee's room apart.

14

Kaylee

It had been a long time since either Haylee or I or both of us had been locked in the pantry for something we had done to displease Mother. Even so, the silence we had suffered back then was not anywhere as intense as the silence Anthony was imposing on me now . We had hated being shut up in the dark when Mother did it to us, but we'd known we would be let out. There had always been an end in sight. It frightened me to think that in his madness, Anthony would never come back, never unlock the door. I was, in the most terrifying sense of the words, shut up in a coffin just like his mother in the bedroom above me.

He was right about how I would be keen to hear the sound of his footsteps. After a while, I couldn't help but listen for them, for some sign of life, even his life of madness. I wondered if I, too, would go insane. Would I reach the point where I would want to hear him walking around his house and pray to hear him on the stairs outside the basement door? Would I grow so tired of talking to myself and walking around in circles that I would look forward to seeing him and listening to him talk to me, no matter what frightening things he might say? How horrible would it be to become that desperate? In what deranged state of mind would I be? This place, despite the furniture, the music, and the books, was destined to become the medieval dungeon I had first imagined.

It was difficult to move around anyway. My feet hurt, and my legs ached, and I hated the sound of the chain dragging behind me over the floor. I slept a lot, not for long periods but in spurts, and every time I woke, I woke with a start, sitting up quickly and listening hard. W as he home? Had someone come? I was getting to know every creak in the house, every moan in the pipes, and the different sounds the breeze or wind made sliding across the two windows. I endured the stings from the soles of my feet and stood on a chair for hours at a time, peering out between the boards that covered those windows, sometimes until it grew too dark to see anything. I was dreaming that the driver of that pickup truck had seen me and had finally worked up the courage to get involved with what looked like someone abusing a young woman.

To keep from going completely nuts, I played the music he had brought down, music I called Haylee's music. I kept it going most of the day and even into the night. There were things to read, mostly children's stories, some of which both Haylee and I had read or Mother had read to us when we were very young. I tried to be creative with the food he had left me, and as it dwindled, I realized I should ration certain things. I hated wearing his father's robe. It stank and make my skin itch. I finally decided to wash it and hung it in the shower While it dried, I walked around with two towels wrapped around me.

I was diligent about caring for my cuts and bruises. Except for my vigils at the window, I tried staying off my feet for long periods of time, which was why I dozed so much. After the fifth day, I realized I hadn't brushed my hair once. When I looked at myself in the mirror, I almost didn't recognize the image staring back at me. I pictured my sister standing beside me, looking at the same image over my shoulder.

You're getting what you always dreamed of having, dear Haylee, I thought. *Right now, no one would call us identical twins. People might not even call us sisters. You would have no trouble getting anyone to believe you were the prettier one.*

Maybe it was the solitude combined with the dreariness of my surroundings, but I thought my eyes looked like weakening lightbulbs. The excitement and pleasure, the curiosities and interests that brightened the candle of life were so subdued in me that I sometimes thought I was looking at a wax replica of myself. It resembled me, but it was life - less, listless, almost comatose.

Meanwhile, Anthony was true to his threat. He must have been on that job he had described as being a good distance away. I didn't hear him come home until late in the evenings, and as if he was carrying out his determined punishment of me, he practically tiptoed when he walked on the floors above. I had to strain sometimes to hear him. My only amusement was to try to determine where he was standing. I realized where the bedroom with the coffin was situated above me and heard him go in there often. He seemed to remain there for a long time each time. Maybe he even slept in there beside it.

After nine days, I had run out of milk, eggs, and bread. I was eating handfuls of dry cereal for breakfast. There was no fruit left, nor was there any cheese. For dinner, I ate out of a peanut butter jar, scraping out every bit. The juice was gone, too. I knew my energy level was diminishing. My sleep, which had occurred in spurts, was becoming longer and longer naps, sometimes taking up half the day.

Finally, I had no interest in reading anything, and I stopped playing music. I no longer went to look out the window through the boards, either.

Loneliness was never sharper, a knife that cut deeply into my heart and made me ache inside and out. I began to imagine that Haylee was here occasionally. She visited to see how I was doing, and whenever she came, she was always dressed in something pretty and sexy, her hair perfect, her makeup just the way she always wanted it to be, despite Mother's warnings about it being too much.

Of course, she was always smiling.

She never spoke. She just stood there looking at me.

"You knew this was going to happen," I told her. "Are you satisfied?"

She didn't respond.

"Why did you do this? Why?" I screamed. When I screamed very loudly, she left, and I went back to sleep, thinking that if Anthony would come home just once when she was here, he would see that there was a Haylee after all.

I wondered if he had ever sneaked down to check on me late at night. If he had, he certainly would have seen how low my food supplies were. How bad would he let things get? Soon I would have nothing. I began to believe that he had com - pletely forgotten about me, that he had told himself it had all been a dream, I wasn' t here. It threw me

into another panic. Maybe this was what had happened with another girl he had captured and kept
down here, and one day he had come down and
found her dead. If she hadn' t starved, she might
have committed suicide. Was that my destiny, too?

The nightmares became more vivid, and they
weren't confined to sleeping at night, either. It
got so that every time I dozed, I'd have one that
involved me dying here, my fingers covered with
the dried blood that had come from my desperate
scratching at the door. When I thought about all
this, especially the possibility of dying down here,
it would make me shiver so much with fear that I
had to wrap the blanket around myself.

The worst part of all this dreary thinking was
the fear that I might die and he might bury me
somewhere and no one would ever know what had
happened to me. He had already done away with
my clothing and would clean away any possible
trace of me. I would disappear . Mother would go
to her own deathbed still hoping that I would come
home. Daddy would end up the same way. Whether
Haylee would suspect that I was dead and gone I
did not know, but I imagined she would ease her
conscience by telling herself that I was off living
as Anthony's wife and by now had a family of my
own.

My friends and teachers would forget me eventually. Oh, maybe once in a while someone would

bring me up. "Remember Kaylee Blossom Fitzgerald and how she simply disappeared? I wonder what became of her."

People would shrug. There were many other things to think about, happier things, and besides, what good did thinking about Kaylee Blossom Fitzgerald do anyone?

Imagining all this gave me the idea of writing a diary so I could prove my existence. Time had become blurred for me. I had no idea what day it was, and after a while, I had trouble remember - ing exactly how long it had been since I had been abducted. I would just use numbers to signify the passage of time, I thought. It didn't matter that I didn't know if it was Tuesday or Wednesday. I re-called movies in which prisoners kept in dungeons for years marked time by scratching lines on a wall. I'd better not do that, I thought. Keeping track of the days would only heighten the pain associated with how long I was here. Why do it? What did the number of days matter now? They all ran together. I was in a day that had no limits.

What I planned to do instead was write about what had happened to me in as much detail as I could and then find a place in the basement to hide it so that years and years from now, after Anthony was dead or gone, someone might stumble on it and then contact whatever family I had and give them the diary. At least they would have some closure that way. It was depressing to plan how to help those who loved and remembered you and no longer to think of ways to help yourself. But what choice did I have?

I was surprised at how exhausting it was to write a couple of pages in the notepad I had found. It was a child' s notepad, with different cartoon animal characters at the top of each page. The paper itself had yellowed with time. Sitting there thinking about what to write was becoming a chore in and of itself. I was afraid of falling asleep with the pad in my lap and Anthony finding and destroying it, so as soon as my eyes began to close, I stopped and hid the pad behind the food cabinet. There was just enough space between it and the wall for me to slide it in. The following day, I'd get it out with a butter knife, convinced that he would never find it if I kept it hidden there.

One morning—I guessed it was morning, since I had fallen asleep in the dark, and when I woke, there was light streaking through the boards—I looked at myself in the mirror and realized I had lost significant weight. There was a vacant darkness around my eyes, and my cheeks were a little sunken. My lips were pale, and my hair was so twisted and dirty I resembled a hag on the streets of plague-ridden London. My complexion was colorless. I thought I could see the tiny blue veins through my cellophane skin.

I truly am dying, I thought. *I'm wasting away.* The light within was dwindling. *It's not my imagination.* I panicked and charged across the room as quickly as I could. With all the strength I had left, I began to pound on the door . I screamed until I had no voice, and then my legs gave out and I sank to the floor. I regained consciousness a few times but remained there, staring at a few dozen small brown ants that were working diligently , gathering up minuscule food crumbs and bringing them as a team to their hole between the floor and the wall. It occurred to me that they could outlive me. In any case, they could come and go as they pleased. They could even find their way outside. Imagine envying an ant, I thought, and felt myself smile.

In moments, I was asleep again at the bottom of the basement door, which was where Anthony found me. I had no idea how long I had been lying there, but I felt my body being moved and opened my eyes to see him carrying me to the bed. He laid me out gently and stood looking down at me. He was in and out of focus for a few moments. My lips were so dry that I couldn't speak without pain.

"I think you're ready," he said, and smiled.

He braced me up on the pillow , moving me around as if I were no more than a rag doll. I felt him brush strands of hair away from my eyes.

"Hello in there," he sang. He pretended to knock on my skull. "Hello. Anyone home? Come out, come out, wherever you are."

I closed and opened my eyes. He was simply standing there and smiling. I was so confused. For a few moments, I thought maybe it wasn't Anthony. Maybe it was someone who had finally come to rescue me.

He put up his hand like a cop stopping traffic. "Don't go away," he said.

Then he left and returned a few minutes later with jars of baby food, napkins, and a spoon. I watched curiously as he undid the tops of the jars and dipped a teaspoon into one. He brought it to my lips. I felt like I was outside myself, watching all of this happen to someone else.

"Open," he said, poking the spoon gently against my lips, and I did.

It tasted like sweet potato. Nothing had ever tasted better. He gave me another spoonful and then held a third spoonful just a little bit away from my lips. My whole body wanted to lunge at the nutrition.

"Now, before you get this, I'd like to hear you say, 'Thank you, honey.' Go on. Say it."

I looked at the spoonful of food and then at him. "Thank you, honey," I said.

He smiled and fed me another spoonful and

another. "I'd like to know how much you love me," he said. "You can say, 'I love you so much.' That would be nice." He waited.

"I need some water. I can't talk," I said in a raspy voice.

"Oh, right. Sorry."

He rose and got me a glass of water , but he didn't give it to me. He held it near me.

"How much do you love me, sweet Kaylee? You can do it. You can make some words."

"I love you so much," I said. My throat hurt. It felt like it was torn inside.

He brought the water to my lips. "Drink slowly slowly. You're doing so well."

Doing so well? Was he seeing me? How could I be doing well? I was only a foot from my grave, so exhausted and defeated that it looked inviting.

"Don't worry. We'll build you up again, and then we'll have our honeymoon," he said. "W e'll have music and great dinners. I'll bring you some - thing beautiful to wear. That's right, something that fits you. Now that you're back and you realize how much we love each other, I'll get you many beauti- ful things, jewelry and shoes, everything that makes a woman feel like a woman."

He spoke the way a parent might speak to a little girl, telling her a story, and as he spoke, he fed me some more until the jar was empty. He opened

another jar of some chicken mixture and fed me
that. I drank and ate, listening to his description of
how we would begin a perfect family life.

"We won't have just one kid, of course. That
was my parents' mistake. I shoulda had a brother or
a sister. It's important. Sometimes I sit in a park not
far from here and watch the mothers and fathers
and their children play together and think, why
can't that be us? Of course, now it can. Someday
soon we'll be in that park with our kids.

"Okay," he said when I had finished the second
jar. "We got to go slow. I know how this should go
when someone's been away a while and then comes
back. It's sorta like a resurrection. It'll take at least
three days."

He laughed, and then he checked my feet and
nodded.

"Coming along," he said. "You did take good
care of them, but it will be a while yet, so we got to
keep you from doing too much for a while longer"

He gave me some more water, and then he went
out and up the stairs. I sat enjoying the feeling
of some food in my stomach. When he appeared
again quite a while later, I had fallen asleep, probably for hours. This time, he was carrying bags of
groceries.

"I didn't want to go out and shop for all this
until I thought you were ready," he said.

I couldn't believe how happy I was at the sight

of him and the food. I watched him putting it all away as he went on about our future. If it wasn' t being forced on me, I thought, it wouldn' t be so terrible a future, with a dedicated husband whose main concern was his family. Was my father's main concern his family? How could he leave us? No matter what my mother had done, why didn' t he think of us first and then himself? Was he sorry now? If he hadn't left, I might not be here. Was he blaming himself? Did his guilt wear on him? W as he crying for me?

Anthony was going on and on about the changes he would make in the house, changes to ae commodate more children, repairs he would make once we had reached a point he called "our gradua- tion," the point when we could move upstairs.

"I know I said we never would, but this place is too small for us, especially when we have more than one child, especially. Mother told me that would be okay."

Mother told you? I thought. *When? Was it when you had another girl down here?*

Or did he believe she had just told him? Was he talking every night to his dead mother in that cof - fin? Was that really why he kept it in her bedroom? I didn't think I was capable of feeling more terror, but suddenly, that thought was like the icing on a cake of horror.

"Don't think I don' t have the money to do all

this, either," he said. "I haven' t spent a tenth of what I have, and who could I spend money on before I had you anyway? My mother never wanted much, and I wouldn't buy my father a toothpick. You know, my mother used to steal money out of his pockets when he came home drunk. 'He'll only waste it,' she told me. Just her and me knew where she hid it, too. And he never realized she was taking his money. He was always too drunk to remember what he did and didn't have. We were a good team once, me and my mother. I bet you wish you had a mother like mine. I know you do. You said so. Well, you don't got to think about her anymore. Just think about us. Okay?"

He looked at me, holding up a fresh loaf of bread in his right hand and a package of ham in his left. How good that would taste, I thought, and nodded.

Why am I listening to him? I really am going crazy, I realized. *I'm being led down a path of insanity that he has cut through the maze of his everyday life, and I'm no longer fighting it.*

I should have hated myself for even nodding at him and forcing a smile. But what else could I do?

It surprised me that I wanted to live and be well again at any cost.

Anthony had left the door open, and suddenly, of his own volition, Mr . Moccasin strolled back into the basement. I was happy to see him. He could have stayed upstairs, but he wanted to be down here with me. I held out my arms, and the cat came to the bed, leaped up onto it, and curled up beside me.

Anthony watched with a broad smile on his face. "Mr. Moccasin knows who he should love. I'll give you some more to eat, let you rest a bit, and then we'll look into cleaning you up," he said.

He made another one of his perfectly trimmed and cut-up sandwiches with ham and cheese and brought it and a glass of orange juice to me. I sat up and ate slowly, closing my eyes with pleasure as each bite dissolved with my slow chewing and swallowing. The juice was delicious. I could feel my strength returning.

He stood back and watched me proudly, the smile widening on his face. "Beauty returns," he said. "Just like in the fairy tale, after a kiss."

He leaned over to kiss me and stood back, beaming. *In his mad mind, he actually does love me*, I thought. When I finished my sandwich and juice, I lay back and closed my eyes. I felt him take away the tray and then fix my blanket. I kept my eyes closed but sensed him hovering closer and closer. He kissed me on the forehead and cheek, patted my hair, and walked away. I opened my eyes and watched him cleaning the dishes. I fell asleep

and didn't wake until I heard him moving around
the basement apartment, picking up things and
mumbling to himself. He was dressed only in his
underwear. My eyelids fluttered, and he stopped.
He seemed to hear them, as if he could hear the flut-
ter of butterfly wings, and turned to me.

"Figured you'd be awake by now   ," he said,
walking over to the bed. "I've got your warm bath
ready. No shower tonight. You need to soak them
sores and bruises some."

He pulled back my blanket, unlocked the ankle
bracelet attached to the chain, and easily lifted me.

"You're a feather," he said, carrying me com -
fortably in his arms. "A feather of beauty."

He started out with me. I glanced back and saw
Mr. Moccasin leap off the bed to follow us up the
stairs. When we reached the top, Anthony kicked
the door to swing it open and then turned left and
took me to the bathroom. An old-fashioned claw-
foot bathtub was filled with water. He lowered me
to the floor gently and took off the bathrobe.

"Hey, I didn't realize you washed this old rag.
Good job." He dropped it onto the floor beside
me. Then he lifted me again and lowered me into
the tub. The water was just a few degrees less than
too hot. He stood back and looked at me. "You did
lose some weight," he said, shaking his head. "We'll
fix that. Good desserts every night, snacks in the
middle of the day, and vitamins."

He reached for a bottle on the shelf to the right of the tub and opened it.

"My mother's bath oils. She had them made special for her by this lady who concocts miracle stuff, guaranteed to keep your skin young. Not that you hafta worry about that," he said. "I just want you to feel good. This will do it." He poured some in and then reached for the washcloth on the rack. "You don't need to do anything. I'll do it all."

I was probably as helpless as when I was first born. I couldn't push him away. There was no point in screaming. The best thing to do was close my eyes and try to imagine that I was somewhere else.

He began on my neck and back and then worked over my shoulders and down the sides of my torso, reaching around to wash over my breasts and my chest. I thought that was it, but he hooked me under my arms and lifted me until I was standing in the water. Holding me around my waist with his left arm, he began washing below my waist, around my legs, and between them. I started crying, or at least I think I did. I didn't sob aloud. But he didn't notice or care. He lowered me again into the water and started to wash my hair.

Suddenly, he stopped and was silent. I held my breath. What was he planning now?

"Just a minute," he said, and walked out of the bathroom. When he returned, he had a good-size pair of scissors in his hands.

This time, there was no question that there were tears streaking down my cheeks. I uttered a cry and held up my hands to keep him away.

He went around and behind me. "Don't get so upset," he said. "Your hair is so bad that washing it won't help. We've got to start over."

I gasped and struggled to get out of the tub, but he forced me back into a sitting position and began cutting away, close to my scalp, and dropping clumps onto the floor. Too weak to do much else, I gave up, closed my eyes, and waited until he was finished.

"I'll clean this up later," he told me, as if I was worried about it.

Or maybe he was telling someone else.

He lifted me out of the tub and began to dry my body. I stood helplessly and waited. Then he lifted me in his arms and carried me out and down the stairs, placing me on the bed and covering me snugly.

"Get some sleep," he said. "I'm going to get you something nice to wear when you wake up."

When he had walked away , I felt around my head. He had cut my hair so unevenly that there were areas where I was almost bald, but there were also other areas where I had half the hair I'd had before. It was shocking but really not much more shocking than anything else he had done to me. I was far too tired and defeated to cry about it now

Mr. Moccasin crawled up beside me. I thought the cat looked sorry for me. He closed his eyes and opened them and then lowered his head to sleep. That was becoming the only solution either of us had to deal with unpleasantness and entrapment. For the first time since I had been brought here, when I closed my eyes, I wished that I would never open them again.

15

Haylee

Twice during the week that followed, R yan came over as soon as he got out of school. If it wasn' t for him, I would probably have gone as bonkers as Mother, or else I would have given in and returned to school earlier than I had intended. Each time he came, I sneaked him up to my room without Daddy, Mrs. Lofter, and especially Mother know-ing he was there, and we made love. It was funny how guilty he was each time afterward.

"Stop looking like you raped the farmer's daugh-ter or something," I told him. "Y ou're supposed to enjoy it."

"I can't help it," he said. "We're having fun and pleasure, while your sister . . . who knows what terrible things are happening to her? And your par-

ents, your mother just a little ways down the hall,
suffering. Practically every time my mother looks
at my little sister, she starts to cry, thinking about
your mother. So yeah, I think I'm taking advantage
of you sometimes."

"You can't think of it that way," I said. "It's just
the opposite. You're helping me. I'm suffering, too,
you know. You can't imagine how it is here for me
until you come to see me. I practically hide from
my mother. She is getting worse, and my father is
simply overwhelmed. Kaylee would never believe
it, but I made dinner three times this week. That
nurse wanted to help, but I told her to concentrate
on my mother. That was what we were paying her
to do. I know that sounds mean, but I can't help
it. It's hard to be pleasant. I'm not even pleasant to
myself."

"It's not mean. I understand. You're so strong,"
he said. "I don't know what I'd be like if my little
sister was abducted."

"I'm pretending to be strong, R yan. It's all an
act I do for my parents' sake. I'm not strong," I
said, and pressed my face against his chest. He hesi
tated and then embraced me again. I lifted my head
slowly and looked into his eyes, mine soaked in
tears that I was sure were so authentic-looking that
it would take a chemist to determine if they were
mine or a crocodile's.

"You're strong to me," he said.

"It feels so good to have someone with your strength holding me, Ryan, especially now."

I brought my lips closer to his, and then he kissed me, and I surrendered myself again to him. At least I was sure that was how he saw it. I never really surrendered myself to any boy. The trick was always to let them believe you did, when you were actually in control, getting them to move the way you wanted when you wanted them to. Some boys I'd met in school were so easy to arouse that I called them the hair-triggers. Kaylee thought that was obscene, but the girls who clung to me and my words were always titillated.

After we finished, I cried real tears, but they were tears of joy . I had hit a new record for or - gasms. He couldn't stop kissing my tears away and telling me that he would stand by me and do any - thing I needed. I luxuriated in his promises the way I might in a warm bubble bath, soaking up every word, every sentence followed by a kiss instead of a period.

We lay side by side, my head on his chest, doz - ing under a blanket of warm contentment. And then, suddenly, both of us woke to the sound of my mother shouting in the hallway. I sat up when she tried to open my bedroom door, shaking the handle roughly. We could hear Mrs. Lofter beside her, urg - ing her to return to her room.

"Where are you girls?" Mother yelled, and she

slapped the door so hard I was sure her palm would
be beet-red. "There are people downstairs waiting
to see you. They're asking about you. I told them
you would play something on the pianos." She
shook the door again.

Ryan sat up, looking petrified.

We heard Mrs. Lofter cajoling her . She lied
and said that Kaylee and I were at a school event.
I imagined it was the first thing that came to her
mind. After a few more moments, we heard them
walk away, Mother whining like a child. Neither of
us spoke until it was deadly quiet again.

"I'm sorry," I finally said. "My mother's not
right in her head."

"Play something on the pianos? Doesn' t she
know Kaylee's missing?" He looked so shocked I
thought I might start laughing.

"It's something Mrs. Lofter calls preventive
disbelief. It's too painful for my mother to face
what's happened, so she refuses to believe Kaylee's
gone, or her brain refuses. Mrs. Lofter's not just any
nurse, Ryan, she a psychiatric nurse."

"But . . . Kaylee's obviously not here. She can
see she's not here, right?"

I shrugged. "It's very complicated. I don' t understand it all myself. I hope, we hope, she returns
to reality soon, as dreadful as that is, but for now ,
there's not much more to do. She's on some medication and has the special nurse. Anyway, you saw

firsthand how horrible all this is for me. Not only is my sister gone, but it' s like my mother is gone, too." I turned onto my stomach and pressed my face to the pillow.

He was all over me, kissing me and swearing he would stay by my side. "I'll be here as much as you want, and when you return to school, I'll be right beside you every moment I can," he said.

I turned around again and reached up to stroke his handsome face. I wanted him here now, but if it was going to be this easy to get any boy I wanted anytime I wanted him, I wouldn' t want R yan haunting me. "We'll see," I said. "You're so sweet. We have to get up, and I'll show you out. I'd rather you not have to face my mother just yet. She'll just get more confused, and my father will blame me."

I could see that facing my mother was some - thing he'd rather not do, either . We dressed and went downstairs quietly, moving as silently as pos- sible, like two burglars. Daddy wasn' t home yet, so no one noticed Ryan. After he was gone, I made myself a snack and then called some of the girls who practically worshipped me. I soaked up their sym- pathy and promises like someone raising funds for a charity. I really called them because I wanted to see how many knew about Ryan Lockhart and me. As I'd expected, Rachel Benton had been moaning to everyone about my stealing her boyfriend. She was in a bind, because she looked bad for complaining about his helping me at such a horrible time for me and my family, and yet she couldn' t help feeling robbed. It was difficult for her to say any of the nasty things I knew she had believed about me even before Ryan had begun seeing me.

Everyone I spoke with wanted to come over to be with me, but I didn't want them to, for two reasons. I certainly didn't want them here when Ryan was here, and frankly, Mother's behavior was embarrassing. I knew I would grow tired and bored explaining it. However, I was sure Ryan would say something to someone now, and it would get out. Few would want to come here once they had heard about her. Eventually, when I was back in school, I was sure my mother's condition would add to the feelings of sympathy my teachers and the other kids would direct my way . I realized, however , that there was just so much of that I could take. After a while, I would want to get back to fun. I wasn't worried. Time would clear the way for me. After all, who wanted to keep saying things like "I'm sorry for you" or "Is there anything I can do for you?"

"Help me get past it," I planned to say. "Don't talk about it anymore. Try to act like nothing's different."

The sooner they did that, the sooner I could.

When Daddy got home, he came directly to my room. I had just finished another phone call and was lying there trying to think of something enjoyable to do. I had no interest in completing the homework that had been sent to me over the Internet. I didn't want to watch television or even put on earphones and listen to music. For the first few days after Kaylee's disappearance, I had thought doing any of that would look insensitive. Sometimes, however, I couldn't help it, and I did turn on the television but with the volume almost too low to hear. After a little while, that seemed boring; even my favorite soap opera held little interest. I used to copy the flirtatious techniques some of the actresses performed. Now it was like putting blanks in a gun or something. I was certainly not challenged by Ryan anymore.

Still, it was painful avoiding everything. I had never been fond of silence, but now I was afraid of falling into thoughts about Kaylee. What I didn' t need to do was nudge my conscience and wake it up. I was comfortable telling myself that what had happened was mostly Kaylee's fault anyway. Who had asked her to butt into my private life? She was more Mother's daughter than I was in that way . She was practically convinced that neither she nor I could have a private life without the other being involved. Well, now she was involved. How did she like it? I had been doing just fine with Anthony by myself. It had been amusing to me, but she wouldn't leave it alone, threatening to tell Mother or even Daddy. I was sure that if she could do it over again, she wouldn't be so annoying.

When Daddy knocked and came into my room, he saw me lying with my arms folded across my breasts and glaring angrily at the ceiling, frustrated. Sex was nice, but it was only adistraction. I was still locked up here. In a weird way, I was as trapped as Kaylee.

I lowered my eyes and looked at him. It was clear he was feeling sorry for me.

"What a mess," he said.

"Something new?"

"No, nothing. So far, everything's been a dead end, but I can see what this is doing to you, as well as to your mother and me."

"I'm just so angry about it, Daddy . If I could get my hands on that horrible man for just a few minutes . . ."

He nodded. "You and me both. Look. Mrs. Lofter is bringing your mother' s dinner to her in her room tonight. I thought you and I should get out. We'll go to a restaurant I know that' s about fifteen miles from here, so we won' t have to con - front anyone we know. What do you say? I think it would be good for us."

"I don't know. I won't be the best company for you."

"Of course you will."

I hesitated. *Don't be too anxious to do it; don't look too excited*, I told myself. "I don' t know," I said.

"I do. Let's do it."

I sighed deeply and nodded. "Okay. I'll put something else on."

"Yeah, wear something you like. I want you to feel good about yourself. We can't live in this depressing darkness day and night."

"But do you really think we should go? I mean . . . poor Mother."

"There's nothing wrong with trying to take a breather, Haylee, so don't feel guilty about it. She'll be fine for the few hours we're gone. Besides, I don't want you getting yourself run down and so depressed you get sick."

"Okay, Daddy," I said, as reluctantly as I could say something I really wanted to say. *Make him feel like he's dragging me out of here*, I thought.

As soon as he left, I practically leaped off the bed. With glee, I began to sift through my clothes, looking for something that would do just what he had suggested and help me feel good about myself. Since we were going to a restaurant where no one would know us, I didn't have to worry about looking too sexy, either. A few months ago, after I had persuaded Kaylee to show her she wanted it as much as I did, Mother had bought us identical dark-blue lace-detail dresses that clung to our bodies like another layer of skin. They were only twenty-one inches long from the waist, which Mother had thought was too short. I'd really wanted the dress, because I knew how sexy I would look when I wore it.

"Don't worry, Mother," I had said. "We know how to bend to pick something up when we wear them."

Reluctantly, she had given in when Kaylee matched my enthusiasm. In her heart of hearts, I knew she had wanted it as much as I did. She was just a lot shier. We had worn the dresses out of the store, and despite Mother's reluctance, she had basked in the looks of admiration we were getting from other women and girls, not to mention the lustful looks from men, even men old enough to be our grandfathers.

"We're making them regret their age," I had told Kaylee. "They're practically undressing us with their eyes."

She had looked back at them and then actually blushed and walked faster.

Something was surely missing from her DNA that was in mine after all, I thought, but it wasn't something Mother would ever let herself see.

Mother had bought us matching shoes, too. Now I got them out of the closet and then played with some earrings until I found the right pair. I hadn't done my makeup for so long I was afraid

I might mess it up, but after I was finished, I had to admit I looked pretty good, actually more than pretty good.

"I'll break hearts," I told my image, which was something I would say whenever I got dressed. I used to say, "We'll break hearts."

It felt so good not having that *We* to start so many sentences.

Daddy had changed and looked very handsome in his turquoise sweater. He had already informed Mrs. Lofter that we'd be gone. Of course, she had his cell number. I felt like I was getting off a sinking ship as we got into his car and drove away.

"You really look beautiful, Haylee," he said.

"Thank you, Daddy. I don't feel beautiful, but I'll try for you."

He laughed, something he probably hadn't done for nearly ten days. "You're always beautiful to me, Haylee. Both of you," he added.

"I know. I feel like I've got to be doubly good at everything, do Kaylee's share as well as my own. With everything!"

He was silent for a while, and then he took a deep breath, turned to me, and said, "I really wanted us to be alone so we could talk about your mother more freely."

"She can't stay like this forever, can she?"

"That's the issue," he said. "Mrs. Lofter has been in constant touch with a Dr. Solomon Jaffe in

Philadelphia, someone with whom she's worked. She was a nurse at his clinic for more than ten years. He's coordinated with Mrs. Lofter on the medica - tion your mother is taking, but if she doesn't make some progress, we're going to have to have Dr Jaffe examine her. It might be a deeper issue than we can manage at home, even with Mrs. Lofter's help, and then there are days when she won't be here, of course. I'd have to stay home when you were at school, or you might miss school."

He paused to let his words set in my mind. My silence was disturbing, but I was wondering if this was all leading to a place I had not intended to go. It was one thing to have people sympathize with you because your mother was distraught over the abduc- tion of one of her children but another to have her declared certifiable. How would I live with that? Not that I would feel so guilty about it, but I was thinking that everyone would look at me differently.

This had happened to Tami Gary when she was in the seventh grade. Her father had left them when Tami was in the fourth grade. Her parents hadn't gotten a divorce. He'd just left, and Tami's mother's family had tried to get him arrested for not pay - ing child support. That had been bad enough, but her mother had been into alcohol and some drugs, maybe as a result, and eventually had been put into a rehab clinic. Tami had gone to live with her grandmother, but I recalled how she had suddenly become so unpopular that she wasn' t invited to anything and barely had anyone to hang out with at school. Her mother had been in and out of rehab until she had eventually been put into a mental clinic, supposedly because of side effects from the life she had been leading, if it could be called a life. When Tami's grandmother had died, Tami had been sent to live with an aunt and uncle on her father' s side, and no one had ever heard from her or about her again. And no one had cared!

"Do you understand what I'm saying, Haylee?" Daddy now asked when I remained silent.

"I think so," I said. "She could go into a nut - house."

"Well, you shouldn' t call it that. Nobody should—and anyway, even if she had to be admit - ted, it could be for only a while."

"Doesn't matter, Daddy. Once she's in there, everyone will think she's crazy."

"Maybe it won't come to that. Maybe we'll get Kaylee back, and things will return to normal," he said.

He wasn't saying it with any conviction. He was saying it the way parents said a thousand different things to you as you grew up. "Maybe Santa will bring you that for Christmas. . . . Maybe we'll go to Disneyland next year. . . . Maybe we'll do that when you're older." There were more maybes in life than anything else. Maybes were mostly empty promises designed to make you shut up, stop your complaints, and leave your parents alone.

If I had to compare the two of them as we were growing up, I'd say Mother was more definite or determined about her maybes. Daddy used maybes a lot, especially just before their divorce. It seemed perfectly natural for him to be using another maybe now.

"We have to be concerned for her ," he continued.

"Can't I just continue pretending along with her that Kaylee is home?" I said. "I'll set the table that way, and I'll invent conversations that Mother can overhear, and . . ."

"The danger comes when she stops avoiding the truth, Haylee. The impact, as we already see, could be severe."

"Severe? You mean . . . she could commit sui - cide?"

"I don't know," he said. "Let' s see what Dr . Jaffe concludes."

"When is that happening?"

"Next week," he said.

"That fast?"

"We'd be sorrier if we waited too long, right?" He forced a smile.

We were close to the restaurant now   , but I wasn't thinking about the impression I was going to make on people, especially men, when we entered.

Daddy wasn't taking me out to cheer me up; he was taking me out to prepare me for more depressing things.

"So you think she's crazy, right? You always thought that, Daddy."

"I didn't think she was crazy, just too fanatical when it came to raising you two. It got in the way of our relationship, but from what I could see, both of you were handling it all well enough and would be okay. This is just something out of the blue that no one could have predicted. We'll handle it. Together." He threw me a typical Daddy smile, full of promises and maybes.

"Okay," I said. It was the automatic answer when we had no choice anyway.

"For now, let's enjoy a great dinner together," he said as we drove into the restaurant's parking lot. "You can tell me all about your love life."

"My love life?"

He pulled into a space and turned off the engine. There was that smile again. "What's his name, Ryan Lockhart? I know he's been coming to see you."

"Mrs. Lofter's a little spy, huh?"

"Just very observant. It's part of her training. It's all right. Frankly, I'm surprised more of your and Kaylee's friends don't come to see you."

"I've been discouraging it for now . . . with Mother and all."

"Right. But you like this Ryan Lockhart?"

"Oh, he's just a boy," I said.

"They're all just boys, and I remember what that means," he said, and opened the door.

"Then maybe you'll tell me what it means, Daddy. Sometimes it's like navigating through a swamp."

He laughed, and we started toward the restau - rant entrance. I had never been here, and I won - dered if it was a place to which he had brought one of his girlfriends. He opened the door for me and took my hand as we stepped inside.

"You're *my* date," he said. "Let's make sure no one misunderstands that." He nodded toward the bar as we walked by . A group of young men had stopped talking and were looking our way. I smiled to myself, thinking that the interest of good-looking new men was something I no longer had to share with Kaylee. Besides, I'd always believed they were looking mostly at me. I gave off the air of maturity they'd like in a girl my age.

My suspicions were correct. The maitre d' knew my father. He had been here often.

"Good evening, Mr. Fitzgerald," the man said, his gaze locked mostly on me. "And who is this beautiful young lady?"

"My daughter," Daddy said.

"You will have to hire the Secret Servicefor pro-tection," the maitre d' replied, smiling.

Daddy held on to my hand as the maitre d' led

us to what I assumed was Daddy's favorite table, off to the side and sort of private. I couldn' t help but enjoy the looks I was getting from men with their dates or wives. I wondered if any of them thought I was Daddy's girlfriend. Whenever he took Kaylee and me out, there was no doubt who we were. We had to be his daughters. But by myself, I was sud - denly more mysterious. It was a feeling I had never had when we were with him.

It was an elegant restaurant, one that Mother would surely call pricey. The waiter gave Daddy the wine list, and he ordered something by the glass. He whispered that he would give me a sip of it.

"I hope you're hungry," he said. "They make a terrific surf and turf here. My favorite and some - thing I know you girls like."

"Kaylee never liked it as much," I said.

He nodded, thoughtful. His wine came, and we ordered salads and the surf and turf.

"Now, I would never dare say this to your mother, even when you two were not around," he began. I had sensed there was more to this dinner date than preparing me for possibly more intense psychiatric attention to Mother. My body tightened as though I were expecting a slap or something. "But I do see some significant differences between the two of you, of course. You are not clones, even though your mother sometimes presents you as if you are."

"I'm glad," I said. "Neither Kaylee nor I want to be a clone."

"And you think maybe that was why she did what she did?"

I shrugged.

"She's never seemed that adventurous to me," he said. "I guess I've really been out of the loop when it comes to you two."

I kept my gaze on my soft drink and waited for him to say or ask something more.

"From what the police have told us about their interrogations of your friends and hers, no one had the least suspicion. Is she that good at keeping secrets?"

"For us, a secret is like a diamond," I muttered. "We've had to share so much in front of everyone, especially Mother and you."

Our salads came. I really shouldn' t have been surprised at his curiosity. He was our father, despite all that had occurred between him and Mother . A father had to have some instincts about his chil - dren. Mother made it seem like he was a complete stranger sometimes.

"Why do you think she claimed it was all hap - pening on her computer?" he asked.

"You're into computers and all that, Daddy . I suppose it's not a big leap for her to think of that first."

He nodded. "Yeah, I guess so. It' s just that I

keep thinking she's always been more timid than you. To me, it seems that she depends more on you to lead when it comes to anything social."

"Maybe that bothers her," I offered.

He looked thoughtful.

"Besides, timid girls are more apt to get into trouble, don't you think? They're more trusting."

"That makes sense. You're right," he said. I felt the tightness lessen in me. "Well, let's stop talking about it. I'm defeating my purpose, aren' t I? This was supposed to be a dinner for relief, a breather . Let's get back to your love life."

"And back to your telling me what 'they're all boys' means?"

He laughed. "I never had a pretty girl for a friend. Don't believe the propaganda. Any boy who wants to be just friends is really trying to figure out a way to be more. Or else, he lacks testosterone."

For a moment, I wasn' t sure whether I should laugh. Then he cracked a smile, and I did.

It was wonderful.

My father was becoming my father.

If Kaylee wasn't gone, it might never have happened.

16

Kaylee

I wasn't sure how long I had slept, but it was dark outside, and whatever lights we had were on. Anthony was back in the basement apartment when I woke, and at the foot of the bed were two bags and a shoe box from a department store I knew well. Mother had bought most of our new clothes and shoes there, in fact. Had Haylee told him that? Had she recited one detail of our lives after another, with him taking notes like a student studying the Fitzgeralds? Did he even know the name of our dentist?

"Ah, finally awake," he said, coming over to the bed. "You took a nice long nap. I've been back nearly an hour, and I have nice surprises for you."

He opened one bag and took out a new bra and

some panties, in mixed colors, and a dozen pairs
of mixed-colored socks. He placed it all on the
bed, laying everything out like a display in a flea
market.

"Just as I promised, new clothes," he said. He
waited for my reaction, but I simply gaped. "Oh,
I know. You're wondering how a man can buy a
woman's clothes for her and get it right, huh? Well,
I have a confession. I kept your old clothes so I
could be sure to get the right sizes when it came
time to start buying you new clothes. I lied to you
because I didn't want you asking for them con -
stantly. Don't ask for them now," he quickly added.
"They're really gone this time, just like I said. But
there's lots better here and more coming."

He reached into the second bag and took out
a light-pink blouse with a frilly white collar and a
darker-pink pencil skirt.

"Look familiar?" he asked, proudly holding the
two up against each other.

I recognized it. Haylee and I had the same outfit. She had either told him about it or worn it so
he could see it when they communicated over the
Internet.

"Time to put some color into the place, dontcha
think? Brighten you up. Of course, Ma wouldn't
be happy about how tight and short some skirts
are these days. This isn't that short, but it's tight.
I didn't want to get you something old-fashioned.

Girls like to keep in style, look sexy right? You told me about some of the other clothes you had and how important clothes and shoes were to you. This is just a start. Every day, I'll bring you something new that's just like what you had, what were your favorite things. Well, I mean almost every day." He smiled. "Listen to me rambling on like this. I get so enthusiastic that I exaggerate some. I gotta work, too. Can't go shopping anytime I want."

He opened the shoe box and took out the shoes, a pair of black flats.

"This is what you was wearing the first night. I wouldn't give them back to you. W e want only new things for a new life, right? Same size," he said proudly, and dropped them back into the box. "I brought one of the old shoes with me to be sure I had a perfect match. Shoe salesman was pretty damn impressed. 'A woman lets you buy her shoes?' he asked. 'My woman's special,' I told him."

I hadn't moved an inch or said a word. I was still wondering how long and in what detail Haylee had been discussing this new life with him. What other secrets about us had she revealed? Her contact with him had probably been going on for some time before I'd finally realized it.

He folded his arms across his chest and leered at me. "You know, the least you could do is say 'Thank you, Anthony.'" He waited for it.

"Thank you, Anthony," I said.

He smiled as if he hadn't forced me to say it. "You're more than welcome, honey. Well, get it all on. Tonight's perfect for dolling yourself up. I'm making us a rib eye with fries and green beans. Of course, we'll have a nice salad with some fresh bread. And wait until you see the chocolate cake I got you for dessert. Your favorite of favorites, seven-layer. We'll get that weight back on you in no time."

He slapped his palms together so hard I was sure it stung, but he didn't seem to care. I winced. The air seemed to be crackling around me.

"Chop, chop," he said, then turned and headed for the stove. I rose slowly. He unchained me until I put on the new clothes. Considering that he had been able to use my own clothes to determine sizes, it was easy to see how much weight I had lost when I was dressed in what he had bought me. It brought me to tears.

He paused and shook his head, smiling with a look of amazement.

"You are the sort of woman who just can't look ugly, even when you've lost so much weight, Kaylee," he said. "I knew that from the first time I laid eyes on you. I've done struck gold," he declared.

How he was able to look at me and say that was not just amazing, it was insane. I saw that he had been taking sips from a bottle of gin as he worked on our food, and he took another sip now.

He wiped his lips and said, "Real beauty cannot be silenced. To you."

He drank again. I stood there, feeling a little weak and wobbly. His smile evaporated. He expected something from me for layering one compliment after another, but I was still too dazed even to pretend appreciation.

"Go wash your hands for dinner ," he com - manded sharply, sounding more like an overbearing parent who was disappointed in his child's lack of gratitude. He nodded toward the bathroom. "Go on. Don't dilly-dally. I'm starving, too. Man needs his strength for a woman like you. It's like breaking in a wild horse or something. It aint easy, but you'll appreciate me when you realize how much I've been doing for you. Damn right, you will."

His voice could change in tone as fast as striking a match. The fire in his eyes quickly followed what he had said. Even if it was just for another second or two, his fixed angry gaze was horrifying. He was like two different people, one sweet and caring and one wrathful and mean. Perhaps when he got like that, he was more like his father as he had described him, vicious and unpredictable. And when he was nice, he was like his mother. I could almost see the two personalities wrestling in his mind, neither staying down too long.

I moved as quickly as I could to the bathroom, hoping that if he saw how dragging the chain was especially difficult for me in my weakened condition, he might be merciful and unfasten it again. Surely he could tell that I didn't have the strength to attempt another escape, but when I glanced back at him, I didn't see any sympathy. He was still gazing at me furiously, as if he imagined having a whip in his hand. Maybe that was coming next.

The moment I looked into the bathroom mir - ror, I lost my breath and started to gasp. Having felt the top of my head earlier, I had some idea of how brutal he had been when he cut my hair , but the sight of it now, the patches randomly interspersed with portions that showed pink scalp, was so ugly and disfiguring I wished he had shaved me until I was completely bald. When I saw myself now , I once again wondered how he could look at me and mention the word *beauty*. Didn't he realize what he had done?

A rush of new terror I didn' t think possible came over me. I thought I had reached the limit of what I could endure, but my pale face became even paler. The contrast with the bright new blouse made it look even worse. Visions of Haylee standing behind me and gaping at me returned. Her smile began and widened. I heard her laugh and saw her run her fingers through her beautiful hair, tormenting me with the sight of her rich, pampered strands.

I couldn't stand it any longer. The little strength that had returned surged down my arm and helped me make a fist. I screamed and screamed and pounded the mirror, pounded at Haylee' s face, until I heard the glass shatter. Blood seemed to leap out of my hand. In moments, Anthony was beside me, his eyes bugging at the sight. I began to sink to the floor, but he grabbed me around the waist and helped me up with his right arm as he turned on the water and ran it over my hand. I watched my blood stream down the drain and wished I could go down completely with it.

There was a shard of glass still in the side of my palm. I gazed at it and then closed my eyes and felt my body turning boneless. Nevertheless, I tried to stay conscious. How many times could I faint and live? I kept myself from going completely dark this time. He had me sprawled on the floor and began to work on my hand wound, cursing and complaining as he did. He was mumbling like a drunken madman. I tried not to think of the pain, to imagine myself somewhere else, but even my imagination was ex - hausted. It was as if I had drained every nice thought, every pretty memory, and every ounce of happiness from my bank of cheerful and blissful times.

"No matter what I do to make us happy , you spoil it," he muttered. "Spoil and spoil, that' s all you can do. That's you, spoiled to the core. I was afraid of exactly this. Y es, I was. My mother told me, warned me, girls, pampered girls, are poison. They'll turn your blood to ice water. They'll make you hate yourself for ever caring about them. And they'll always make more trouble for you than they're worth."

He began to imitate a woman' s voice. " 'They don't love you. They never love you. They love only what you can do for them. Their love doesn't come to you; it bounces off you. Y ou become a reflector . . . they'll just be looking at themselves. They'll see and want what's good for them only. Stay away from pampered girls. You hear me, Anthony?'

"I heard, but I didn't listen good. What you go and do this for? I got this great dinner planned. I bought you new clothes, new shoes, and your fa - vorite things to eat. Why did you do this to me?"

He plucked a shard of glass out of my palm and then washed my hand roughly, mumbling and repeating his mother's words like some chant. He smeared disinfectant cream over the deep cut before he wrapped my hand in gauze and bandaged it so tightly that I couldn' t move my fingers. Then he stood up and looked down at me with such disgust I couldn't imagine him wanting to keep me any longer.

These have to be the final moments. Surely he'll either let me go or kill me, I thought, but I was almost too tired and defeated to care which it was.

"You ain't getting another mirror, Kaylee. And you ain't gonna spoil my dinner . No, ma'am, no. You'll sit there at our table, and you'll eat every   -

thing I put in front of you with your other hand. Whatever you don't eat, I'll stuff down your throat either tonight or for breakfast tomorrow . That's what my father did to me many times, made me eat for breakfast what I didn't eat for dinner. You hear what I'm saying? Do you?"

He straddled me, both hands clenched into fists that looked like mallets, his knuckles strangely bruised, like those of someone who had been punching walls. The muscles in his neck were tight, embossed against his skin. His jaw looked locked open. My imagination was going wild. I thought I saw two tiny eyes gazing out at me from the dark - ness of his mouth.

I nodded.

"Say it!"

"Yes," I managed. Every time I thought I would simply give up and die, the fear within me boiled higher and higher. I didn't want any more pain. I couldn't refuse to speak to him. I had tried that and failed. He would simply imagine my words, imagine them the way he wanted them to sound. I couldn't deliberately starve myself. My body wouldn't let me. I couldn't defy him in any way , and yet somewhere so deep inside that I had never gone there before, I felt the twitter of resistance, a part of me still alive. I couldn't give up, no mat - ter how futile it looked. I was in that strange place where you could only shut down your mind and try to step outside yourself, no longer caring what happened to your tortured body but still dreaming of escape.

"You get yourself up and go sit at the table. Don't do anything else to get me mad," he warned. "My patience is on empty. And I'm not putting on any of the music you like. This ain't a romantic dinner now. It's just a dinner, tossing food at you like feeding hogs. Don't get me mad again."

He stared down at me, imprinting his threat on my forehead with his angry eyes. I closed mine and waited, half expecting him to stamp on my face and maybe kick the last drop of life out of me.

He returned to his dinner preparation, mum - bling to himself as he worked. I sat up slowly . He hadn't picked up the pieces of the mirror, so I had to be careful where I put my left hand as I stood. My right hand was pounding with pain, but I walked out and sat at the table. He began to bring food, but not pretending to be a waiter this time. He was more like who he really was, my prison guard, my abductor. He served the salad and then sat and glared at me, defying me not to eat.

I began. It was impossible to use my right hand, and I was clumsy with my left, but he didn' t say anything. He watched me unhappily . I was eating, but his rage was not subsiding. Maybe the end really was near, I thought.

"Nice new clothes, the best steak, good food,

plans to fix up our place with you picking out what colors to use, planning new furniture, new flooring, all of it, and none of it making you happy ," he recited with the speed of an automatic weapon. "Ah, why waste my breath?"

He stabbed at his salad, nearly splitting the dish in two, and began to eat. It sounded like he was growling when he chewed. He poked at his lettuce and tomatoes, nodding as if he had been listening to someone speak. Suddenly, he threw his fork down and sat back.

"What's it gonna take to make you happy, Kaylee? You told me things you like, and I made sure you got them. Love ain' t a one-way street, you know. Yeah, I remember you said you was spoiled and I might have to be a little tough with you, but you were just being honest, and don't forget, you invited all this. Did I tell you to meet me? Did I keep contacting you, or did you keep contacting me? I told you, I warned you, I don' t like just fooling around, and you said you weren't. You swore. You even got mad at me for even thinking you were. And now this behavior? You think a man is just another toy for you to play with? Is that what you think? I ain't no toy—no, ma'am."

He folded his arms across his chest and sat back, scowling at me.

Did I dare try again? Did I have the strength for it?

"That wasn't me," I said. "I told you, that was my twin sister. Her name is Haylee. You were supposed to meet her, not me."

He didn't speak; he simply shook his head, looked up at the ceiling, nodded again as if he heard someone speaking, and returned to eating his salad.

After a few quiet moments, he spoke, but he looked down at the table as if he was speaking his thoughts not to me but to himself.

"It's just gonna take time. Patience, like Ma always said. 'Patience paves the way to satisfaction. Impatience lets the air out of your tires.'"

He rose and went to the stove to finish fixing our dinner. Everything he did was still lined with anger, as he slammed pans and cursed under his breath. I kept my head down. I was eating and swallowing, but I wasn' t tasting anything. I was trying to get it down as quickly as I could, think - ing that my eating would calm him and give me the strength to resist again. When he brought my steak, he stood over me and cut it into small pieces for me. I kept my eyes down and ate. He did the same and stopped talking. We were both almost done when I heard what sounded like a doorbell. He paused and listened. It was there again, definitely a doorbell.

Did I dare hope? I had never heard the doorbell ring.

He looked at his watch, thought a moment, and then smiled and nodded to himself. Why was he happy that someone had rung the doorbell? W as he bringing someone else down here? He stood up.

"Just finish eating," he said, "and don't make any loud noises, either." He walked out, closing the door behind him. I heard him run up the stairs.

I listened as hard as I could. If I heard another voice, I decided I would get to that door and that stairway and, with all the strength I had left, scream and scream for help, no matter what.

But I heard no one. Less than a minute later , I heard him coming back down the stairs. He opened the door and stood there with a large carton in his arms, and he was smiling again, smiling as if noth - ing that displeased him had ever happened.

"Federal Express. This was easier to get that way. It's not exactly something a husband goes to the stores to get for his wife anyway ," he said, crossing over to the table, "even if she is a special woman. It's addressed to you."

He pushed everything aside and placed the carton on the table. I saw the name he had created for me, Mrs. Kaylee Cabot. It was from an online clothing store. He took the steak knife and sliced the top so he could open the carton and take out its contents. He lifted them all with both hands and dropped them in front of me. I was confused for a moment. What sort of new clothes were these? He stood there smiling like someone who couldn't wait to see the reaction to his gift. I lifted the first garment with my good hand. Impatient for my understanding, he seized it and held it up with both his hands. The realization of what it was washed over me like a cold wave in the ocean.

It was a maternity dress.

"It won't be long now," he said.

What won't be long? I wondered. He had not yet raped me. Did he believe I was somehow pregnant? Was this part of his imaginary world?

He dipped his hands into the pile of garments and showed me each one.

"Three different colors, but each one a color you favor, right?"

Did I dare say it? Would I be bringing on my own rape? "But I'm not pregnant," I said.

"Well, you're gonna be, ain' tcha?" He folded the dresses and put them back in the carton. "Just a matter of time," he muttered. "Everything grows better when it's planned well. I'll have everything ready way ahead of time. It'll get so you wont think of anything else but our child. I told you that, and I believe it. That's the cure to being selfish, having someone besides yourself who matters more. Ma was never selfish. Of course, men can be. My fa - ther proved that in spades, but I swear , I won't be. No worry about that, Kaylee Cabot. Say ," he said, "you want to keep your middle name? I kinda like it . . . Blossom . . . Kaylee Blossom Cabot. Sounds almost like a song, don't it? You know what? If we have a girl, maybe we'll name her Blossom.Whatcha think?"

I didn't answer.

"Yeah, it's a little too soon to plan all that. Probably be a boy anyway."

He closed the carton and brought it to the right corner beside the bed.

"For now, we'll keep it here," he announced. "And now, to further celebrate, we'll have that chocolate cake I promised you."

He went to the counter and took the cake carefully out of a box. I watched him cut it up with that same meticulous attention to the size of the pieces that he gave to the sandwiches he made for me. He brought the slices over and sat.

"Can't help liking the name Blossom Cabot, though. Maybe I'll wish for a girl. Don't matter to me if my father's name is kept going with a male child. Yes, sir, time to think about it seriously now."

"I thought you said that your mother told you a woman in pain won't have a good baby," I said.

He nodded and smiled. "You remember Ma's words? Yeah, sure, but you ain't gonna be in pain much longer, even with that stupid cut on your hand. Your feet are almost healed, and in less than a week, I'll have you looking just fine," he said. "Don't you worry your little head about it. Dr . Daddy is here. Hey, guess what I'm gonna bring down tomorrow. My crib. That' s right, my own crib. Ma wouldn't let my father throw it out or sell it or anything. It's still in my room. I'll take it apart to get it down and put it back together here. You'll watch me do it, and you'll look at it every day and think about our baby crawling around in it. There's lots more I'm gonna do. I've been studying up on what a newborn baby needs."

He nodded toward the wall on my right.

"I'm gonna build some more shelves over there, shelves just for baby stuff."

When he was happy and reasonable like this, despite what it suggested for me, I wasn't as afraid to speak. "Babies need sunshine and fresh air most of all," I said.

"Oh, sure. By then, I'll have the backyard fixed up, too. I got lots to do but never before had a good reason to do it. Now I do. W e do. So stop your worrying, Kaylee Blossom Cabot. You're in good hands now." He started to eat the cake and nodded for me to do the same.

I did.

With every bite, my will to survive and escape inched its return. *Why shouldn't it?* I thought as the level of my energy rose. *I'm smarter than he is. I can escape. All I have to do is convince myself, and a new plan will come.*

He smiled at my enthusiastic eating of the cake. "Want a little more?"

"Yes, please," I said.

"That's what I like to hear, more please and thank you. You're going to change. You're going to be perfect, a perfect little wife and mother."

He went to get me more cake.

Yes, I will be someone's perfect wife and someone's perfect mother, but not your wife and not your child's mother.

In my mind's eye, I saw Haylee listening. As the determination returned to my face, she began retreating.

She even looked a little sorry and now a little frightened.

Oh, don't worry, I thought. *You will be sorry. You have good reason to be frightened.*

Anthony returned with my second piece of cake. I ate it faster than the first.

"Well, I'll be a dog in heat. You want to be better faster, too, don'tcha? You want that baby even more than I do."

I looked up at him.

And smiled.

This had to lead to another way out of my prison. I was already thinking of ways to use it.

17

Haylee

"I'm moving back into your mother's bedroom tonight," Daddy declared as we drove home from the restaurant.

"Really?"

"Mrs. Lofter has given us all her time with-out taking any time off for herself because it was important in the beginning, but we can't expect her to be at our house day and night seven days a week."

"Oh."

So he wasn't falling back in love with her or anything like that, I thought. It was something tem-porary.

"Does Mother know you're doing that?"

He looked at me as if I had just arrived on the

planet and then shook his head. "I'm sorry , Haylee. I know it's difficult for you to wrap yourself
around it, but your mother doesn' t know what's
happening right now. She's in a sort of limbo state
of mind. I doubt she'll think anything of my moving back in . . . or maybe it will nudge her back into
reality. Like shock treatment or something."

"Then what? I mean, when she realizes again
that Kaylee is really gone?"

"We'll see, but if she should regain her bearing
and her strength to the point where she can handle
things again, I'll move out, not just out of her room
but out of the house."

"Out of the house? I'll be alone with her?"

"You were before this happened."

I turned away and stared out the side window .
I would never say it, of course, but Mother' s psychological breakdown was a bonus. She'd had such
a firm control of our lives before all this. She practically knew how many breaths we took daily. From
the time Kaylee and I could move around the house
by ourselves until Kaylee' s disappearance and
the aftermath, I felt we had lived in a Big Brother
world, only it was a Big Mother world instead.
She had homeschooled us until the third grade
and then reluctantly gave in and let us attend a real
school. But when we were at that school, she was
still watching us closely. She had taken a teacher' s
assistant job just to spy on us.

To do what I considered normal things, I'd had to devise ways to sneak around, and I'd had to do it for the two of us. Kaylee was never very good at coming up with clever deceptions. I was the one who had to invent the excuses and the good lies. She was the timid and reluctant one. No other girl my age had such an added burden. There were many times when Kaylee had stupidly revealed the truth and ruined things for us, or maybe she'd done it deliberately because of her fat conscience. I prob-ably had fewer hairs on my head than the number of times she'd gotten me angry at her since we were born together. I wouldn't doubt that she'd angered me in Mother's womb, too. Mother used to com-plain about all the kicking we did. I'm sure it was all my kicking. Kaylee was too considerate to kick while she was inside Mother.

"Hey," Daddy said now. I turned back to him. "I wouldn't be too optimistic just yet."

Optimistic? It was just the opposite. He should have said, "I wouldn't be too depressed yet." After all, what did "the point where she can handle things again" mean? It wasn't simply going to be a return to the past. It couldn't be with Kaylee gone.

Oh, no. I imagined new restrictions, especially on my social life. For one thing, Mother might come up with the insane idea that whoever took Kaylee would come after me, too. Wouldn't he want both halves of a perfect young girl?

Besides that irrational fear , she'd conclude that since Kaylee wasn' t here to do something, then I couldn't do it, either. Night after night, I'd be sitting at home having to console Mother . She wouldn't simply accept that Kaylee was gone and there was nothing more to do, no reason to punish me by restricting my life. Perhaps she would stop pretending Kaylee was here, yes, but she wouldn't give up on her returning. If I happened to die be - fore her, Mother would tell the undertaker to wait before burying me: "Her sister is on the way home, I'm sure."

One insane moment after another was sure to occur. Could I imagine bringing a friend home, even if she let me, especially a boyfriend? After ten minutes with her, whoever I'd brought would find an excuse not just to leave but to flee. Eventually, I'd feel like I was the one who had been kidnapped. Maybe I'd think I would have been better off and become jealous of Kaylee again.

Daddy had said that he would move out, so I'd have no ally, no one to support me and tell Mother to loosen her grip on me. Everyone would tiptoe around her and not dare say , "Don't let Haylee suffer any more than she' s already suffering." Re - membering how Mother had reacted to such sug - gestions, even when they involved something small that I wanted or something I could do and Kaylee didn't want or couldn' t do, I was confident she would get very upset with whoever had said any-thing like that. He or she, including Daddy, would find himself what Kaylee used to call persona non grata. She was always showing off how much more she knew than me.

Mother would have no one, and I'd have no one. The house would be full of echoes. My phone would stop ringing. I wouldn't get another party invitation. It would be like our house was covered in one of those tents they use when they have to kill termites, only in my case, we'd be killing contact with any normal person. That was the future that Daddy was suggesting without even realizing it.

I wasn't going to let that happen.

"Have a good time?" Daddy asked when we got home. He sounded unsure. I hadn't said a word to him most of the way. "The food was very good, wasn't it?"

"Yes, it was all great. Thank you, Daddy."

"I had a good time, too. I forget sometimes how great it is to be with my young ladies," he said.

What young ladies? I thought. *You were only with me.* Maybe he was catching Mother's insan-ity. Soon he was going to be the one who needed a psychiatric nurse.

When we entered the house, we found Mrs. Lofter waiting. Apparently, Daddy and she had already made the plans he had described to me. She had a small suitcase beside her.

"Everything all right?" Daddy asked quickly. I didn't think he had expected her to be waiting like a relay runner, anxious to get going.

"Yes. She's asleep. There were a few phone calls that went to your answering service. I didn' t pick up any. I was sure the police had your cell number."

"Yes, of course. Thank you, Mrs. Lofter ," Daddy said.

She looked at me. "Y ou look very beautiful, Haylee," she said. She said it kindly , but I didn' t want to soak up a compliment the way I ordinar - ily did. Kaylee used to say I resembled a ravenous newly born baby bird being eagerly fed by its mother. I was gluttonous when it came to compli - ments. She'd made it sound sinful, but I'd smiled and said, "Pile them on. There's never enough."

Now I quickly put on my guilty face for Mrs. Lofter.

"I can't feel beautiful without my sister beside me, as dressed up as I am. It' s the way we always are."

"Of course," she said. "I understand it' s very difficult for you and your father, too. You have to keep strong." This time, she did sound suspicious and critical. "I'll be back tomorrow morning," she told Daddy. "Have a good night." She flashed a smile my way and left.

"We lucked out getting her," Daddy said. "I'm going up to check on your mother and prepare for bed soon myself."

"Let me know if you need me, Daddy. I'm not tired yet. I might do some of the homework that was sent to me over the Internet."

"Sure thing," he said. "That's a good idea, too. You have to get back to school soon, Haylee. It won't be easy, but you have to find the strength."

"I'll get my strength from you, Daddy," I said. I said it so sincerely that I believed it myself.

He smiled, kissed me on the cheek, said good night, and went up ahead of me.

I checked the phone messages. My suspicion about them was right. There were two calls from Mother's friends, but the rest were all my and Kaylee's friends. I decided not to call anyone tonight. I had no intention of doing any homework, either . The things Daddy had told me were gnawing at me and putting me in a bad mood.

After getting a drink of water, I followed Daddy upstairs. Just as I was turning toward my bedroom, I heard his voice, and then I heard Mother's. Curious, I went to their bedroom door to eavesdrop.

"Are the girls asleep?" she asked him.

"Yes," he told her.

"I had a bad dream. We lost one, and when that happened, the other died of unhappiness. She just withered like a rose."

"It was just a dream," he said. "Don't worry."

Don't worry? What would happen if he told her the truth, forced her to face it? Wasn't that the shock treatment he had said she needed? I was torn about it. I convinced myself now that I was much better off with a mother who was lost in a fog. At least then I could do whatever I wanted, even when I did return to school. If she asked me about anything I was planning, I could say, "Oh, Kaylee wants to do it, too" or "Kaylee wants to wear this, too."

Ironically, more than ever, I could make Kaylee do what I wanted. The thought brought a smile to my face. My gloomy mood dissipated like drifting smoke, and I was suddenly full of new energy.

Maybe I'd give Ryan a call. A little love talk before I went to sleep would be perfect, just the way to drive off any troubled thoughts that threatened to ruin my plans for the future. He answered on the first ring. Wherever he was, he had his cell phone right next to him, probably hoping I would call.

"Hey," he said. "I was just thinking about you."

"You're always thinking about me."

He laughed. "You're right. How was your dinner with your father?"

"Peachy keen. How did you think it would be? He took me out to get away from the situation with my mother, but that was practically all he talked about."

"Oh, I'm sorry."

"No one knows how it's going to end. She could be like this for a long time, and even if she wakes up and realizes what's happened, she could be worse in a different way."

He was silent. My talk of tragedy was too heavy

"But I'll be fine as long as I have strong people beside me like you."

"You will. I swear."

"I might return to school sooner than I planned."

"That might be very good for you. I'll pick you up in the morning if you like."

"I like. Until Daddy gets me my own car. I expect he will now."

"Just say the word."

"The word."

He laughed. "When should I come see you again?"

"Call me tomorrow," I said. "Maybe the same time. We'll be together in the same place, unless you're getting bored with it."

"Are you kidding? I'd claw up the wall to your window."

I smiled. I really did have more power over boys right now. They'd never disagree with me or disappoint me. The girls who normally envied me would eat their hearts out watching me capture the interest of whomever I wanted, whenever I wanted.

Of course, I knew it wouldn' t last forever. I'd get tired of it myself.

But what lay ahead after this was what I had always dreamed of having anyway.

I talked a while longer, listening to him describe what some of my and Kaylee's girlfriends were doing, soaking up the sympathetic talk about me and my family. He also told me how nervous the parents of other girls had become, some tightening their restrictions on their social activities. The principal had apparently asked all the teachers to address the dangers attached to flirting with or encouraging strangers.

"I guess the Fitzgeralds are famous now," I said. "But not in a way we wanted," I quickly added.

Hearing all this had tired me out again. I said good night and hung up. Then I got ready for bed. Before I turned out my lights, I heard what sounded like whimpering coming from Kaylee' s bedroom. I went to the door to listen, but I heard nothing more. My imagination was running wild again. *Snuff it out like a lit match and go to sleep*, I told myself.

There was a lot left to do now that I understood what turns my future could take.

Daddy was up before me and down in the kitchen preparing Mother's breakfast. I was still in my pajamas, but I wanted a cup of coffee.

"Hey," he said. "Up early?"

"It's hard to sleep late. As soon as my eyes pop open, I think about Kaylee. Sometimes she wakes me up."

He nodded, a pained look in his eyes. Actually, Kaylee almost always woke me up on a school day. She'd make sure to get to me before Mother could, because if Mother thought one of us was oversleeping, she'd assume the other was, and then she'd restrict what we did at night even more.

I poured myself a cup of coffee.

"I'll be home later than usual today," he said. "I've got an appointment in New Jersey that I cant postpone any longer. Mrs. Lofter should be here soon, definitely before I leave."

Having her around for another day was de - pressing. Whenever she wasn't tending to Mother, she'd be watching me with those suspicious eyes. Suddenly, my miraculously getting the strength I needed to return to school seemed like a good idea.

"I'm thinking of returning to school tomorrow, Daddy," I said.

"I think that's a good idea. There isn't much you can do here, and the moment I get any information about Kaylee, I'll contact you."

"Promise?"

"Absolutely," he said. "Probably before I tell your mother." He gave me a quick kiss on the cheek as he passed by with Mother's breakfast tray. "Eat something substantial," he called back.

"I will."

I toasted a slice of bread and smeared it with jelly. As I sat there eating, I thought about what I would be wearing when R yan arrived later. I was surprised at the sound of the front door opening and realized that Daddy must have given Mrs. Lofter a key to our house. Was I better off with her here snooping around or with Mother recovered enough to no longer need her?

Mrs. Lofter mistook my angry musing for de - pression and sadness. I saw the look on her face when she stepped into the kitchen carrying her small suitcase. "How are things?" she asked.

"No different from the moment you left."

She nodded. "Your father is upstairs?"

"He just took Mother her breakfast."

"Listen, Haylee, I don't want to tell you what to do and what not to do, but in my experience with situations that were somewhat similar for other reasons, it became best for the young people to try to get on with their lives until things sorted themselves out. You might not think she realizes it, but your mother senses your sadness and that affects how hard she's taking it, too."

"You want me out of the house?"

"It's not that I want you out of the house, no. I want you to try to get into a normal routine. And I know how difficult that will be," she quickly added.

Normal routine, I thought. If she had any idea what our normal routine was, she would never even think to suggest it.

I sighed as if she had placed a heavy burden on me, on top of all that I was already carrying.

"I suppose you're right," I said. "I'm think - ing of inviting someone over after school. He can bring me my homework and tell me what' s been going on."

She widened her eyes a little. "Oh, you have a steady boyfriend?"

"No," I said, perhaps too sharply . "He's not a steady boyfriend. I think that's juvenile."

"Oh?"

"Girls who settle on one boy, swear to be loyal or something, are insecure. It' s easy and comfort - able."

"I see. Well, that's certainly another way to look at it," she said. I thought she was close to laughing at me.

We heard Daddy on the stairs.

"Whatever," she said. "If it helps you get back into things and keep your mind off all this trouble."

Thanks for your unwanted approval, I thought, and took my cup and dish to the sink.

She went to meet and talk to Daddy. I saw them turn and head for his old office-den. Secret talks, I thought, and started up to my room.

"Who's that?" I heard Mother call when I drew close to her bedroom door.

I paused, thinking. I checked the stairway , listening for Mrs. Lofter or Daddy , and then I went into Mother's bedroom. She was sitting up in bed, her breakfast tray on the bed table Daddy had set up for her.

"Good morning, Mother," I said.

She started to smile and then stopped. "Where's Kaylee?"

"She's in the bathroom taking a shower . I'm going to take one now, too."

"Good."

"Daddy's taking us to school."

"Good."

"We'll stop by to say good-bye. Don't worry."

"That's my good girls."

"Oh, yes, Mother. That's Haylee and Kaylee."

She stared. Was she coming back? Did she realize I was humoring her? "I'm still a bit tired," she said.

"There's no reason to hurry yourself, Mother . We're taking care of everything, sharing all the chores like always. I'd better go shower . We're wearing what you set out for us today . We both like it."

She smiled. "Of course you do. My girls," she said.

"Your girls," I replied, and walked away.

I took a shower and started to get dressed, thinking more and more about Daddy's advice and Mrs. Lofter's, too. I could easily tell my classmates that I'd been practically tossed out of the house, that, as Mrs. Lofter had suggested, my moping about, crying over Kaylee, was not helping my mother but was making things worse for her . Everyone would understand, and that would practi - cally double the doses of sympathy I'd receive.

Thank you, Mrs. Lofter, I thought.

I decided I would ask Daddy to drop me off at school today. I could be late. That would be even more dramatic. And of course, I would have R yan take me home. I really didn't want to spend another day in this doom-and-gloom atmosphere. It was as if the whole house had turned into a funeral parlor. I opened my closet and considered my choices. I had to show some restraint and not wear something too loud and cheerful, especially not something too sexy. After all, I was still like someone in mourn - ing, wasn't I? I settled on a rather drab black dress that Mother had bought us to attend a wake for the husband of one of her friends a little less than a year ago. *Thanks for dying, Mr. Whoever*, I thought. I had hated every minute of it and had forgotten her friend's last name. Every once in a while, I had poked or tickled Kaylee, who had been sitting there with her appropriate demeanor and pretending she didn't hate every second of it like I did.

I had always thought the dress was unattractive and did nothing for our figures. When I'd complained to Kaylee, she'd said, "It' s not supposed to be attractive and sexy, Haylee. Think of it as a costume or something."

"Ha ha." She could be so condescending. No one else saw that as well as I did. Little Miss Perfect had her own nasty streak at times.

Now, right after I put on the dress, I heard a commotion in the hallway . I opened my door enough to peek out and saw Mrs. Lofter with her arm around Mother's shoulders. They were standing in front of Kaylee's bedroom door. Mother, still in her nightgown, was crying hysterically . Daddy was running up the stairs. He joined them, and he and Mrs. Lofter practically carried Mother back to her bedroom.

Mrs. Lofter glanced back at me and shook her head. I closed my door and went to do my hair and put on a little makeup. Minutes later, I heard Daddy knock on my door and step into my bedroom. I came to the bathroom door.

"What's happening now?"

"Your mother got it into her head that I took you and Kaylee to school without either of you stopping by to say good-bye to her and show her how you looked."

"That just came to her?" I asked, afraid he knew what I had told her.

"It's like that right now ." He realized I was dressing. "Going somewhere?"

"I thought you were right, and Mrs. Lofter told me the same thing when she entered the house and saw me in the kitchen. I'll go to school today. You can take me on your way to work, right?"

"Sure." He lingered.

"What?"

"Mrs. Lofter thinks we should have Dr Jaffe see your mother sooner. I might put off this appoint - ment I have in New Jersey for another day . We'll see. Mrs. Lofter is speaking to him a little later this morning. How long before you're ready to go?"

"Ten minutes," I said.

Unexpectedly, his news filled me with trembling. It was as if I had begun an avalanche by rolling a snowball down a hill. As much as I hated the world in which we had been living, it was the only world I knew. I could sense that it was coming apart at the seams, and although I imagined only good things for myself in the future, I suddenly wasn't as confident as I had been.

Daddy could read the fear in my face. "Hey ," he said, coming toward me. "Don't be so worried. You're not alone by any definition of the word. We're in this together, you and me. Whatever we have to do, we'll do."

He drew me to him to give me a loving hug and then kissed me on the forehead.

"Don't think that every moment I'm not think-ing as hard about you as I am about your mother. I know this is as devastating for you as it is for any-one. More so because your sister was, is, so much a part of you and you of her. I'll be here for you. Don't worry," he promised.

I was crying. *What is this?* I wondered. *Am I really crying this time? It's the Kaylee in me, damn it.* No matter what I did, we were part of each other. Maybe in time, she would dwindle, but right now, she was here, standing beside me, crying for us all the way I imagined she would. She would even be blaming herself.

Well, take the blame, I thought, and wiped the tears from my cheeks.

"I have to redo my face," I told Daddy.

He smiled. "And what a pretty face it is," he said. He kissed me again and left.

I returned to the bathroom and stared at myself in the mirror, wondering if I had enough water in me to generate all the tears I was planning to shed when I met my girlfriends and Kaylee's at school.

On my way out, I hesitated at Mother' s door-way. Mrs. Lofter stepped out of the bathroom and saw me.

"I'm giving her a bath," she said. "It' s calming. Your father says you're going to school?"

"Yes. I'm taking your advice," I quickly added, making it sound clearly like if anything went wrong, it would be her fault. "I'm not really ready for it, but you certainly know more about these things than I do."

The smile around her narrowed eyelids was the kind of smile I often saw and feared. It usually indicated that the smiling person was amused at how deceitful I was. Usually, I turned away quickly, but I wouldn't let Mrs. Lofter make me feel ashamed or guilty.

"Don't you?" I followed.

"Everyone's different, of course, but I think it might be good for you, yes," she said. "I'm sure you'll try your best."

She returned to the bathroom to tend to Mother

It was as if a wall of ice had formed between us. I hurried downstairs, rearranging the look on my face so Daddy could see how painful this was going to be for me.

He had just hung up the phone. I paused. He shook his head. "The police."

I held my breath.

"Nothing concrete yet," he said.

I lowered my head. *She will never come back*, I thought. *Has it truly sunk in? Will I be waiting for the phone to ring forever, no matter where I am, even at college, even married with my own family?*

"Ready?" Daddy asked.

"As I'll ever be, I suppose." I followed him out to the car and got in.

"I forget what time to pick you up," he said.

"No worries, Daddy. I have someone eager to bring me home."

He laughed. "I should have realized that."

Once we were away from the house, I said, "Mother promised Kaylee and me that we would have our own car. Most of the kids our age in our school do."

"Oh. Well, if that's something she promised, it's the same as if I promised," he said.

"That's sweet, Daddy."

"Besides," he added, turning to me, "just think what a nice welcome-home present it will be for Kaylee."

"Yes," I said. "Just think."

I looked forward, thinking about the new future opening up for me.

Welcome to your new life, Haylee Blossom Fitzgerald, I heard the voice inside me say.

And I added, *Yes, and it's* my *new life. No sharing ever again.*

18

Kaylee

"I need a real nightgown," I said, daring to say it in a more demanding voice now . If I whined, he would think I was just showing him how spoiled I was, something Haylee had apparently admitted she was. No, what I had to do was cleverly disguise my disgust for him and slide into his fantasy gracefully, to convince him that he had won my love. Despite how crazy he was, I felt this was my last chance.

I had tried to resist, I had tried to escape, but now he had to believe that I wanted a baby with him, a family with him, and a new life.

"New nightgown?"

"I don't sleep well enough to get better faster. You need to get me something that fits me, something new. Something I like and feel comfortable wearing. I like . . ."

"I know what you like," he said quickly, surely trying to convince me of how clever he was and how perfect he was for me. "Y ou were wearing one, the same one, when we spoke on the Inter - net three different times." He thought a moment, looked at his watch, and then nodded. "Okay. I'll clean up the dinner dishes later . You rest until I return," he said.

"Thank you."

I rose slowly and started toward the bed, de - liberately dragging my chained foot, exaggerating the effort until I caused myself to fall forward. He rushed to my side.

"I'm sorry!" I wailed. "My leg just gave up with the added weight."

He studied me while he squatted beside me and then reached into his pocket, took out a key, and undid the ankle bracelet.

"Thank you, Anthony," I said.

He helped me to my feet and held my arm as I walked back to the bed and lay down. He fixed the blanket around me and kissed me on the forehead. "Feels like you might have a little fever ," he said. "I'll get a couple of aspirin."

He went into the bathroom and returned with the aspirin and a glass of water. I took them and lay back again. He studied me a moment, his face full of concern. *Milk it*, I thought. *Milk it and survive.* "Thank you. I do have a little headache."

"Okay. I'll be back as soon as I can. While I'm shopping, I'll get you some of those weight-gain bars to eat, too. Just rest."

I nodded, and he rushed off. Mr . Moccasin leaped onto the bed and stood there looking at me as if he knew what I was up to. I reached for him, and he moved closer so that he could rub his head against my palm. Then he settled beside me. I did doze off. An hour or so later , Anthony returned with another bag and took out a nightgown exactly the same as one of Haylee's and mine, pink with a frilly white collar and frilly sleeves.

"This is it, right?"

"Yes," I said. Had she dictated everything, down to the exact clothing manufacturer, or did he have a very good memory, almost a photographic one?

He handed the nightgown to me, and I sat up. He pulled half a dozen chocolate weight-gain bars from his pockets.

"Nibble on these between meals," he ordered. I nodded and gathered myself to my side. "I'd better get those dishes and pans cleaned up. Ma would have my hide for leaving a mess."

He returned to the sink. I put on the nightgown and lay back. As he worked, he whistled. He looked happy now, content in the imaginary future world

he was designing for us. I closed my eyes and pre -
tended to be asleep when he finished and turned
back to me. I kept my eyes closed when he put his
hand on my forehead again. He stood there for
quite a while watching me sleep, and then I heard
him walk out of the basement apartment.

I had to keep him off balance, I thought. No
more tantrums and no more threatening him. The
more he believed that I was succumbing to his de -
mands and desires, the better chance I would have
to try another escape. I put the weight-gain bars on
the table beside the bed.

He returned hours later. I heard him lie down
beside me. I had turned onto my side so that my
back was to him. He reached out, touched my
shoulder as if to convince himself I wasn' t a fig-
ment of his imagination, and then fell asleep, snoring away. I tried not to move very much. I knew I
needed to get stronger, so I slept as well as I could.
I woke before he did and went to the bathroom. He
had swept up the broken pieces of mirror . When
I came out of the bathroom, he woke. He looked
stunned for a moment when he saw me, almost as
if he had forgotten everything, including who I was
and why I was there. Then he smiled, sat up, rubbed
his cheeks, and said, "Good morning."

"Good morning."

He got out of bed—naked, of course—and came
over to give me a hug and a kiss. I was surprised

myself at how oblivious I could be to his nudity. I, too, could see only what I wanted to see and not see what I didn't want to see.

"I don't think you have any more fever . I'll whip up a good breakfast for you."

He went to the bathroom and afterward began to make some eggs and bacon. Just like the night before, he whistled while he worked and then began to describe the things he was going to do. Today he would, as he had promised, bring down his crib and put it together . Assuring me that he had planned for this for a long time, he said he had a list of items any newborn baby would need. He was going to start shopping to set up the nursery in the corner of the basement apartment and work on the shelving. As he went on and on, I wondered if he had ever mentioned any of this to someone else.

"Do you have a best friend?" I asked him as he set the table for breakfast.

"I did, but we fell out. Never lend money to a friend," he told me. "Ma warned me about that often, but I didn't listen."

"Don't you have any other friends, someone you told about us?"

"Naw. Everyone I've worked with is a creep, an irresponsible bastard. I know guys who leave their wives and kids fending for themselves. Selfish bastards. Besides, most wouldn't appreciate what we have and what a girl like you means. They'd ask only about the sex. C'mon, sit and eat," he said. "Stop worrying about me. W orry about yourself. You're days away from being better and strong enough to get pregnant. That' s what we want, right?"

"Yes," I said quickly.

He smiled, and I sat at the table. How ironic it was now for me to be hungry , to eat well, and really try to get healthy again. I had no idea when he would decide that I was ready to make his baby, but the healthier I became, the closer I came to the day he would rape me. What was my choice? Stay sickly? Maybe it wouldn' t matter. Tomorrow, in fact, he might look at me and say it was time, and I would never have the strength to fight him off. If I tried to do that, there was no question in my mind that he would become very violent.

I recalled the conversation Haylee and I had had about rape, and now that I had tried to escape and failed, now that I was physically weak and feeling defeated, I realized I would probably do what she'd said she could do: accept it by trying to imagine I was with someone I liked. Ironically , Haylee had put me in a place where I could survive only if I was more like her after all.

When we were little, we used to play the switch game. We'd take each other's name and pretend we were each other. Mother had even caught us doing it but thought it was a sweet and loving thing for us to do. It had seemed to confirm her belief in what we were.

"You could easily be each other," she'd told us once after seeing us do this. "You are the same person. You like and dislike the same things. No sisters will ever love each other as much as you two love each other, because it's like loving yourself. That's why you must try never to fight or argue with each other. You never have to be jealous of each other, and you must always want the best for each other because it's the best for yourself.

"People will see this about you, and they will be amazed. They will understand why I think you're so special. My girls," she had said, hugging us to her. "My wonderful, unselfish girls."

I remembered looking at Haylee and seeing the unhappiness in her face. It was one thing to pretend and play a game, but the game always ended. She didn't really want to be me. I never said it then. I even tried not to look it, but I felt the same way. I certainly felt it stronger and stronger as we grew older. I didn't really want to be her.

Nevertheless, I supposed we had spent most of our youth trying to get us to be more like each other, me like her, her like me. It had been a struggle we knew enough not to let Mother see, but it was always there. Haylee loved to say , "You'll realize I'm right." She was so confident that I would become more like her, whereas I was never confident

that she would be more like me. The older we be -
came, the more I was convinced that we were very
different people, despite the things Mother had said
or had pointed out to us and everyone. Half of the
things we did that made us seem so perfectly identical were things we did just to please her anyway.

Whenever Haylee did get me to do something
I didn't want to do, she'd looked so pleased. She
wanted to be more in charge, more powerful, more
everything, but she was smart enough not to try
to compete with me in some things, like school   -
work, especially math and science. She was content
using me to keep her grades high enough to satisfy
Mother. If she couldn't compete in something, she
would dismiss it as not very important.

There was never a question about which one
of us was tougher, shrewder, and more conniving.
Haylee always had been, and the truth was, I had
depended on her strength often. She would defend
me as hard as she could defend herself. Sometimes I
didn't like the way she went about it, distorting the
truth and lying about any girl who tried to hurt me
or was jealous and cruel toward me. If that didn' t
work, she would get in her face in the locker room
or the girls' bathroom and threaten her so crudely
and firmly, the girl couldn't apologize and stay out
of my way fast enough.

In some ways, then, I supposed Mother was
right. We were two halves of one perfect girl. I

provided what she needed, and she did the same for me. But, like her, I wanted to be completely myself. Right now, I had no choice. If I didn't become Haylee when I needed to, then yes, I would suffer more. She was winning in so many ways after all.

In the days that passed, I ate well, nibbled on the weight-gain bars, and felt myself getting stronger and stronger. Without the chain anchored to my ankle, I moved about more, exercised, kept myself clean, tried to occupy myself with my diary , and tried to come up with a new plan of escape. Anthony brought down the crib and put it together . He wanted me to admire how well it had been kept for so many years, something for which he praised his mother. He was talking about her now more than ever. Sometimes he would spend hours describing how she had brought him up in a house with so much conflict, all created by his father. He wanted me to understand how much she had protected him. He vowed to be as protective of our child as she had been of him. He was determined to be the opposite of his father in every way.

I was tempted to tell him, to suggest that he was being more like his father by imprisoning me, but I didn't dare. As time passed, he dwelled more and more on our having a baby, being surprisingly detailed about how we would bring up our child, what things he would teach him or her, ranging from manners to basic survival in nature. He listed what sorts of toys we would buy, always something educational, and he promised we would always eat dinner together like a family should. He promised that he would make sure to read our little boy or girl bedtime stories and showed me the books he had on the shelves, stacked in the order in which they should be read.

Almost always, he would end by telling me how important it would be for our child to have a brother or sister , which he had told me about before but was now planning to the point of how soon after the birth of the first child we should work on the second. He claimed that he had done a great deal of reading about it. Maybe it was his hor rible upbringing and his loneliness that made him so determined to have a successful family . It truly amazed me how out of the mouth of a madman trickled promises that any good parent would want to see come true.

As the days went by , I struggled to think of ways I could hold him off. Although I didn't have a mirror, I could look at my body and see that I was regaining weight quickly. When I would fin- ish eating, he would force me to eat a little more or have another weight-gain bar before going to sleep. I was beginning to feel like a farm animal being fattened up for slaughter, only in this case my slaughter would be sexual intercourse and, as he predicted, a few times a day. He talked about that and his sexual powers as if he was a horse put out to stud.

His conversation circled back to the plan to improve the basement apartment. Once I was strong enough to get pregnant, I was obviously strong enough to help redo the walls and floors so we'd have that togetherness he thought was so important. The day he brought down materials to begin the new flooring, I knew my time was nearing. If the sex was not starting this very evening, then surely it would start the next.

To keep me happy, he did what he had promised and began bringing home more clothing, shoes, new makeup and colognes, even some costume jewelry that included matching necklaces and ear-rings. Every evening after the first two days of what I would call forced feeding, he would take me upstairs to have a bath. Now he would let me bathe myself. He would stand guard at the door or stand beside the bathtub and talk as I washed myself. I sensed that he was measuring my recuperation. I could see it in the way he studied my hips, ribs, arms, and legs. I was somewhere between embar-rassment and self-denial.

He treated me with a strange, almost asexual respect, not mauling me or doing anything that could be considered sexual. At times, I felt as if he thought someone was watching us to make sure he behaved. I was always anticipating it, but it had yet to happen. If anything, I continued to feel like some sort of animal being prepared for slaughter . The tension and expectation were maddening at times. Whenever he did touch me, as innocent as it was, my body would get as tense and taut as a bow and arrow. I would close my eyes, hold my breath, and think, *Here it comes*. But it had yet to happen.

Nevertheless, there was no doubt that it would. To him, the event and the date were almost holy, so it couldn't be impulsive. Finally, on the afternoon he had me assist him in laying the carpet, he de - clared that I needed only one more day to recuperate. I tried not to look frantic, but my heart began to pound. I gazed at the door and at him bent over, measuring something. He did concentrate when he worked, but did I dare try another run for it? Even with my strengthened legs and better shoes, I'd never make it, I thought. This time, if I tried and failed, it would surely be worse for me. Instead, I forced a smile, nodded, and continued to help him with the work.

The following morning, our lovemaking was all he talked about at breakfast.

"I'll be hurrying home from work today ," he vowed. "We'll have a nice dinner, with some wine and music, and make love a few times. I can be quite the stud when I have to be."

All I could think of was to keep him talking. "Have you had many girlfriends?"

"More than my share. Of course, none of them could hold a candle to you. I don' t mind confessing that I was with some who could have used a bag over their heads. Good sex but no romance, understand? I'm a little ashamed of those times. My mother could sense when I had been out with some tramp. She'd say things like, 'Y ou smell like you been with trash, boy.'

"Of course, my father would laugh and say   , 'Who else would go out with him?'"

"How horrible for you."

"Yeah, how horrible," he said, nodding, his face filling with rage. I said nothing, and he looked at me and quickly smiled. "No bad thoughts, hear? We have no bad thoughts today or tonight. Bad thoughts can trickle down into your deepest soul and contaminate your child."

"Okay. No bad thoughts."

"Good. You don't do too much today . Have a good lunch. Listen to music. Read and think of me, okay?"

"Okay," I said. I was hoping he didn'   t hear the panic in my voice. He seemed not to, but then again, he never saw or heard what he didnt want to see or hear.

After he left, I sat on the bed and contemplated my fate. What was left to do? I could try to get that door open again. Of course, if I didn' t and he saw chipped wood when he returned, he'd know that I had tried, and that could bring the worst. But being forced to have his baby was the worst anyway. Perhaps it was time to choose between death and what would come day after day now.

Last year, there had been a suicide in our school. A boy named Hampton Hill had shot himself with his father's pistol in his father and mother's bedroom. He had been under a lot of abuse from other boys in his class because he seemed ambivalent about his sexuality. Things had become worse when one boy accused him of making sexual advances. Some parents had apparently complained that their sons were uncomfortable with him in the locker room before and after gym class. We had heard that his own father was belittling him for not being in an after-school sport and for not having friends, especially girlfriends. Haylee had said that was why he used his father's gun and killed himself in his parents' bedroom. He'd wanted to get revenge.

"Some revenge," I had told her. "He's dead."

She'd laughed. She always laughed at a lot of things I didn't think had an iota of humor in them.

I wondered if she was going to laugh now.

I picked up the bread knife and stared at it for a few moments. I could try to kill him. I had thought about it a few times, but killing someone, even someone like him, seemed more difficult than killing yourself. And what if I failed? He might not kill me; he might torture me for weeks and weeks until

I died, just as I had almost done before. No, suicide was a better choice now.

Where would I want to die?

I looked about the dismal basement apartment to consider my choices. Do it in the bathroom, maybe over the sink with the water running? Sit at the dinner table with my arm extended? Maybe on his newly laid carpet? No, I thought, it would probably be best to lie down on the bed and close my eyes. I pulled back the blanket and fluffed the pillow, thinking that I might as well be comfortable.

What do people who are about to commit suicide think about just before they do it? I wondered. If they were angry at someone or something, they'd probably concentrate on that. If they were depressed, they'd probably see it as the doorway to a place where there was no depression. If they thought so little of themselves, as Hampton probably had, they'd see no reason to continue being who they were. Maybe they thought they'd become someone else, someone better, in another life or somehow brought back in another body. Maybe Haylee had been right about Hampton after all, and that applied to most suicides. They just wanted someone to feel terrible, to get some sort of re - venge on people or a world that had treated them so badly.

Should I think about Haylee? Should I fill my heart with hate and curse her as I slowly let the life drip out of me? Who would blame me? She certainly would do that if our roles were reversed. And yet there was the Kaylee in me remembering the good times we had together, our duets of laughter and squeals of delight, the two of us holding hands and walking together, falling asleep in each other's arms when we were little, crying when one of us was in pain, maybe because we feared the same pain was about to happen to whoever didn't have it yet but still crying just as hard as whoever was suffering. Sometimes we surely did that to please Mother, to assure her that we did more than sympathize with each other; we empathized.

And what about those times when we got the things we both wanted, the dresses, the shoes, the toys? We gave each other conspiratorial looks of satisfaction. Either she or I had convinced Daddy or Mother to buy us whatever we longed to have. We learned how to play on our "twindom," as Haylee liked to call it. "W e'll do some twindom today," she might say, and then we would plot and plan, perfecting the way we would mimic each other when we wanted something.

Once we were truly sisters, I thought. Should my last thoughts be about her then or be ugly hateful thoughts about her now?

Most people didn't choose how they should die or where they should die. No matter how firm they were in their acceptance of what was inevitable for everyone, they refused to believe it would happen or happen too soon. Something would save them; someone would save them. And when death did come calling, did they surrender, or did they fight until there was no more strength, no more breath, and no more hope? Suicide was the last thing they would ever consider.

"I'm not going to die," Haylee had once told me. "I'll make myself so ugly and mean that God won't want me back."

Well, maybe you have succeeded in doing just that, oh sister of mine, I thought.

Thanks to her, I didn't have to find a reason to die today. I had only two choices, and I wouldn't accept the second choice. I would not bring a child I could never want or love into this world. I would not be so wounded that I would have no hope of any other life or happiness. No one had found me. No one seemed to be trying, and with all my courage and determination, I had to accept that I could not escape.

I brought the knife to my left wrist. I would slice deeply and then drop my arm over the side of the bed so I wouldn't have to watch myself bleed. I would just feel weaker and weaker and maybe get sleepier and sleepier. It would be easy, almost as if it wasn't really happening, once I was past the initial sting of the knife.

Shouldn't I be thinking a little about Mother

or Daddy? Was I afraid that if I did, I wouldn't cut myself? Despite everything, I didn't want to imagine the pain and sorrow they would experience. Of course, I was confident that Anthony probably would bury me somewhere on his land, where no one would ever find me. To them, I would still be alive. They could keep convincing themselves of that and hold off the funereal thoughts.

This was so much better for everyone.

No more good-byes, no more regrets. I would finally escape.

I pressed the knife to my wrist and closed my eyes, but just before I started to slice my skin, I felt something and saw that Mr. Moccasin had leaped onto the bed. This time, he had a just-killed mouse in his mouth and was sitting there with it as though he wanted me to praise him for his hunting skills. He dropped the mouse at his feet and then turned and leaped off the bed.

Normally, I would have screamed or gotten sick to my stomach, but as if the cat had heard every one of my thoughts, he came up with a possible way for me to stay alive and be untouched, at least for a while longer.

I sat up and poked the mouse with the front of the knife. Where I poked it, a tiny pool of blood appeared. I could never guess where I got the nerve to do it, but I reached out and picked up the dead rodent, squeezing it like an orange. Then I dipped the tips of my fingers into the blood and began smearing it on my nightgown, between my legs. After that, I put the dead creature under the bed, washed off the knife, and put it back. Then I waited.

The moment Anthony stepped into the base - ment apartment, I started to cry . He stood there confused until I pointed to the bloodstain.

"My period has come," I said. "W e have to wait."

His mouth dropped open with surprise.

"You have to get me something."

"Yes," he said. "I know where my mother kept her supplies. They're old, but . . ."

"That's fine. Please," I said, and he turned and hurried up the stairs.

I looked at Mr. Moccasin, who was sitting there watching me and looking as contented as could be.

I started to laugh. I couldn't help it. I had been so tense and frightened of Anthony's reaction.

I laughed until I began to cry, which was how he found me when he returned.

For the time being, he was full of sympathy and confusion, and I was suddenly full of new hope.

19

Haylee

Everyone's eyes were on me when I walked into my first-period class. There wasn't a celebrity on television or in the movies who could have captured this much attention, I thought. Next thing you knew , some of them would ask for my autograph to prove that they really did know the famous Fitzgerald twins.

I looked straight ahead as I entered the room, keeping my face full of tension and pain and clearly appearing, I was sure, like someone who didn' t want to be there, be anywhere, for that matter. I'm sure they saw how subdued my makeup was and how what I was wearing was something I wouldn't have normally chosen. I had no jewelry on, either , no earrings, bracelets, or necklaces. Some of the girls actually looked like they were going to cry for me. Even the boys seemed embarrassed by their own emotions and quickly looked away or down.

"Sorry, I'm late, Mr. Madeo," I said to our English teacher, and I sat at my desk with obvious reluctance and pain. I glanced at my sister's empty desk while doing so and thought I heard an audible gasp from Melody Wilkes, who sat right behind Kaylee.

"It's all right, Haylee," Mr. Madeo said. "We're talking about the second act of *Macbeth*. It's on page 235 of your textbook."

"I haven't gotten a chance to read it yet," I said. "Sorry."

"That's fine. Just listen for now."

He looked totally off balance, which was something new for him. It would be new for all my teachers as they worked through how to speak to me. They'd all be afraid that they might cause me to start crying. I kept my eyes on my textbook for most of the period, but I didn't read a word or hear much of what Mr. Madeo or anyone in the class said. I could feel everyone looking at me. Maybe they were afraid I would start sobbing uncontrollably whenever I chanced a glance at Kaylee's empty seat. Once or twice, I took emphatic deep breaths and pressed the back of my hand to my mouth as if I was trying not to throw up.

Seconds after the bell rang, the girls were

around me, offering to do all sorts of things for me.
I thanked them all, and then, like a princess walking down a red carpet, I made my way through the
halls to my next class, keeping my gaze forward but
collecting the looks of surprise and interest from
all the others who saw me. Many started whispering to one another. The word of my arrival flew
through the building, and before the bell rang for
the next class to start, Ryan was there at the door,
wanting to know why I hadn't had him pick me up
this morning.

"It was a last-minute decision," I said. "I didn't
think I'd have the strength to do it, but my father
and our psychiatric nurse thought it was best if I
tried to get on with normal life for now ." I said it
loudly enough for all the students around us to
hear.

"Well, I'm taking you home," he insisted. "And
I'll be there every morning to take you to school."

"Thank you, Ryan. You are so sweet and de -
pendable," I said, touching his cheek. He turned a
shade of crimson. I left him looking a little stunned
and took my seat again, this time in science class,
one I hated. You had to pay too much attention and
take too many notes, something Kaylee always did
for us. Again, as it would do in every class, Kaylee's
empty desk shouted out more loudly to everyone
because I was there.

Ryan had moved so slowly after talking to me

that he was late to his next class. When I saw him later, he said his teacher had warned him that he'd be in detention if it happened one more time. I told him he just couldn't let that happen. Who would take me home? I made sure that everyone nearby heard me say that I didn't want to put any more of a burden on my father's shoulders. We were the center of attention. Those around us stopped talking to hear every word. I felt like there was a spotlight constantly on me.

Time for a close-up, I thought, and smiled to myself.

I didn't know when I'd had a better time in school. There were so many girls around me in the cafeteria talking all at once that I could barely get a word in, much less my food. That was fine. My silence and lack of appetite confirmed everyone's suspicions about how much I must be suffering. Ryan was at my side, but there were other boys looking at me now, and whenever I did sneak in a smile, it was for one of them.

"I can't imagine how terrible this is for you and your family," Amanda Sanders told me as we all left the cafeteria. "I'm planning a house party this Saturday night and thought maybe you could come. It would help take your mind off it for a little while. Of course, I understand if you don' t think it's proper or anything and . . ."

"No, it's a good idea," I said, nodding. "My father wants me to slowly get back into things. Thank you."

"I'll be sure to invite Ryan."

"Oh, invite as many boys as you want," I replied, then forced a smile and left her fumbling for the right words to say. She didn't want to sound too happy in front of me.

Everyone was tiptoeing with words and smiles, unsure how to act with a girl whose twin sister had been abducted and could very well never be seen again. It amused me to see how this was true even for my teachers, the principal, and the guidance counselor, all of whom tried extra hard to make me comfortable.

That first day, Ryan was a chatterbox when he took me home. Everyone knew that he had been visiting me, but seeing us together in school heightened his importance in their eyes. He described how he was always being interrogated about me and what he knew about my sister's disappearance.

"What did you tell them?" I asked. "I hope you didn't tell any of your friends too much about us."

"Oh, no, no. They wouldn't understand," he said, making it sound like only he and I could.

"No, they wouldn't. They would get the wrong idea, and I would have only more pain. That would be the cruelest thing you could do."

He swore on the head of everyone he loved that

he wouldn't provide a detail about our time to -
gether. "All I tell them is that I'm happy I can keep
you company."

"And how difficult it is for me not to cry all the
time?"

"Yes," he said, even though he hadn't said that.
Now I was sure he would.

"And how I was so depressed for a while that I
actually thought about killing myself?"

"No. Did you?"

"Of course, Ryan. Kaylee and I were two parts
of one person. It' s as if you lost half your body .
What would you think of doing?"

"You don't think like that now, do you?"

"Sometimes," I said. "But not when I'm with
you," I added quickly, and washed the look of fear
from his face.

I could see his mind working. He was terri   -
fied of how my suicide would affect him. He'd
be wondering if he could have done something to
prevent it, maybe told someone. If I did it, he could
be so full of guilt he wouldn' t know what to do
with himself. "Look," he said. "I know you can' t
be yourself, enjoy yourself as much as you used to
right now, but I promise I'll make sure you have a
good time no matter what. Whatever you want, you
just tell me, okay?"

"That's very sweet, Ryan. You know I've decided to try to go to Amanda's party this Saturday.

At least, I told her I would, but I keep thinking that I won't want to go when the time comes."

"Sure, I understand. But I'll pick you up and stay right at your side all night. If you feel bad being there, I'll take you home, even if it's after only five minutes."

"We'll see," I said. "I probably shouldn't have promised her I'd go."

"Everyone will understand if you change your mind. Don't worry."

We pulled into my driveway. Mrs. Lofter's car was there. Ryan started to get out to rush over and open my door. He was treating me like fragile china. If I wanted him to carry me to the doorway, he would.

"Wait," I said, before he got out of his car

"What's wrong?"

"I just remembered that my father and the nurse took my mother to a real psychiatrist today."

"Oh."

"I don't know what to expect, Ryan. Besides, I think the emotional strain of going to school was much more than I anticipated. I'm just going to go in and go to sleep for a while as soon as I can," I said.

"Right. Well, I'll call you later."

"Thank you," I said, and got out. I waved and smiled at him before I entered the house.

By now, I hated the heavy silence that greeted

me at home. Mother was often sedated and asleep. Mrs. Lofter would nod off in Mother's room or go to hers. Sometimes I heard her playing the televi - sion with very low volume. Daddy was at work more often now. I never thought I'd be so happy to go to school, but the funeral-parlor atmosphere was starting to annoy me. Intending to go up and watch some television, I turned quickly toward the stair - way, but Mrs. Lofter came out of the living room, surprising me.

"Was it difficult?" she asked.

"Was what difficult?"

"Returning to school," she said, her eyes wide with surprise that I hadn't known what she meant.

"Of course," I said, making it sound like her question was pretty dumb. "Everyone, even my teachers, was overwhelming with pity and sympa - thy. I couldn't even talk without choking up. I cried in the girls' room about a dozen times."

She nodded. "It's good for you to keep busy nevertheless."

"I know," I said, following that with a deep sigh, one of my best, actually. Anyone might think I would close my eyes next and float to the floor like a leaf in the fall, too overwhelmed with the winds of sorrow to resist being torn away from the branch. I started again for the stairway , walking with my head down, my shoulders slumping with the weight of my sadness.

"Just a moment, Haylee."

I turned, surprised at the commanding tone of her voice. "What?"

"I'm still here because I've been waiting for you," she said quickly, stepping closer. "I promised your father."

I looked up the stairway . "What's happening now? Has there been something new about Kay - lee?"

"No, nothing that I know . Your father is with your mother," she quickly continued.

"With my mother? Where?"

"Dr. Jaffe thought it best if we admitted her to his clinic now . Being here in this environment at this time is putting too much stress on her and reinforcing her condition. She'll get more intense and frequent treatment at the clinic. You'll be able to visit her when Dr. Jaffe thinks it's appropriate."

"When he thinks it's appropriate? I can't visit her now?"

"Not yet. He wants to give her a few days to ad just. He thinks that seeing you without your sister would only exacerbate her problem."

"Exacerbate?"

"Intensify the situation. I know it's going to be hard for you, but we have to think of what's best for your mother now. I'll be going in a little while. Perhaps I'll come back when she's released. I can stay until your father comes home, if you like."

"I think I'm going to throw up," I said. "I shouldn't have eaten lunch."

Before she could say another word, I charged up the stairs and ran into my room, slamming the door behind me. I stood there for a few moments listening. As I expected, she started up the stairs behind me. I went into the bathroom and began to run the water in the sink. I heard her knocking but ignored it for a moment, looking at myself in the mirror. I was a little stunned that it was all happening so fast and happening the way I had decided would be best for me, but it was difficult to hold back my excitement. Mother was being committed to a clinic. Daddy would be busy with his work and with Mother's treatment. I strongly doubted that any of our relatives would come to spend time here. Nana Clara Beth wasn't going to like visiting Mother in a mental clinic. She'd find every excuse there was to avoid it. I'd really and truly be on my own ... finally.

"Haylee?" Mrs. Lofter called, knocking again. "Are you all right?"

"Yes. I'm just going to rest for a while."

"Very smart," she said. "I'll stay around for a while longer in case you need something."

"I'm fine. You can go," I said. "Go," I whis - pered. "Get the hell out of my life."

"I'll go soon," she insisted. I heard her descend and then flopped onto my bed and lay there looking up at the ceiling. Of course, I had to show Daddy how devastated I was, but I also needed to be strong for him, for both of us. If I wallowed in self-pity, he would think I was too immature to handle all the added responsibility that I was looking forward to enjoying.

I waited a good hour . During that time, the phone rang once. I wasn' t surprised to see that it was Sarah Morgan, Kaylee's best friend.

"Yes?" I said coldly, instead of hello.

"Hi, Haylee. It's Sarah."

"Yes?"

"I tried to talk to you three times today , and each time I started to cry and thought I would only make it more difficult for you."

"Yes, you would have," I said. "There's enough crying going on in my family to fill a swimming pool."

She made a small guttural sound, which I knew came from fighting back tears and sobs. "I'm sorry I didn't speak with you and offer to help you any way I can."

"There's really not much anyone can do for me."

"Well, if you need any help with your home - work or . . ."

"I'm only in school because the doctors and nurses and my father think it' s best for me right now. I'd rather lock my door and crawl under my blanket."

For a moment, she couldn' t speak. "If there' s anything . . ."

"When you do today's math homework, copy it for me," I said. It was like offering a small bone to a starving dog.

"Oh, yes, sure. Absolutely. And I'll be happy to make sure you understand it later."

"That's not important. You can hand it to me in homeroom."

"Okay," she said. She paused, gathering her courage. "Is there any . . ."

"There's nothing. I can' t talk anymore, Sarah. Kaylee and I were always together after school doing our homework."

"I'm sorry," she said. Now she was really crying.

"Homeroom," I told her, and hung up.

I waited another ten minutes, dabbling a bit with my hair and choosing something to wear that I liked more, and then went downstairs. Mrs. Lofter was still there, sitting in the living room.

She looked up quickly when I entered. "How are you?"

"I'm surviving, Mrs. Lofter . I don' t need a babysitter. I have to get myself together and help my father."

She nodded and rose. "I'll keep in touch with him and Dr. Jaffe," she said. "I left my number on the kitchen counter should you need me for any - thing."

"How kind," I said dryly. "Do you always take such a personal interest in your patients and their families?"

"Only the ones who need it the most," she said. "Don't take on too much, Haylee. You're like a pot of boiling milk emotionally right now."

I stared a moment and then nodded. That was exactly what I was, a pot of boiling milk, but I wasn't boiling for the reasons she thought.

"I've got to start on dinner," I said. "Thank you."

I turned and went into the kitchen. I had de - cided to prepare pasta with eggplant, something I knew my father liked. Kaylee usually ran lead when we were surprising our parents by making them dinner. I let her, but I knew how to do it all just as well as she did it.

I heard Mrs. Lofter leave, and then I took the slip of paper with her cell-phone number and put it in a drawer. I'd have to be really desperate before I'd call her, I thought, and went to work. An hour later, Daddy arrived. I had all the ingredients out, the salad prepared, and the table set. When he saw me, he simply stood there looking at me.

"Mrs. Lofter is gone," I said. "She told me ev - erything. She was very comforting."

"Dr. Jaffe thought she was right about step - ping up your mother's care. I know how hard this is going to be for you on top of everything else, but . . ."

"We'll be okay, Daddy. We'll be here for each other. I'm upset that I can' t see her yet, but Mrs. Lofter explained it well. I just want to be sure you don't get sick yourself."

"I won't. So? What are you doing here?"

I described our dinner.

"Okay, fantastic. I'll shower and change and help."

"There's nothing for you to do. Just go into the dining room when you come down. I made that chocolate cream pie you love," I added.

"You did?"

"It wasn't that hard. I used to do it with Kaylee. Mother likes it, too."

He shook his head, smiling. "Y ou are one ter-rific kid, Haylee."

"I'm more like you, Daddy . I've always been more like you," I said.

He had to hug me before going up to shower and change. I looked to my side, just where Kaylee would have been standing, and I smiled. I always knew he would love me more. Maybe I'd said it. Sometimes we both voiced thoughts as part of the normal way we treated each other, so often that nei-ther of us knew what we had thought and what we had said. We were, after all, so identical back then.

It brought a smile to my face to think, *back then*. Everything about us from now on might very well become *back then*.

At dinner, Daddy described where Mother was and what sort of treatment she would be getting. He was very impressed with Dr. Jaffe and had spent almost as much time talking to him as Dr. Jaffe had spent with Mother. He kept assuring me that it was going to be temporary.

"He'll bring her around," he said. "He's a very gentle man. I'm sure by the time he's finished with her, she'll be strong enough to take on her responsibilities here again. I spoke with the police," he added. "They have assigned three officers to do nothing else but check on every registered white van in a fifty-mile radius. It's painstaking old-fashioned police work, but they're determined."

He paused, ate, and then looked up.

"Lieutenant Cowan and Detective Simpson are convinced that Kaylee did not run off, by the way"

"How can they be so sure?"

"She left too much behind. She didn't give any of her friends the slightest hint, and there's been no sign of her in any bus depot or airport."

I nodded and then looked up at him. "She and I often talked about running away, Daddy, especially after you and Mother divorced. Mother became even more intense about how we were to behave, what we could do without each other , and what friends we could have. Up to the very night we went to that movie theater , she insisted that we dress similarly, and nothing Kaylee liked that I didn't, or vice versa, was ever made for breakfast, lunch, or dinner. It was no secret that you got so disgusted with it all and that was probably what drove you away."

He lowered his head, nodding softly. "We can't blame her, though, not now. Dr. Jaffe suspects that her sense of guilt is partially responsible for her current condition."

I didn't say it, but I thought, *Good, she should feel guilty, very guilty.*

"Let's do the best we can," he said. "How did it go for you today at school?"

"Difficult, but I'll manage."

"Sure. You're a very strong young lady."

"I've been invited to a party on Saturday," I told him.

He looked up, brightening. "Oh? You're going, right?"

"I don't know if I can," I said. "Every time I think about it, I get a sick feeling in my stomach."

"Oh, no. You've got to overcome that, just the way I've overcome my reluctance to get back to work. Otherwise, we're letting this creature kidnap all of us," he said.

"I never thought of it like that."

"Well, that's how you should think of it. Okay? You go."

I nodded. "Okay, Daddy."

"And by the way, this dinner is terrific."

He smiled and reached for my hand. I clutched his, and for a long moment, it was as if there was no one else in this family and never had been.

That feeling seemed to unlock the small chain of reluctance I had fastened around anything fun I might do for the rest of the week. Every passing day, I grew more outgoing in school and began to talk on the phone more and more to the girls I liked, none of whom was close to Kaylee. Although Ryan was like a strip of flypaper, attaching himself to me whenever he could, I managed to slip away from him enough to toy with two other good-looking boys in the senior class, Eddie Hayman and Luke Stillwell. I suggested to both of them that Ryan was becoming an annoying mother hen.

"He always reminds me of how horrible things are for me. He's very nice and considerate, but he doesn't give me a chance to relax, put it all aside for a while. Every doctor says that's best, or you'll just be another burden for your parents and your family."

They both agreed and promised that they would be at Amanda's party.

"We'll have something to help you escape for a while," Eddie promised with a wry smile. "Ryan never would."

Ryan was terribly jealous of my spending any time with them, but I told him they were just being nice.

"Everyone likes to help, R yan. It's not fair to deny them the chance. It's selfish, in fact."

"Oh. I never thought of that," he said.

"Well, think of it."

They both started calling me every night, and before the end of the week, I was spending hours on the telephone and on the computer again, some times messaging with both of them at the same time. With most of Kaylee's friends like Sarah filling in to help me with the schoolwork, even cheating on pop quizzes to get me passing grades, I felt happier than ever. Saturday night was promising to be a great time.

The only dark spot came when Daddy came home on Friday to tell me that Mother had suffered something of a setback, just when Dr . Jaffe had thought she was making progress. Apparently, she was practically catatonic.

"Maybe I should go see her, then," I said.

He surprised me by nodding. "Dr . Jaffe and I discussed it today. He agrees. We'll go on Sunday if there is no improvement in her condition."

"Okay, Daddy. I'll do whatever you and the doctor decide."

He smiled, then hugged and kissed me.

It was hard to describe to anyone my age the feeling this gave me. Every friend I or Kaylee had took their parents' love and affection for granted. Kaylee and I were afraid to compete for it, and our parents, of course, Mother especially, were so careful about how they showed it. When you had to share love the way we did, it was better not to have it at all. Now, however, I had it all.

I had never spent as much time preparing myself for a party or a date as I did on Saturday. Anyone would think it was my very first. Daddy surprised me Saturday morning at breakfast by telling me he had called Mother's hairstylist and made an appointment for me for late morning.

"If you want to," he said. "I'll take you and come back for you."

I had never been to a hairstylist without Kaylee or even shopped for new clothes without Kaylee. I was strangely nervous about it. Of course, I knew everyone at the salon would be catering to me and careful about what they said concerning Kaylee's disappearance and Mother's condition. Ordinarily, that would make anyone uncomfortable, I supposed, but getting my hair done, and the way I wanted, not the way Mother wanted so Kaylee and I would look alike? Oh, yes, I wanted to burst out with a big "Thank you" and kiss Daddy His face lit up. He wanted me to forget about cleaning up the kitchen. He'd do it.

"Just go get yourself ready ," he said. "This is your day, Haylee. You deserve it."

How wonderful that sounded. *Your day, Haylee*. Not *Your day, Haylee and Kaylee*.

I rushed upstairs to thumb through my maga - zines, deciding what changes I wanted to make with my hair. I ripped out the picture of the hairdo I wanted. Mother had refused to let us cut our hair much, but I wanted to look older and sophisticated. I chose a slicked-back bob for a short hairstyle, which meant I'd have a pound of hair cut off.*Good riddance*, I thought as I bounced down the stairway to meet Daddy and go.

Dawn Selby, Mother's hairstylist, was quite surprised when I showed her the picture. She looked at my father, who was preparing to leave. He saw what she wanted and said, "Just do whatever she wants."

Dawn nodded. It was one of the most silent sessions I'd ever had at the salon. She was very nervous and talked mostly about her own hair, but she did a perfect job. I looked exactly the way I wanted. *If and when Mother sees me now, even if she is getting better, she'll probably have another nervous break-down*, I thought.

Daddy liked it. He said exactly what I wanted to hear any man say: "You've got the face for it, Haylee. It complements your beauty."

What a surprise I would be to all the others at Amanda's party. At least now they could freely talk about other things without thinking about Kaylee. On the way home from the salon, I was tempted to ask Daddy to buy me something new to wear .

He saw me gazing at a display of clothes in the department-store window we were passing.

"What about something new to wear?" he said, slowing down. I guessed I was pretty obvious about it. It would be the first thing I had ever owned without Kaylee owning it as well.

"Really? That would be so sweet, Daddy."

"Let's go for it," he said, and turned into the parking garage.

I knew exactly what dress I wanted, something Mother would never approve. I had longed to have it and went right to it. It was a body-hugging lav - ender dress with a scoop neckline, sleeveless with mesh cutout sides, short with a curve-hugging, tight fit. Daddy looked quite shocked when I stepped out of the dressing room.

"Is that legal?" he asked, smiling.

"All the girls have dresses like this, Daddy ," I said, even though I was probably going to be one of less than a handful in my school who'd wear something like this to a party.

"Are you sure?"

"I've always loved it. It's so comfortable."

"I bet. It's like another layer of skin. Okay," he said. "But I feel sorry for Ryan. He'll spend most of his time fighting off the competition."

On the way out, we stopped at the shoe department and bought me a pair of matching open-toed shoes with a two-inch heel. The moment I got home, I started on my makeup and then got dressed almost an hour earlier than I had to, just so I could be sure I had done everything I wanted. Both Eddie and Luke started a Skype call with me, and I de - cided to let them see me first.

They both whistled and whooped. I teased them for a while and then checked myself out one more time. One thing was for sure, I thought, I looked nothing like Kaylee now.

When I finally came downstairs, Daddy looked like he had lost his ability not only to speak but to make a sound. I turned around for him and struck a pose like someone taking a selfie.

"Haylee, what can I say? I walked out of here one day when you two were little girls and un - fortunately had to return for a terrible reason, but I've found you're a beautiful young woman. Y our mother was right about how you two would be."

"Thank you, Daddy, but I probably shouldn't even be going to this party , much less getting so dressed up for it."

"Nonsense. I want you to have a good time. We've got quite a difficult road to travel ahead of us, I'm afraid."

We heard the doorbell. It was Ryan. He had no idea about the changes in my appearance. When I opened the door, his mouth fell open, making him look dumb.

Daddy came up behind me. "Y es, this is the same girl, Ryan," he said.

"Hi, Mr. Fitzgerald. Yes, she's . . . beautiful," he said.

"And I wasn't before?"

"Huh?"

Daddy laughed. "Okay, you two. Have a good time, but I want her back here by midnight at the latest, and I mean latest, Ryan."

"Yes, sir."

"Don't you want a jacket, Haylee?" Daddy asked.

"I won't be outside long, Daddy. I'm sure Ryan has his car warmed up."

"Yes, sir, I do," Ryan said.

It was cold, but I didn' t feel like wearing any - thing over my dress. R yan reached for my hand. I looked back at Daddy. Despite all the nice things he had said, his face was full of worry.

Midnight, I thought. *Who am I, Cinderella?*

Not tonight.

20

Kaylee

His mother's sanitary napkins were quite old. The box was damp. I was afraid they might crumble or come apart in my fingers, but of course, it didn't matter. I went into the bathroom and put the first one on. I didn't expect that he would check every day, but just to be sure, I asked him to bring me a separate garbage bag. The whole subject ap - peared to embarrass him, and he quickly did what I asked, and he took my nightgown to wash for me. I put on the robe he had bought me, and the next day, he went out and got me three new night-gowns.

Eventually, I flushed the dead mouse down the toilet. I promised I would tell him when I was ready to make our first child, and he left it at that.

I tried to buy more time by explaining when a woman ovulates and when she doesn' t, stressing that it would be a waste of time to try too soon. He listened, but I had the sense that he already knew everything about it. I was glad I didn' t have to lie about any of it.

He didn't want to talk about it very much anyway. I found it ironic that after all the other things he had done to me, this one thing, a woman's monthly period, was difficult for him to discuss without showing embarrassment or disgust.

I took as much advantage of it as possible, moaning about severe cramps and sending him out to get me some over -the-counter medication designed to ease the side effects. Every morning, I would lie scrunched up and make him get me glasses of water, cold compresses, another soft pillow, another blanket. I had him running up and down the stairs before he had a chance to have a cup of coffee.

In fact, I complained so much every morning that he was eager to leave for work.

"This should end soon," he told me in an omi - nous tone.

"Oh, how I wish," I said. "Usually , my men- strual bleeding lasts a full week, but sometimes it's lasted a day or more longer than that."

It was actually Haylee who had done research about it, always afraid she might get pregnant because she got "too hot and heavy" on a date. She knew most of the facts before we were twelve.

He accepted everything I told him and always tried to change the subject. When he came home from work, I made sure to be in bed moaning and groaning. He looked a little suspicious until I told him I had missed school many times because of a severe reaction to my monthlies.

To avoid me and my talking any more about it, he went right to preparing our dinner, which I usually asked to be brought to me in bed, and then he cleaned up and dove himself right into laying our new carpet. He didn't ask me to help him, not even to hand him a tool. I thought his behavior was even weirder than most of what he had done already. He looked like he didn't even want to look at me while I was supposedly bleeding. He avoided touching me, and a few nights, he didn't sleep with me, either. Of course, I wondered how long I could stretch it out and what I could come up with once this was supposedly over.

In the meantime, I studied ways to escape. He was careful to take his tools with him when he left, and he always locked the door behind him. I again debated the idea of forcing the lock open with a kitchen knife. The frightening thing was that if I did manage to get it open, what would I do if the door upstairs was locked? Could I get them both open before he returned? I kept track of when he came home from work the best I could, not having a watch or a clock, but I thought I had a fairly good estimate of how much time I'd have.

On the sixth day of my supposed period, I decided I had to try . I could think of no other way to put him off after my period ended. It was ironic that I was really due to have my period, but it hadn't come yet. The girls in my class had spent a unit of health education with our school nurse when I was in the eighth grade. Most had gotten their first periods by then, but there were at least half a dozen who hadn't. One girl had been having hers for almost two years already , and there were stories about girls who had gotten theirs when they were in the fifth grade. A few girls in our class were quite irregular at the start. There were some months when they didn't have their periods at all.

I knew that dramatic weight loss and stress, especially very dramatic stress, could cause you not to have a period. Both reasons certainly applied to me now. I had been practically anorexic down here, which certainly had a big effect on my estrogen level.

One possible good result of all this was the di - minishment of my chances of getting pregnant. Of course, that was the most important concern for me, but the idea of his forcing me to make love to him once, twice, even three times a night any day now turned my stomach. How could I not become disgusted with my own violated body? I would always feel a little dirty, I thought. The psychological damage would be greater than the physical damage.

Girls were losing their virginity all sorts of ways when they were my age or a few years older. They were date-raped or drugged at parties, and many were too ashamed to admit it or to report what had happened to them. Some could live with that self-denial and maybe even have somewhat normal romances and lives, but those who did reveal it didn't fare much better. Yes, the rapist might be punished, but the stigma was there. What man could date you and not think about the fact that you had been raped? Surely he would wonder if you would be normal. Would you think about it every time your boyfriend and you made love willingly?

If I did escape, what boy would want to have any serious relationship with me, even a year or more later? I knew they would all look at me and wonder how badly I was mentally wounded. I would surely need serious therapy . I might even have to stay in a clinic for mentally disturbed peo - ple. Of course, I wondered what Mother was like now and how I would confront Haylee. I couldn't imagine how she had gotten herself out of being to tally blamed for this. On the other hand, maybe she was clever enough not to get blamed at all. W ould I make sure she was? Could I care at all about her ever again? I could easily imagine her explaining everything I did or said afterward as being a result of my abduction and torture.

"You have to excuse her for being hysterical," she would say, and somehow, knowing my sister, I believed she would get people to feel sorrier for her She'd put on a good act for everyone. She always did when she had to, and she always got away with it.

I was fighting for so much more than my reputation or my future relationships with boys and even my girlfriends now. It was for my very life and soul. Over and over, I told myself, *You can't let this happen. You can't become pregnant with his child. You might as well return to suicide.*

My hands were trembling as I began to work on the tooth of the door lock. Mr. Moccasin sat directly behind me, watching me work, as eager as I was, I thought, to get out. I worked and worked on it, never quite getting it to back out of the notch fully before it slipped back again and again. My wrists began aching from the effort. I had to rest and try again. The butter knife I used eventually bent. I'd have to hide it, I thought. The moment he saw it, he would know what I had done with it.

I scoured the place for something better and realized that the pair of scissors he had left in the bathroom cabinet would be stronger than the butter knife. I hurried back to the door and tried again, coming very close the first time. I wasn't doing very much damage to the doorframe, either . If I failed

this time, he might not notice, I thought. Encour -
aged, I worked harder until I got the tooth of the
lock out far enough for me to pull the door at the
same time and open it.

I stood there, my heart thumping as I gazed up
the short stairway, barely lit with the illumination
spilling in from the partially blocked basement windows of the apartment. Cast in such dark shadow ,
it looked ominous. I estimated that it was early in
the afternoon. He never told me what job he was on
or how far away he had to go, but I was confident
that I still had hours before he would be back. This
time, I made sure to dress and put on a good pair
of shoes. Mr. Moccasin didn't wait. He was out the
door and sitting on the top step by the second door,
waiting patiently for me to open it.

"I promise to let you out of the house, Mr. Moccasin," I said as I joined him.

Slowly, I turned the doorknob and pushed, but
the door did not open. It was as I had feared. He
had locked this one, too. The good thing was that
it was the same type of door lock. I returned to the
basement apartment, got the scissors, and hurried
back up. This door was harder, probably because it
wasn't used as much, and because of the dim light, I
couldn't see it. The tooth of the lock hardly moved
when I jimmied the scissor blade against it, but I
worked on it with my shoulder against the door

The longer it took me, the more panicked I

became. At any point, I could retreat and lock the basement apartment door behind me again without him knowing what I had done. That might give me the opportunity to try the following day. But what if he didn't go back to work? What if his job was finished and he was with me all the time up to when he believed we could begin to make our baby?

I had to get this lock open. I had to.

I pressed and pressed, until the palm of my hand burned. My chest ached from the effort. A few times, I cried out in frustration, but finally, the stubborn tooth of the lock moved enough for me to slip the blade of the scissors between it and the notch. I pushed and turned the handle. The door swung open.

And facing me, her thin, pale, blotched face as wrinkled as a sock, was an elderly woman whose hair had thinned to the point where she was almost bald. Her scalp was peppered with black and brown round, raised moles. She was sitting in a wheelchair Her twisted, almost colorless lips separated to reveal a mouth with missing teeth. The teeth that were there were yellowed and blackened, and her tongue looked like a sliver of raw fish. Her eyes seemed like two bubbles with gray heads about to pop.

I screamed at the sight of her and, panicking, stepped back a little too far. As I fell, I reached for the thin railing and caught myself, but the momentum twisted me around awkwardly, and my legs fell downward. Mr. Moccasin leaped out of the way as my lower back slammed against the edge of the step, knocking the breath out of me.

I heard the door above me slam shut.

For a moment, I lay there waiting to see what parts of my body would telegraph the pain. My wrist had twisted when I seized the railing. The pain in my back was sharp, but I somehow hadn' t broken a bone. For a few moments, I gasped, and then I slowly pulled myself up. The pain in my back shot down through my legs, but I was able to walk. Mr. Moccasin stood just inside the basement apartment doorway and watched me, frightened. I stumbled forward, descending, and went directly to the bed to sprawl out and catch my breath. I hadnt closed the door. What would be the point of trying to hide what I had done? She would tell him.

The shock began slowly to wear off. Had I imagined it? Was that Anthony's mother, still alive? She looked half-dead if she was. Why hadn't I seen her the last time?

I struggled to sit up. My back felt like I had a bad scrape. I was sure I'd turn black and blue, but at least I hadn't damaged my spine badly. I sat, catching my breath, and rubbing the base of my back.

The bedroom with the coffin must not have been hers, I thought. She was probably in another room, and when I was up there, she was asleep. How old was she? Surely she had known I was brought here. Who was crazier, Anthony or her?

Why had he kept her being alive a secret? Now
that I had seen her, would he be so enraged that
he would kill me immediately? Should I go back
up the stairs and try again? I could easily get past a
woman in a wheelchair, especially one who looked
as decrepit and old as she did.

It was getting later . I had to decide quickly .
Gathering my strength and courage, I returned to
the still-open basement apartment door and located
the scissors where they had fallen on the steps. Mr.
Moccasin, more cautious this time, did not follow
me up. He stayed at the bottom and watched me go
up the stairway. I was in pain, but I was determined.
I began to work at the tooth of the lock again.

Perhaps because of the pain throbbing up my
back and the sharp stinging in my wrist, which had
twisted when I grasped the railing, it was taking me
much longer. Twice I felt myself grow dizzy and
had to stop to steady myself on the stairway . The
effort and the tension were overwhelming me, but I
had to keep going, trying.

I thought I had it when the door swung open.

But it wasn't my doing.

Anthony stood there glaring at me. I cowered
against the wall. His scream was the scream of a
wounded animal. I raised my hand to stab him with
the scissors, but he simply scooped me up, shoving
his right arm around my waist, and then twisted
me around, slamming my hand against the wall and

sending the scissors bouncing down the steps. Mr. Moccasin fled into the apartment.

Anthony closed the door behind me and carried me ahead of him as he descended. I struggled, but his arm was too tight, and his grip too strong. He had me back in the basement apartment and closed that door behind us, too. Then he walked with me to the bed and threw me facedown. I was sure I was screaming, but I didn't hear the sound.

Moments later, I felt him seize my right wrist and wrap some masking tape around it and then around the head of the bed frame. He did the same with my left wrist and stepped away. I couldn't see him, but a second later, he was tearing off my skirt and panties. I felt him grab the sanitary napkin.

"You liar," he said.

"I'll never have your baby. You're crazy. Your mother must be crazier. I don't care what you do to me. I'll never have your baby."

"No," he said. He came over to the side of the bed and seized what he could of my butchered hair to turn my head so I had to face him. "I don't want you to have my baby. You wouldn't be a good mother. You're a liar."

He let go of me and walked away. I lowered my head and closed my eyes. I was so tired that I didn't even feel the pain anymore.

At least it's over, I thought. *At least it will end.*

21

Haylee

Amanda Sanders's parents had one of the biggest and most expensive houses in our area. It was more rural, with farms on either side of the property. I had been there once before with Kaylee when Amanda's parents had celebrated her sixteenth birthday. They had acres of land, a pool, a tennis court, and a very large, Queen Anne, Victorian-style house that my mother envied. It was Wedgwood-blue and single-story but nearly twice the square footage of our home, and it had a full-width asymmetrical porch that she loved. I wasn't all that interested in house styles, but I had to admit I was impressed with the variety of shapes in the roof, with part being a steeple and with attractive front-facing gables. It looked important and even historic, even though it wasn't really that old.

What was inside, however , was more impres -
sive to Mother. They had a larger dining room than
ours, with obviously more expensive furniture,
curtains, and chandeliers, and they had art every -
where in the form of oil paintings and sculptures.
The living room had a fireplace that took up an
entire wall, and the kitchen looked like it belonged
in a restaurant. Everything in it was technologically
up-to-date.

But what impressed me most was the basement,
which ran the width and length of the whole house
and was their party room and media center , with
stacks of sound equipment and a large screen for
projecting movies and television. Amanda's father
was an audio engineer for one of the bigger televi -
sion stations, and everything in the party room was
state-of-the-art. Mother had told us that everyone
who had been there said that when the Sanderses
threw a party, it was a party.

This weekend, Amanda's younger brother, San-
ford, was on a Boy Scouts outing. Her parents had
given her permission to have a party for no more
than twenty-five of her friends, so her invitation
was cherished. She was being rewarded for good
grades and some favor she had done regarding her
brother. The reasons didn't matter to me or to anyone else. A party was a party . Some wouldn't care
if it was a wake.

Amanda's parents let her cater her party with

what looked like a limitless budget. It was as elaborate as most people's special events. It looked more
like a wedding reception. She even had a profes -
sional DJ, and although her parents obviously
locked away their alcoholic beverages, including
beer, that didn't stop some of the boys and even
some of the girls from bringing something "hot" to
drink. Amanda had promised not to permit smok -
ing, of any kind, but the basement ballroom had
access through a short set of cement steps to the
rear of the house, and anyone could go out there
and do what he or she wanted. Enough kids would
be smoking pot to get the birds high.

I felt like a magnet when Ryan and I entered.
Not only did most of the girls turn away from
whomever they were with and rush to me, but boys
were ignoring their girlfriends, too. The compli -
ments came flying at me from all directions.

"I love your hair!"

"I was going to try that hairdo. You look beautiful."

"I love what you're wearing."

"You're like a movie star! Who did your makeup?"

I stood there, changing from a magnet to a
sponge, soaking up all the envy and admiration.
Ryan had a hard time keeping me to himself. He
went to get us something to eat and drink and then
wanted to dance. Everyone on the dance floor made
room for us—or for me, I should say . Dancing

with Ryan was like dancing with myself. He could barely keep up, and since this was the first time we had danced together, I discovered he wasn' t very good. A bad partner could make you look bad. He was trying too hard and wore an expression so serious that he looked comical.

Off to the side, I saw Eddie and Luke smiling at me. I turned my back on R yan and indicated to them that he was a drag. Luke held his jacket open and pointed to his inside pocket to illustrate that he had something that might help. I winked at him and continued to dance, or try to dance, with Ryan. More couples stepped onto the dance floor, and some of the boys were dancing so close to us that I was practically dancing with them, too. In their minds, I think I was. Their girlfriends weren't exactly pleased. They practically had to seize their faces to get them to look at them and not at me.

When we stepped off to have something to drink, Amanda hurried over to tell me how great I looked and how happy she was that I had come.

"There's nothing I can do staying at home," I said.

She nodded and then looked at Ryan as if she had just noticed he was with me. "Hi, R yan," she said. "Got everything you want?"

"I have Haylee. That should do it," he replied, and Amanda laughed.

Luke and Eddie slowly made their way toward us, slipping in and around people like they were weaving a web to trap everyone.

"Hi," I said.

"Hey," Luke said.

"Hey, Ryan," Eddie said, insinuating himself between Ryan and me. "You guys having a good time?"

"We just got here," Ryan said sharply.

"It doesn't take long to realize if you're going to have a good time or not," Luke said, and Eddie laughed.

"This party's going nowhere," Eddie said, looking around. "Too civilized."

Luke laughed again.

Ryan glanced at me and smirked. "Anything is too civilized for you savages," he told Luke.

Luke and Eddie laughed again. It was easy to see that they were already high on something—something good, I thought.

"You get bored, come see us," Eddie said. They walked toward the food.

"They're bad news," Ryan said. "It's only a matter of time. Everyone knows they run the drug store at our school."

"Do they?" I saw Paulie Marcus pour something in the glass of punch he had gotten for Melanie Roth. I moved in their direction. Ryan tagged along. I poured myself a glass of punch and held it out toward Paulie. He glanced around and then took out a flask and poured some in.

"What is that?" Ryan asked him.

"Vodka. Doesn't smell as much on your breath," Paulie told him. "Want some?"

"No. And don't give her any more, either," he ordered.

"Hey," I said. "Don't tell people what to give me and what not to, Ryan. I like a little of it. You should drink some, too. Loosen up."

He blushed but shook his head. "We're going to get Amanda in trouble," he muttered.

"Oh, please. She knows what's happening," I said. "Chill, Ryan."

I emptied my glass in two swallows.

Paulie smiled but looked fearfully at Ryan, who was a good twenty-five pounds heavier than he was.

I winked at him and put the glass down on a table. "Let's dance again," I told Ryan. "You need the practice."

While we danced, Paulie smiled at me and then poured another good couple of shots of vodka into my glass. I didn't think I'd ever danced as hard or as well. I could feel the boys undressing me with their eyes, and Ryan looked more and more uncomfortable. Occasionally, I stepped off the dance floor, quickly grabbed my glass, and poured some more punch into it so Ryan wouldn't know what I was drinking. Paulie refreshed it twice for me.

Ryan looked disappointed with the party. He wasn't having a good time dancing with me. At times, he looked like he was moving in slow mo - tion. At one point, when Charlie Levine started dancing very close to me, I turned and started danc- ing with him. His girlfriend, Lois Christopher, was shocked. I nodded toward R yan. She glanced at him, shrugged, and moved over to dance with him. He looked stunned, but continued to go through the motions. What else could he do? He didn't want to make a scene. I was the one making scenes.

One song ran into another, and I never stopped. When Charlie was tired, someone else took his place. Ryan finally stepped off and went to the food table to get something else to eat. I saw Rachel Ben ton, his former girlfriend, approach him and start a conversation. It didn't bother me at all. I was hav - ing too good a time to care. The faster I danced, the more I drank, and the more I flirted and boys flirted with, the more it helped me forget the past weeks of depression. I decided I was through punishing myself. With Mother off my back, that wasn't going to be difficult to do.

Ryan was too engrossed with Rachel to notice when I slipped off the dance floor and joined Eddie and Luke.

"So whatcha got?" I asked.

"Some very good X," Luke said.

He held his closed fist close to my hip. I put my

hand there, and he deposited a pill into it. Eddie handed me his cup of spiked punch, and I washed it down quickly.

"Let's party," I told them, and they both joined me on the dance floor. It was no problem for me to dance with two boys simultaneously.

I was vaguely aware of the time as the party continued, but I tossed it off like a gum wrapper and kept dancing and drinking, and when I felt myself slowing down, I took another pill from Luke. Ryan hovered, looking more and more dis - tressed and lost. Suddenly, I found him annoying. His look of concern was becoming more and more irritating. At eleven thirty, he pushed his way past some kids dancing around me and grabbed my wrist.

"We've got to go. Y ou've got to be home by midnight. We promised your dad."

"Forget it," I said. "Cinderella has left the building."

"What?"

My laughter made others laugh. R yan stood there looking foolish.

"Haylee!" he cried, holding his arms out. "I promised I'd bring you home by midnight."

"Oh, have a drink or something," I told him. "I don't have a curfew anymore."

He backed away, obviously angry. I saw him talking to Rachel again, both of them now glaring at me, and then, a little more than half an hour later, I noticed they were both gone.

"The prince left," Eddie told me.

"Not the princess," I replied. "I can' t let my fans down."

He laughed. We danced for a little while, and then he leaned toward me and said, "W anna cut out? I know a cool place where they play jazz and no one cards you."

"Sure. I'm not that crazy about jazz, but I am crazy about not being carded."

He laughed, took my hand, and led me to a side door. With all the commotion around us, it was easy to slip out. We went up the steps and across the side of the house to his car. I felt like I was floating, and it felt better than anything. He gave me another pill when we got into his car, and we drove off.

We never made it to his cool jazz club. On the way, we turned off the main road and parked on a dirt lot where someone was preparing to start construction on a house. He told me it was where his father was working. I really didn' t listen that much to what he said. I was laughing a lot and didn't put up much resistance when he started to make love. It seemed like the perfect way to end a great night.

Both of us fell asleep after that. I was the first to wake up, and I punched him when I realized that it was four in the morning. He groaned and took

forever to wake up, but he finally did. He thought
it was funny.

"I'm going to get into a lot of trouble," I said.
"I'm more than four hours late now!" The reality of
what was happening sobered me quickly. "Get me
home. Fast," I ordered.

I tried to straighten myself up enough to look
okay as we drove to my house.

"Don't your parents care that you're out this
late?" I asked him.

"My parents? Hell, no. My mother's probably
not even home yet herself, and my father lives
somewhere else."

"Great," I said.

My heart stopped and started when we ap -
proached my house. There was a police patrol car
in the driveway and a familiar black car beside it.

"Oh, shit," Eddie said. "I have some stuff in the
trunk."

"Just pull in and pull out quickly after I get
out," I said.

The moment he pulled into the driveway, however, two policemen stepped out of their car and
walked toward us.

"Don't say anything," Eddie ordered.

In the back of my mind, I thought that someone
named Ryan Lockhart might have already done the
damage.

I got out of the car . Eddie started to back out,

but the first officer put up his hand and moved quickly to get alongside the car . I heard him tell Eddie to step out.

The front door opened, and Daddy appeared. Even though I'd suspected whom the black car belonged to, I was shocked to see Lieutenant Cowan beside him.

They must have learned something about Kay-lee, I thought. Why else would he be here? I had often rehearsed my reaction to bad news. I was ready to hear it.

Daddy didn't move from the front entrance to let me in when I approached. He stood there with his arms folded across his chest and glared at me. He looked different and not like someone who had just been given tragic news about his daughter. He looked angry, and I had never seen anger planted so deeply in his face. *If he's gotten bad news, that only intensified his disappointment in my staying out so late and not calling*, I thought. *What else? Get ready for tears.*

"I'm sorry, Daddy," I began. "I lost track of time and . . ."

"You had me in quite a panic, Haylee. I called Ryan at one thirty. His parents weren't too happy," he said. "He told me you wouldn't let him take you home when he told you it was closing in on midnight."

"I was having so much fun! I couldn' t remember when I had fun last. Nobody had to go home so early. It wasn't fair," I whined.

Lieutenant Cowan stood staring at me in a pe - culiar way.

"Eventually, I called Amanda Sanders' s home. The party was long over. She told me no one saw you leave, but you weren't still there."

"I'm sorry," I said. I couldn't think of anything else to say. I glanced back and saw that the second policeman was at Eddie's car, and Eddie was stand- ing to the side with his hands behind him. The other policeman was searching his car, and he opened the trunk.

Oh, no, I thought. *That Ryan. He must have told.*

"So naturally, my first fear ran toward what had happened to Kaylee. Maybe this abductor was interested in her twin sister, too. I called Lieutenant Cowan, who got right on things for us, and then it occurred to me to check your room to see if you had any phone numbers or notes that would give us a hint about where you might be."

He paused. It seemed like minutes, but it was only some very long and deep seconds.

"I noticed that you had left your computer on. Pretty dumb to use a computer for what you were doing, especially when you have a father in the software business, Haylee. I had no other ideas and didn't want to start calling around at that hour, so I began surfing through your computer. That's when I called Lieutenant Cowan."

I felt like I was shrinking, and in moments I would be only inches tall.

"Why did you do this to your sister, Haylee? Why did you lie about who was communicating with this man?"

I bit down on my lower lip and stared at him.

"The trace is happening now. We already know his name is Anthony Cabot, but that' s something you could have told us right away, isn't it?"

I started to shake my head and then stopped. It was difficult even to consider lying.

"It won't be long before we find out if it's too late. Detective Simpson is on his way with the po - lice. Do you have any idea what you have done? To your sister? To your mother? To me? Even to yourself?"

"You don't understand, Daddy," I said defi- antly. "You never did."

"Frankly, I don't want to understand," he said. "I don't even want to try."

"You are an accessory to your sister' s kidnap- ping," Lieutenant Cowan rushed to say . He was practically steaming with impatience.

I started to shake my head, but he stepped for - ward and shocked me by putting handcuffs on me. "Daddy!" I cried.

Daddy made no move to help me. "Pray that

she's all right," he said. "Pray for yourself and for her. That's what your mother would say. And how right she would be right now ." He stepped back into the house and closed the door.

Another patrol car arrived, and a female police officer got out quickly to join us.

"She's all yours," Lieutenant Cowan told her.

As she led me away, I saw the police put Eddie in the back of their car.

Just before the female officer guided me into the rear of her patrol car, I stopped and turned back to my house.

Where the word came from I didn't know. I wasn't expecting to shout it. I had never said it like this, even when I was little. Neither had Kaylee, I thought, but this time I did.

"Mommy!"

22

Kaylee

He brought one of the kitchen chairs up next to the bed and sat without speaking for a long time. I was very uncomfortable and tried to pull myself into a crouch, but every time I bent my legs, he reached out and grabbed my ankles, pulling my legs straight again. Finally, I gave up and pressed my face into the blanket. Maybe I could smother myself to death, I thought, but every time I held my breath, my lungs burst with demand, and I gasped.

"Untie me!" I screamed.

He didn't move; he didn't speak.

I cried and pleaded until I was hoarse and then just lay still, waiting. So much time went by that I actually dozed off. When I awoke, I listened for some sound of him, but it was deadly quiet. Then

I realized he was still there, still sitting in that chair looking at me. I tried to turn my head enough to look at him, but I couldn't.

"What are you doing? What do you want?" I cried.

"I wanted you to have our baby ," he said. He sounded so different to me, like he was talking in a tunnel. I felt him reach out and touch the sole of my right foot and then my left. "Y ou were ready, but you lied."

"Untie me," I said, no louder than a whisper . "Please."

I heard him moving around, and at one point, I was able to catch a glimpse of him. He had some of the clothing he had bought me in his arms.

"What are you doing?" I asked.

"You don't need any of this anymore, and I can't give it to her."

"Who?"

"My next girlfriend," he said. "Just like you, she deserves her own things."

"Who's telling you to do this? That' s your mother upstairs in the wheelchair , isn't it? Y ou never told me she was still alive. You made it sound like she was dead. Why?"

"It's none of your business now. You don't exist anymore," he said.

He continued to gather things. I heard him leave the basement apartment and didn't hear him return for some time. When he did, I heard him packing the things he had gathered.

"Are you going to let me go?" I called. "Anthony, are you letting me go?"

He didn't respond. He continued what he was doing. I dozed off again, and this time, I was able to draw my legs up into a crouch. I couldn't turn, not with my wrists bound to the bed frame.

Every once in a while, I called out to him and asked again and again, "Are you going to let me go?"

Finally, I heard him approach the bed. He came around on my right and looked down at me.

"You're going to go," he said. "Yes."

Then he walked away . I heard him leave. My mind was racing with possibilities. He was gone a long while. And then it came to me in a resound - ing clap, a realization that was like a stake driven through my heart.

He was outside.

He was digging my grave.

It was a fear I'd had from the moment he had abducted me. I would die, and no one would know Forever and ever, no one could be sure. Maybe that was good. I would be alive in their memories from time to time. People would see someone similar and think, *That might be Kaylee Blossom Fitzgerald. Should I tell someone?*

You're alive in a little way, then, aren't you? I

thought. *When he returns, I'm not going to beg for my life.*

I didn't want to say anything more to him or hear his voice. I wanted to think only of people I loved who loved me, of friends, of music. I didn' t want the last thing I ever heard to be the sound of this horrible man's voice. At least I could choose that. I closed my eyes and tried to think of all the best times of my life.

I could hear footsteps above me. Maybe his mother was just senile. How could she approve of what her son was doing? She looked ancient.

Suddenly, I heard more footsteps and then some shouting. The footsteps grew louder . They were coming from the stairway.

Someone screamed, "She's here!"

I heard more people and then I saw the blue uniform and looked up at a policewoman. She was ec - static and hurriedly untied my wrists. When I turned, I saw two paramedics come charging through t he doorway and rush over to me. I couldn't speak. Was I dreaming? They were working on me quickly   , checking my blood pressure, looking for injuries, and discovering the blow I had taken to my lower back when I'd fallen on the stairway. Another pair of paramedics arrived with more police and a young man in a jacket and tie. He stood by while the para - medics took my vitals.

The look on my face convinced them that I was in a state of shock.

"You're okay now, Kaylee," the policewoman said. "You're going to be all right."

I looked at her , and then, to be sure I wasn' t dreaming, I reached out to touch her . She smiled and grasped my hand gently.

Maybe I was in shock. I started to laugh, and I laughed so hard that I started to cry uncontrollably, enough to warrant one of the paramedics giving me a shot of something. Almost immediately, I calmed and closed my eyes.

I felt myself being lifted from the bed and gently placed on a stretcher. They started to take me out of the basement apartment. I was still awake enough to remember.

"Wait!" I cried.

They paused.

"Don't forget Mr. Moccasin," I said, pointing at him.

The last thing I remembered was the policewoman smiling and lifting the cat into her arms.

Epilogue

Kaylee

They kept me in the hospital for nearly a week, because they wanted me to have counseling in ad - dition to stabilizing my body. It seemed to me that they checked out every inch of me. They even had a dentist come see me. Daddy had a stylist brought in to cut my hair so that it would grow back evenly He promised to take me to find a suitable wig for the time being, even two if I wanted. He didn't tell me everything until the third day.

I didn't say anything or ask any questions. I was sorry about Mother. Daddy was hoping that when I was well enough to visit her, she might begin a real recovery herself. For the first few days, I slept a lot, but whenever I woke, he was sitting there, waiting. At times, I was vaguely aware of him talking to someone. One day, I saw him talking to two men in jackets and ties. I knew they weren't businessmen. They had to be policemen.

The therapist who was sent to treat me was a woman named Dr. Sacks. I gathered from her introduction and things I heard about her later that she specialized in helping rape victims. I made a point of telling her that I was never actually raped. The pride I took in the clever ways I had avoided that was amusing to her. She kept promising me that I was going to be just fine.

"The mind has ways to file away such a horrible experience," she assured me, but she also pointed out that I might have nightmares for some time.

We also talked about my being what she called psychologically gun-shy.

"Your trust of strangers, especially men, will be difficult to achieve, maybe for your whole life, but all of us are a little paranoid. Paranoia isn't necessarily a bad thing if it's controlled. You'll just be a lot more careful than most people."

Of course, I knew that many of the things she told me were things she was saying simply to help me feel better about myself and my future.

She wanted me to tell her in as much detail as I could what had happened to me. "It's better to get it out," she said.

I did tell her a great deal, and I did feel better

after telling her. Arrangements were made for me to see her periodically after I was released from the hospital. It made sense to me. I didn't have another woman in whom I could confide. My grandmothers were not useful for this, and with Mother still suffering herself, there wasn't anyone. There were things I didn' t want to tell Daddy or didn' t feel comfortable telling him. He understood. Actually, I think he was happy that I couldn' t tell him these things. He was afraid of his own nightmares.

I asked about Mr. Moccasin. Dr. Sacks thought it was very nice that I cared, but she didn' t recommend that I keep him.

"He's too tied to it all," she said. "He'   s too much of a reminder and will revive images that you would rather forget. He'll be fine, I'm sure."

I was sorry about that. Mr. Moccasin had become my only friend and companion, but I understood what she was saying.

It wasn't until the night before I was going to be released from the hospital that Daddy talked about Haylee. She was in a county jail, and the at -torney Daddy had felt obligated to get for her was moving to have her psychologically evaluated and transferred to a clinic.

"The legal system works slowly, but frankly, I'm happy she's in a real jail for a while," he told me.

I'm not, I thought, but I didn't say it. No one,

especially Daddy perhaps, would understand how I could feel so sorry for her. But it was like Mother always told us—we felt each other's pain. I wanted to believe that she had felt mine while I was trapped. I wanted to believe that she was sorry. How could I believe any of that if I let myself hate her?

I said nothing.

I would never know how I really felt about her until I faced her again. That would take time.

"Everyone's asking about you," Daddy told me the day he took me home. "Your grandparents are coming to see you, and my brothers and their families will be coming for the first vacation they can get. We'll be like a family," he joked.

I was very nervous about going home. I was afraid that the moment I entered the house, I would burst into uncontrollable sobbing. I could see Daddy was nervous for me, too.

The moment we entered, I expected to see Haylee. I couldn't help that. It was so unusual for me to be home without her. Daddy followed me up to my room. I stood in the doorway and looked at everything as if for the first time.

"Why don't you just rest for a while?" he said. "I'm ordering in some Chinese for us."

I looked at him.

"Okay?"

"Yes. You know what we like," I said. It would be what Haylee liked, too.

He realized what I was saying and nodded. Then he reached out to hug me.

He's hugging only me, I thought. *Haylee's not going to be hugged.*

She had gotten what she wanted after all.

We were completely apart.

Two days later, after he had gotten me a wig to wear, so similar to my real hair that no one could tell the difference, Daddy took me to see Mother. She was sitting in her room at the clinic, looking out the window. It was a very nice room, with flowery wallpaper. She was wearing a familiar housecoat she had worn when she was doing housework, and her hair looked like it had just been brushed and pinned.

"Hi, Mother," I said, and she turned to me. She stared at me for longer than I expected.

Daddy was at my side.

My first thought was, *She's not sure who I am. Mother is not sure.* She never made a mistake when it came to who we were. I especially wanted her to know who I was now.

I held my breath.

She smiled. "Kaylee," she said. She held out her arms, and I started for her.

Then she suddenly dropped them, her smile evaporating. "Haylee," she said, shaking her head.

I looked at Daddy and then turned back to her

"She was bad. She's in the pantry," she said.